DISMAL KEY
by
Mitch Doxsee

SYP Publishing
www.syppublishing.com

Published by;
Southern Yellow Pine (SYP) Publishing
4351 Natural Bridge Rd.
Tallahassee, FL 32305

www.syppublishing.com

This is a work of fiction. Names, characters, places, and events that occur either are the products of the author's imagination or are used fictitiously. Any resemblance to actual persons, places, or events is purely co-incidental.
The contents and opinions expressed in this book do not necessarily reflect the views and opinions of Southern Yellow Pine Publishing, nor does the mention of brands or trade names constitute endorsement.

ISBN-10:1940869005
ISBN-13:978-1-940869-00-1

Author Photo: SYP Publishing/Terri Gerrell
Front Cover Art: www.ebooklaunch.com

Printed in the United States of America
First Edition
December 2013

For Rebecca, Luke,
And the little one yet to be named

Dismal Key | Mitch Doxsee

Acknowledgements

I would like to thank God and his Son. Rebecca, thank you for believing even when I no longer did. Grandma and Grandpa, I truly, truly miss you. Your support in life and college, airboat rides, and endless days of fishing have made me who I am today. Mom, thanks for being a huge advocate of this book. Mark, thanks for the emails; they are greatly appreciated. I still won't let Luke look at them, though. Wyman, Diane, and Hyslop, thanks for giving me a great head start on my master's. Teddy and Nancy, thank you for keeping me out in the Ten Thousand Islands when I'm there. It is always a respite from a busy schedule. Moreover, it will always be home. I need to go redfishing soon.

To my advanced readers who gave me their unabashed opinions: Julie, Jimmy, Audeline, and Missie. Your opinions were invaluable during the revision stage. To all of those who bought *Dismal Key* when it was an eBook, I truly thank you.

To my work family at Dalton Middle School, thanks for all your support and encouragement. Moreover, thanks to my students for all your enthusiasm while I was writing *Dismal Key*. Your excitement fueled me.

And last but not least, Terri and Southern Yellow Pine Publishing, thanks for this wonderful opportunity.

Prologue

The End

McKlusky and The Jamaican

My first encounter with a shark was at the age of ten off of Marco Island. You'd think I'd have shit myself, but I loved the damn things too much. Instead, I just floated there, eight feet under the warm August water slowly turning round and round, watching the sleek figure swim circles around me. The lemon shark's yellow eyes looked me over. Deciding I was nothing worth eating, the shark gave a quick flick of its tail, rocketing into the murky water that makes up Florida's southwest coast.

I didn't quite envision my second encounter with a shark, six years later, playing out as it did. Unlike the lemon, this shark searched for the source of blood that polluted the water as it swam behind the lights of the yacht, floating yards in front of me. The blood seeped from my hand and back in a diluted red stream straight to the tiger shark's nostrils. To a shark, this amount of blood is like smashing a kilo of cocaine in front of a junkie's nose. In the shark's case, it wanted to eat, not go on a binger of drugs and sex-fueled promiscuity.

"Look at that monster circling." The Jamaican stared down at me from the yacht's helicopter pad. His dreadlocks hung like snakes by his face, the wind striking them at his neck.

I began to tremble. The funny thing about the Gulf of Mexico in July is that it can suck the heat from your body at night, especially when you've lost the amount of blood I had.

"What are you gonna do, McKlusky? They're all dead. Ain't nobody here to help? You stay out of our business from now on, boy." His spit misted in the night air.

It's true. They were all dead, and I'd soon be too. I stared up at The Jamaican. I should've killed him when I had the chance.

1

The water rose like a moving submarine breaking the surface. I braced for the impact of the shark's jaws. My body was hit. The jaws were painless, but only for a moment.

Part 1

The Beginning of the End

Chapter 1

McKlusky

McKlusky is the nickname my grandfather gave me at the age of five. Grandpa loved an old movie called *White Lightning,* starring Burt Reynolds. Burt played a moonshiner and ex-con called Gator McKlusky who is forced by the federal government to ensnare a corrupt politician. When Grandpa bought his first VCR, he snagged a copy of the movie with it. He lay back on the couch, and I sat down on the floor and watched the movie with him. When the cars jumped and exploded, I imitated the action with my Matchbox cars heaped in a pile in front of me. Grandpa got such a kick out of it he started calling me McKlusky; so did everybody else.

I was what you'd call an average sixteen-year-old: not a school athlete, but not the dregs of the school either. I simply existed. That is, until the summer when I set foot on Marco Island, the island of my birth. As soon as my feet stood on the bow of my grandfather's boat, it was as if roots in my feet sprouted to drink the salt water, tying me to the environment like the many mangrove islands that formed impenetrable mazes all the way to the swamps of the Everglades.

But at the end of August, I returned back to a small town in New Jersey to live with my mother and stepfather. All the life that had filled me in the summer was gone, leaving me to go through the motions of school and trying to avoid the occasional beating by my stepdad.

It's not that I didn't love my mother; I did. I just think she made a bad choice in the man she married. I paid the cost by being away from the ocean. The only time I felt some harmony is when I practiced at the Dojo trying to master the Filipino art of Kali, a fighting style that incorporates precision knife fighting, whips, sticks, and hand-to-hand combat. The physical exertion kept me sane, kept me from going off kilter.

I used my training, once, against the school drug dealer. I helped his girlfriend pick up books that tumbled out of her hands while she rushed down the hallway late to her class. He walked over in a tight t-shirt displaying his self-inflicted Emo image. His arms bulged, hanging by his side. Thick greasy strands of hair that he would whip back, every so often covered his eyes, revealing a blistering garden of pimples on his forehead. I stood up to leave, and he grabbed my collar and shoved me against the concrete wall.

"I'm gonna kick your scrawny little ass for talking to her." His breath reeked of marijuana and Doritos.

His girlfriend frantically gathered her books, pleading for him not to hurt me.

"Shut up, bitch." He pushed her to the side. She stumbled to the floor with one of those sickening hallway squeaks only a buffed floor can make. Choking me with my collar, he flung me beside her. My forearm, breaking my fall, repeated the squeak. By no means was I skinny. I pushed close to six feet, pretty well built too, but I wasn't as big as this six-foot-three steroid fueled bully either.

Pissed off, I looked around for the teachers. They were always around to catch me without a hall pass, but apparently, not during a fight. I pushed myself back up off the floor and turned to face him. Then it happened. He swung. The druggie's right hook headed toward my face. Instinctively, my right hand came up and pushed his punch past my body. The momentum of him missing me spun him around. I snapped him in a chokehold and heard him gasping for air. I squeezed, the beat of his pulse pushing frantically against my forearm. When he went limp, I let him fall.

I didn't worry about the drug dealer attacking me again. He was soft, ravaged by the drugs he took. And I didn't miss school or my pseudo friends when I left them for the summer, most were *Jersey Shore* cast member wannabes anyway. Nor did I dream of returning to New Jersey in time for the blistering gray winters to milk the moisture from my body.

Marco Island was my oasis. The place I went to rebuild and get back to who I was. A blonde haired, blue-eyed somewhat handsome boy, I liked to think, who loved the smell of salt air and the burn of the sun on his skin.

6

Chapter 2

Jada and The Hippie

Jada loved the rhythmic beat of running. She could keep time for a symphony by the impact of her feet hitting the ground. She even enjoyed looking at her legs and seeing her muscles contract with every stride. The burning in her lungs and the quickness of her heartbeat made the stress of her parents' divorce disappear into the Tennessee mountain trail. She enjoyed getting out of the Chattanooga Valley, which trapped the haze and pollen, up to the Hiwassee River to clear her lungs.

Jada was built like a runner: strong legs, slender midsection, and a small top. At seventeen she was the best distance runner that Chattanooga had seen for years.

Jada had gone four miles up the trail and decided to head back when she ran into The Hippie, his beard twisted in braids.

"Hey-hey, Miss," he said, his voice raspy.

Jada came to a stop, giving herself some distance from the man. She still jogged a slow trot in place to keep her heart rate up.

"I'm sorry to bother you," The Hippie said, "but can you tell me how to get down to the bottom? I sort of lost my way."

Jada stopped her trot, catching her breath. She inhaled the smell of patchouli, drifting off the man's clothes, and tried not to gag. "Well, you're on the main trail now. Just keep heading down, and you'll hit the road."

"Thanks. You run up here a lot?"

"Sometimes," Jada said. The Hippie's eyes darted back and forth from her face to her chest. She shifted uncomfortably, crossing her arms over her breasts. "Well, I gotta go."

"Thanks for your help. Have a good run." The Hippie watched her as she started running. He slung his backpack off and rustled through it.

Jada stretched out her strides. A sting on her shoulder sent a paralyzing spasm down her spine. Her vision blurred causing her to snag

7

a foot on an exposed root. Collapsing onto the trail, she raised herself to her knees, barely able to crawl. Her thoughts raced faster than she did.

Move! Get Up! She was vaguely aware of the footsteps coming toward her. The crunching of the dirt and leaves congealed with the static screeching in her head, making it impossible for her to hear the radio that crackled behind her.

"I got one," The Hippie said. "A good one, too," he added delighted with himself.

"Bring her to me, Richard," The Jamaican said. "I'm heading up now."

The Hippie grunted. He preferred not to be called Richard, but he really had little say-so in his life now. He hovered over Jada, who now struggled to prop herself up on her elbows. The Hippie plucked the dart out of her back and placed it in his pack. He thought about taking her himself and playing his games with her in the secluded forest of the mountaintop. But if he ruined her, she'd be worthless. He grabbed Jada, sliding his hand gently around her exposed waist. He lingered for a moment feeling her body underneath his, the slight expansion of her stomach pressing against his hand as she breathed. He thought again how easy it'd be to take her. His body shuddered, ready for the pleasure. He reached down the front of his stomach to his pants, but it was not there. He was no longer allowed to carry the knife. That which had become a part of his sexual experience had been stripped from him, like ripping his member from his body.

"Wh-a-aa-t arre," But Jada's lips felt like weighted ropes had been strung to them.

The Hippie threw Jada over his shoulder as he carried her to the cliff. The sun scattered over the mountains, smudging the trees in soft hues of yellow. The Hiawassee River cut itself on the rocks below, bleeding out frothing streaks of white.

The air shredded underneath The Hippie, popping in a rapid percussion of beats. First the blades and then the body of the helicopter rose in front of him, its side door open. The Jamaican sat in the pilot's seat.

"Get in," The Jamaican ordered over the radio.

"Karam, have patience. I'm not going to do anything to her," The Hippie said, making his best attempt to sound reassuring.

"Then get in. We have two more." Karam words cut with the beat of the blades.

The Hippie smiled and stepped onto the skid of the helicopter and laid Jada on the floor. Sliding the helicopter door shut, he buckled himself in.

Looking at Jada's body lying helpless on the floor, The Hippie smiled. He leaned back, closed his eyes and thought of what he would've done to her in the old days, when he worked independently and alone.

Chapter 3

Becker

John Becker inched toward the edge of Boony Doon Cliffs in Santa Cruz County, California. The wind blowing off the Pacific ripped through his black hair.

Becker held Carlos by the throat. The back half of Carlos' feet came precariously close to slipping off the cliff and tumbling him into the waves crashing against the rocks below.

"Where?" Becker yelled one more time.

"Hombre, come on!" Carlos said.

"Where?"

"Please! You're the FBI. You can't do this."

Becker kicked Carlos' ankles, dangling them off the cliff. Carlos screamed as gravity pulled at his feet. Becker dug his other hand into Carlos' shirt, stopping the Mexican's decent.

"Okay, okay." Carlos' mouth clamored for words. "Just pull me in. I'll tell, dude. I swear I'll tell."

"Carlos, I'm not stupid. Tell me first." Becker paused, "Hurry, my arms are getting tired."

Carlos glanced at the churning water below. A stream of urine colored his tattered jeans dark and dripped out of his pants. The water leaking from his eyes sheared off his face as the wind's violent gust burst up from the ocean's surface. "It's...it's in the Ten Thousand Islands. The drop off point is there. I swear, please." His words trailed off into a whine.

"Where in the Ten Thousand Islands?"

"I don't know." Carlos sucked in jagged gasps of air. "That's the drop off. They're looking for a site there—I was supposed to meet them. Please, man!"

"Okay," Becker set Carlos' feet back on the edge of the cliff.

"We're cool, right, man?" Carlos asked, his voice timid and hopeful.

"Almost." Becker's eyes pierced into Carlos'. "That girl a few years ago, you know, the one who disappeared during the bonfire? She was my sister."

"Oh, man, no, no, no. Hombre, come on." Carlos shook his head, taking another look down at the waves hammering themselves on the side of the cliff. The smell of feces rotted the air. He grabbed Becker's forearms and wrestled for a hold on his shirt, pulling in desperation. "She's probably still alive, man. I know where she is. I know where she is."

Becker jerked Carlos closer. "I already know where she was. I found her."

"Please, man. It was..." Even in his frantic state, Carlos thought better of saying, it was just business. "I can give you names."

"I know the names." Becker smiled. "I found you, didn't I? I just needed to know the drop off point."

"Okay, okay, the drop off—I gave it to you. You're FBI. The badge! You got the badge around your neck."

The badge in the middle of Becker's chest glistened its dull polish in the half-moon. A menacing grin consumed Becker's face. "I know. The only problem is, it ain't real, hoss."

Carlos' eyes widened. "No, man, no!"

Becker pulled Carlos in and set his feet on the ground.

"Thank yo..."

Becker shoved his arms out, launching Carlos off the cliff. Parallel with Becker for the briefest of moments, Carlos' arms and legs thrashed like those of a young child thrown in the deep end of a pool. Becker almost thought it comical.

Gravity grabbed Carlos, and he flipped back, his head taking the lead in the plunge. Carlos' screams became distant, being swallowed up by the surf. Becker stood there for a second until he heard the thump.

Satisfaction spread across Becker's face.

Chapter 4

Kaitlin

Kaitlin staggered down the beach in Hilton Head. The sun had long set behind her to the west. She didn't like the spinning in her head. She was there with a group of friends, and they were all taking shots of tequila. Her boyfriend, Sam, was the worst of all. They'd talked before about waiting, but he always got too aggressive when he was drunk. He tried to fondle her several times, until she slapped him across the face and stormed off, hoping the slight breeze offered by the Atlantic would calm her fuzzy head.

She knew she was attractive, not in a snobbish way either. It was one of those things she realized when she turned fourteen and boys gravitated toward her. But she would be heading to the University of Florida in a couple months to major in pre-med. The last thing she wanted was a child on the way, and she couldn't spend all of her time partying. Sam trying to get her drunk and into bed wasn't going to help her meet her goals either.

Kaitlin was observant, but she didn't see the man approach her from behind, or the black Zodiac anchored a hundred yards offshore cocooned by the night. The hit on her back knocked the breath out of her. A calloused, rough hand covered her mouth, snagging her soft lips and muffling her shrieks. The man was too strong. He felt like a solid piece of iron as she pulled against his wrist and arm. Her nails dug into his forearm and snapped against skin that was tough as tanned leather, hardly leaving an indentation. The water frothed behind her kicks.

Once at the Zodiac, the man lifted himself into the boat with one arm. He pulled Kaitlin by her hair out of the water. He dragged her over the side of the boat like a giant tarpon. The back of her legs squeaked on the wet rubber as they slid over the side.

The 90 horsepower engine sputtered. She inhaled the fumes of smoking oil and gas, which rubbed her throat raw. An accent she couldn't place spoke behind her. "You be quiet now. I won't kill you today, woman," The Jamaican said.

She felt the needle stab her arm. The stars spiraled into a revolving spectrum of trailing light—and then black.

"Where to now?" Richard asked.

"The girls go to the mangroves. We go to Panama City to meet the ship. There is one more girl. I tried something new in getting her."

"You already have her?"

"No. She is meeting me of her own free will."

"Ha! Wait until she sees you. She'll change her mind," Richard mocked.

Karam tightened his grip on the steering wheel and cursed Richard under his breath.

Chapter 5

McKlusky and Grandpa

The sunrise flooded Marco Island, reflecting specks of orange off the condos' windows. My grandfather piloted the Flounder as the sun burned the mist that weighed down the engine's exhaust. The Flounder wasn't much in comparison to a lot of boats. She was built more for power than speed. But what she was, was a twenty-five foot custom hull, whose big block inboard engine could bully its way through the backwater mudflats of the Ten Thousand Islands. While not the most comfortable ride offshore, she still smacked apart the four-foot waves we were going through. Each one of those waves seemed to pay Grandpa homage—cushioning its blow on his feet—while they punished me, jolting me from side to side.

Some people described my grandfather as a "pro linebacker." With broad shoulders and his legs like giant oaks, that was not a farfetched comparison. In the old days of Marco before the condos, hotels, and Yankees, the sheriff would stop by Grandpa's house if any real trouble erupted on the island and bring him along on the call. When Grandpa stepped out of the patrol car, the drunk or wife beater, usually one and the same, stopped his rampage and decided it wasn't worth dealing with him. The sheriff referred to my grandfather as his personal bodyguard. However, he was best known for navigating the labyrinth of the Ten Thousand Islands. Many considered him the best around because he has the expertise that one just gathers over a lifetime, not just by moving to the area and fishing the channels like the Yankees do. Customers paid him good money to rent his knowledge of the Gulf. I have been with him from Naples to Islamorada to Fort Jefferson and the Dry Tortugas, and especially inside the Ten Thousand Islands; he knows them all like the back of his hand.

He fished those mangroves since he was a little boy. He and his brother used to spend days from home in their homemade plywood boats camping on the different islands and living off the land. Even though he only had a sixth grade education, my grandfather was not dumb. He was a different smart. The kind of smart that could read the tides and know where the fish were going to bite for the day; the kind of smart that could bring a small boat through a fierce storm safely and set the passengers' minds at ease while doing it. Also, the kind of smart that could navigate by the stars without the aid of a GPS.

Years of hard living had made Grandpa rough, strong, and steady. He loved to fish and bend the ocean to his will, but he loved his family more, especially my grandmother.

The Flounder lurched to the starboard side nearly flipping me over the side of the boat.

"Grab the net, McKlusky."

I grabbed the dip net and jumped on the port side of the boat. The crab, getting ready to make a dive, fiddled on top of a cresting wave. It was too late. Grandpa had already circled the boat around at half throttle, and I scooped the crab in the dip net.

"Put 'er in the well, boy." He screamed over the Flounder's engine as he brought it back to full throttle.

"Another one on the port side," he yelled again.

He jerked the throttle back and made a 180-degree turn and one more crab sank to the bottom of the livewell.

"How many is that, boy?"

A few of the crabs had eaten the shrimp we had picked up at the marina. They held them up in their claws daring me to reach in and try to take it.

"It looks like we have about two dozen, Captain."

"Why don't you reach your hand in there and see." He smiled putting the boat back in gear. He laughed; I cussed.

One of his favorite practical jokes, to pull on me when I was younger, was to have me pull a plug on the livewell that had turned a murky white from a lack of water circulating through it. He would leave a few hungry crabs in there to "surprise" me when I went to drain the well. Their claws attacked my fingers out of hunger and desperation. I would howl.

Grandpa would laugh his robust laugh that could shake the seas and make you smile at the same time. "If you're gonna be dumb, you gotta be tough, McKlusky," he would say.

"Two dozen should be enough," Grandpa said.

"Captain Harvey!" The fat man yelled in his New York accent. Most people referred to my grandfather by his last name of Harvey or Captain instead of his first, Doyle.

My grandfather's charter for the day was a robust New Yorker and his family. They met us at the dock earlier in the morning. The man eyed me up and down when I checked out his daughter. I'd thought she was cute, nice rack, butt — all the stuff a sixteen-year-old looks for in a girl. I allowed my mind to ravage her until she started complaining about the time of the morning and the smell of the bait. Okay, I still ravaged her, but I shut out the whining.

"Captain Harvey!" he yelled again. His cheeks puffed out as the wind from the moving boat rushed into them.

"Yes, sir?"

"Will you be making anymore turns like that anytime soon?" the man asked, agitated.

The Yankee had been in mid drink of his Coke when Grandpa turned the boat. It had spilled down his new Guy Harvey t-shirt, leaving a brown stain from the collar of his chubby neck to the top of his rounded belly. What he didn't know is that my grandfather would be more than happy to have him swim the 22 miles to shore if he didn't like the turns. Despite the fact that my grandfather is a fisherman for hire, it is still his boat, and he runs it how he likes.

"Not any more. We're here," Grandpa said as he eased off the throttle. We arrived at the Kidd, a wrecked shrimping boat that had sunk off the coast of Marco several years ago.

We were after permit. Permit are one of the best fighting fish on light tackle. During the summer months, they infest the communication towers and wrecks off Marco, sometimes swarming in schools of hundreds.

"Get on the bow and let the anchor down, McKlusky." I did. Grandpa tied hooks to the rods looping the knots while scanning the storm clouds piling up just where the horizon begins to dip. With a frown and a shake of his head, Grandpa finished rigging the rods. I already spied flashes of yellow and silver underneath the surface. The permit were awakening for their morning feeding. Grandpa baited the spinning

16

rods with crabs and cast them behind the boat. I grabbed a rod with a jig and headed toward the bow. On my second cast, my rod began to scream. I walked it back to Grandpa, and he gave it to the fat man. A permit also grabbed one of the rods with a crab and began to rip off line.

The man's wife grabbed the rod. Her bleached blonde hair fell over her face, obscuring her gaudy makeup and fake tan. She gripped the rod and reeled against the running permit.

"Don't reel while the fish is taking line," I instructed her. "It'll break. Wait until he tires a bit and then reel." I tightened the drag for her.

The stout man huffed as he fought his fish.

Another rod took a bow, and the daughter got in on the action. All three fought their fish, crossed lines, and moved under each other. They followed instructions well when they got tangled, or as Grandpa called it, "a cluster fuck!" The daughter even looked like she was having a good time though she kept complaining about sweating. All three landed their permit.

Permit after permit kept hitting the crabs and my jig. A puddle of sweat soaked into the fat man's shorts, outlining the top of his crack. The woman nearly fainted sitting in her chair, her polyester shirt gluing itself under the fold in her neck. What was supposed to be a full day charter turned into a half a day, because the man and his wife were worn-out. They rubbed their arms and worked out the cramps in their hands. This suited Grandpa just fine. He was getting worried about a tropical depression out in the Gulf that had started to kick up some waves. The news said it shouldn't make landfall near us, but Grandpa said they were full of crap. So we headed back to shore.

After Grandpa cleaned the permit for the New Yorkers and I scrubbed the Flounder, we headed home. The house wasn't far. Nothing is on an island that is three miles wide and six miles long. We lived in the center of the island in a modest house my grandfather built when he and my grandmother married. When they first moved into it, sand blanketed the area and grass struggled to grow. If it did get started, sandspurs suffocated it.

The area is called the Marco Highlands. It's the area of the island that the snowbirds who live here for half the year refer to as the poor—where the workers live. The people who bag groceries, mow lawns, and do other services. However, it is where most of the actual history of the island lives too.

My family settled Marco Island in the early 1900s when my great great grandfather, Jack Harvey, migrated from Islip, New York in search of clam beds, which he found. He started canning the clams, and this brought people to the island to work. But the clam beds eventually dried up from disease. So his offspring abandoned the canning business and became fishermen, crabbers, or outlaws—or a mixture of all three. When you live this close to the water, the life of a pirate is never far away.

"It was a hot one today," Grandpa said as he flung open the front door.

"I'll have dinner ready in minute," Grandma said. "Grab you and your grandpa something to drink, Henry." She started to heat the grease in the pan.

Yes, Henry Harvey was my real name. My family had a twisted sense of humor. I stared at my grandmother for a minute.

"Oh, I'm sorry," she said. A slight smile spread across her frail lips. "I mean McKlusky."

"No problem, Delores," I said mockingly.

"You watch your sass, young man." She shook her spatula at me. "By the way, Chloe called for you."

"Yeah, I've been meaning to call her since I got here," I said.

"You should've called her before now. You don't treat a friend like that."

"Don't you start, Grandma." I gave her a hug and grabbed the drinks. "I'll call her. Besides, it's Chloe. She's more than capable of coming to see me."

Grandpa came in the kitchen and pinched Grandma on the butt.

"Stop that!" She swatted his hand with a dishtowel.

"What's a matter?" Grandpa said, shrugging his shoulders.

After all these years, they could still flirt with each other like the day they met. It made me laugh and feel fortunate that there was a stable relationship in my life.

Grandpa lay on the couch to watch the world news, as is his evening tradition. He had the TV blaring when the phone rang.

18

"Boy, bring me the phone," Grandpa said. I grabbed the cordless and tossed it to him. He caught it midair with the reflexes of a cat. He looked at me, "Your ol' grandpa's still got it, ain't he, boy?" Not waiting for my response he answered the phone.

"Hello? Yeah, this is Captain Harvey."

I heard the voice on the other end but couldn't make out what was being said.

"Well, it's all pretty much a remote location. Tomorrow? Probably not. Going to storm—I know what the weather says but they're full of it. I'll tell you what; I'm available for the next few days. I'll keep it open for you until the storm passes. And if it doesn't come, I'll see you tomorrow morning. Alright, take care now."

Grandpa hung up. "McKlusky, you feel like helping on the boat some more?" Grandpa flung the phone back at me, and I snagged it. "Who's still got it?" I said. "Hell yeah, I want to help."

"McKlusky!" My grandmother yelled from the kitchen. "Don't use that kind of language in this house!"

Grandpa shook his finger at me to make fun of Grandma.

Grandma stormed out of the kitchen with her spatula still in hand. "Don't you mock me, Doyle!" Grandpa jumped up on the couch. "Neither one of you is too big for me to whip."

Grandpa and I held the laughs back until Grandma went back in the kitchen.

"Are we permit fishing again?"

"No," Grandpa said. "Some guy wants to go sightseeing, explore a few islands and take pictures. It ain't going to happen tomorrow like he thinks, but it will in a day or two. We'll take some rods. But fishing or cruising, his money is as good as any."

"Hell yeah, it is," I said. Before I realized I had cussed again, Grandma's spatula came flying out of the kitchen. The grease that had clung to it splattered on my arm.

Chapter 6

Becker

John Becker hung up the phone in his Atlanta apartment. He sat back in his chair scoffing at the fact that an aged fishing guide could predict weather better than the computer models at CNN. The bags sitting by the door from his trip to California did not need to be unpacked. He took the FBI badge out of his pocket and flung it into his desk drawer with his ATF, DEA, and other assorted government agency badges.

Becker looked out his high-rise window and grumbled at the humidity pressing down the smog around the city buildings. He pulled out an NOAA map of the Ten Thousand Islands and blurred over the hundreds of islands, channels, and narrow waterways that covered the southwest coast of Florida. "Damn confusing from the looks of it," Becker said.

He'd thought about exploring the area himself with a GPS and rental boat. However, the more research he accumulated on the tangled mess of mangroves that formed the Ten Thousand Islands, the more he knew he needed an expert to navigate him through them.

Becker found stories of boaters fishing in what they thought was deep water, only to be stranded when the tide quietly sneaked out, leaving them dry, stuck until the incoming tide floated their boat again. Stories of people being lost for days, until a local found them, littered South Florida newspapers. He read of boaters, tearing their hulls or propellers on hidden oyster bars, or running full throttle into a sandbar hidden under the black water. In deadlier cases the boat's passengers were launched out onto a sandbar. They either suffered broken bones, concussions, or even death.

In his research, he also found that one of the men who kept finding the lost boaters in the expanse of brackish water was Captain Harvey. He even talked to his former mentor, Kirk Dupree. Kirk went fishing with Captain Harvey on a yearly basis.

"He is a great fishing guide," Kirk said. "Are you going to do some fishing? Becker taking some time off from his personal vendetta?"

"Maybe," Becker said.

Kirk's voice took a serious tone. "I don't believe you, John."

Becker remained silent.

"Listen, you and I both know why you're going. You're getting close aren't you? Tell me. How'd you find out who did it?" Kirk paused. "He gave you the names didn't he, when you found her?"

"You know how it is, Kirk." Becker was becoming annoyed. He'd just wanted verification that Harvey knew the area, not a bombardment into his personal life. Kirk had proved a good friend in the past; he oversaw Becker's training in the CIA. And Kirk was the single reason the CIA didn't lock Becker up for treason.

"I know how it is, Becker, but let me give you some advice. Harvey is a great guide. He can get into parts of the Ten Thousand Islands that no one but him has set eyes on since the Calusa Indians lived there. But if you try to take over that boat or get him caught up in your personal business, he'll leave you stranded on a sandbar. If he's in a good mood, he'll leave you with a flare."

"What makes you think he can handle me?" Becker said.

"Harvey is a little more than he seems. Also, God help you if his grandson is with you and something goes down."

"His grandson," Becker grumbled. "That's all I need is some kid getting in the way."

"It's not an option. The kid works on his boat during the summer. He's about sixteen by now, ornery little bastard with a sailor's mouth."

"Maybe I should just get someone else." Becker tightened his hand around the phone in frustration.

"You can, but he knows every island, sandbar, and oyster bar there is."

"Thanks. I appreciate the advice." Despite Kirk's help in the past, Becker fumed at how much Kirk actually knew about his business.

"You're welcome. Be careful. Hey, you might even try having a little fun. Why not ask Harvey to put you on one of those bull redfish he can find? You might accidently enjoy yourself—if you can put the past behind you."

"I'll try," Becker said more annoyed than reassured. Becker hung up the phone.

He picked up Doyle Harvey's file off of his desk and flipped it open. He had not only picked Captain Harvey because of his knowledge of the Ten Thousand Islands, but also because of his military background. Captain Harvey had been Sergeant Harvey in the Army. He joined at the age of seventeen during World War II. Because of Harvey's accuracy with a gun, he was trained in a unit whose mission was to sneak into Japan and kill top military officials. Harvey had nearly completed his training when the atomic bombs were dropped on Hiroshima and Nagasaki, bringing an abrupt end to the war. "Not many secrets you can hide from me, Kirk," Becker said.

Becker didn't feel threatened by Kirk's warnings. As a Marine, he had been recruited by the CIA to wreak havoc on the Afghani opium farmers who funded the Taliban. One fishing guide and his grandson weren't going to be a problem for him.

He put Harvey's file down and picked up another one. Two faces stared back at him, Kaitlin Rowe and Jada Howard. There was supposed to be a third. But he had interrupted Carlos' acquisition by splattering him into the Pacific.

Becker didn't buy the assumption that their disappearances weren't related. No bodies had been found, no trace evidence, no clothes, hair, and no signs of a struggle. The two girls disappeared, as if they never existed. If Carlos' boss was looking for a site, then that meant he was also looking for a crop of girls to keep there. These two girls fit the type he had seen on the DVDs: young, beautiful, and talented. Neither fit the profile of a runaway, nor did either seem the suicidal type.

Becker's iPhone dinged. Another Amber Alert. This time the girl's name was Amber. The face of sixteen-year-old Amber Lee appeared on his phone. She was last seen the night before in her hotel bedroom in Panama City, Florida, where her family was vacationing. When they awoke in the morning, she was gone.

Becker grabbed his bags and went back to the airport. He checked into his beachfront resort on Marco Island early that evening. Storm clouds the color of a dirty grill already stacked up offshore.

Chapter 7

Amber

Amber sat on her bed in the Holiday Inn in Panama City. Her computer rested on her lap. She waited in anticipation.

"He Li Na, you no talking to boys are you?" Her mom asked in her broken Chinese-English accent.

Amber hated that her family was traditional Chinese. Moreover, she hated her Chinese name. She picked the name Amber when she first started school. Her parents had come to the United States from a medium size industrial city in Northeast China called Jilin before Amber was born. They had fled the country in the early '80s illegally and then found asylum under the first Bush Administration after Tiananmen Square.

"No, Mom, I'm looking for fun stuff for us to do in Panama."

"Okay, honey. I love you. We talk about what we do tomorrow."

"Love you, too, Mom."

Amber did love her parents, but she didn't understand why they didn't want her growing up a typical American teenager. Her parents, after all, fled China for more freedom. Even if they still held on to traditional Chinese customs, Amber did not. She was a full-blooded American teenager who loved rap music and rock, crushed on boys, and loved American food.

Being sixteen and not having kissed a boy or even been on a date bothered her. She wanted something to whisper about to her girlfriends during lunch period and something to write about in notes to her friends. All of her friends had already had their first kiss; some had even gone further than a kiss. Amber didn't want to go that far, but she wouldn't be opposed to a good make out session, maybe even second base.

It wasn't that Amber wasn't beautiful. Her silky black hair and exotic black eyes had drawn the attention of many of her male classmates, but her parents wouldn't let her go on dates.

"You no need go on a date," her mother and father would say. "You need to stay home and help around the house. We'll find you a nice Chinese boy one day. You no worry about it. Mr. and Mrs. Chun have a nice boy. Maybe you marry him."

Amber didn't want to help around the house, and she sure as hell didn't want to marry Bobby Chun. He always picked his ears and looked at the wax on his pudgy little finger. When he hobbled down the street, he sucked the snot from his nose into his throat and spit it on the ground. She found Bobby foul. She'd walk straight from her house and ten blocks to the Brooklyn Bridge to jump off if her parents tried to make her marry him.

Nope, Amber liked white Americans—more specifically surfer boys. She liked looking at the pictures of the surfers in California and Florida, with their blonde hair, blue eyes, and sun kissed skin. This was one of the reasons she was excited about being in Florida. Moreover, she found that most American boys were attracted to Asian women. An "Asian fetish" she heard one of her friends giggle as she told Amber why so many boys liked her. Whatever you called it, the boys paid attention to her.

Earlier that day at the beach, she got an eyeful. She enjoyed watching the boys from her lounge chair, skimboarding the waves. She snuck glances underneath her sunglasses so her mother wouldn't scold her. Getting away from her parents was on the top of her list. Second was getting rid of the one-piece purple floral bathing suit her mother had bought her.

Before they left Brooklyn, Amber took some allowance and went out and bought a two-piece black bathing suit. Keeping her mother from checking her suitcase was like keeping the Mongolians out of China, she thought. But she was successful.

At one point, her mother stormed into her room. "I check to see if you have everything you need."

Amber jumped on the suitcase, quickly closing it up. "Mom! I've packed everything. I'm old enough to pack!"

"You no yell at me young lady. You're Chinese. You respect your parents," Amber's mother chastised her, waving her finger. Then she threw up her hands. "Fine, I no check. If you forget something, you go without."

Amber breathed a sigh of relief. Her parents would've canceled their trip or left her with relatives if her mother uncovered the suit under the hideous one-piece.

Amber liked the way she looked in the suit. Her body was toned from the rigorous workouts she did for swimming. She admired herself in the department store mirror when she tried it on. It made her long, sleek, powerful, legs and arms stand out. The beginnings of a great six-pack had begun to sprout on her stomach. Swimming was the one thing her parents let her do because she'd won a lot. This brought pride to the family, or as her father called it "face."

Amber jumped off her bed to dig the two-piece from the bottom of her suitcase. Then her computer dinged. Amber leapt back on her bed and sat Indian style staring at the computer screen. It was him.

- *amber, r u there?*

She typed back, her fingers shaking, trying to find the right keys.

- *yes!! ;) did you make it to panama city????*

Amber waited, her eyes desperately trying to make his reply appear quicker. She'd met Mike on a swim forum a month ago. They chatted and eventually became friends on Facebook. Amber would browse Mike's pictures and look at his sandy blonde hair, deep, crystal, cryptic, blue eyes, broad shoulders, and blinding smile. Being from Oklahoma, Mike might not be a surfer, but he looked like one.

They chatted through Instant Message sometimes until two in the morning, Amber typing as quietly as possible. She mentioned to Mike that her family was heading to Panama City for a week of summer vacation. A week later, Mike told her he had convinced his parents to go there at the same time.

Amber about launched through the ceiling when she heard this. She knew Mike would be her first kiss. That they would fall in love, get married, and live the American life. It was all too perfect. Plus, he swam for his school. This at least offered some common ground; it was after all what brought them together. So why not make it their first date too.

- *yep, we just arrived about an hour ago. i wish i could see you now.*

- *i know mike but the parentals will hear me go. we need to meet as we planned. i told my parents i was getting up early to do laps in the*

25

hotel pool to stay in shape. meet me down by the beach in front of my hotel.

- k, i will c u 7 in the morn then.

- k, bye

See her he would. She'd bought the two-piece for him.

Amber awoke early the next morning, threw on her bathing suit, and put on a pair of cut off shorts and shirt to cover it. A sense of freedom and rebellion rattled inside her as she quietly slipped out of the hotel room.

The sun had already begun to rise in the east as she hustled down to the beach. She looked at her watch, 6:45. She had a few minutes. Shuffling her feet in the warming sand, she tried to decide if she should strip down to her bathing suit or just take off her shirt and leave on her shorts. Or maybe she should just stay the way she was. But wanting to make an impression when he first saw her, she decided no shirt and keep the shorts on—sexy yet not slutty.

Amber waited. Mike never showed. She went through every scenario. Maybe his parents wouldn't let him go out. Maybe he saw her from afar and didn't think she was pretty enough. Maybe he overslept.

Tears muddled her cheeks. Hurt and anger made her feel like throwing up. She stripped off her shorts and lunged into the water. Swimming always made her mind go blank. Right now she didn't want to feel, so she focused on each stroke, moving her arms and legs faster and faster until it felt like she broke each wave into tiny particles of mist.

She didn't become aware of the yellow cigarette boat until it pulled up beside her and she hit the hull with her hand in mid-stroke. The rush of the water around her ears drowned out the sound of the engine. A giant calloused hand reached down as she looked up, her mouth gasping for air. She was grabbed by the hair and yanked into the boat. As she kicked her legs like a flopping fish, she shrieked, but The Jamaican cupped her mouth and pushed her down on the deck of the boat. Terror choked back her cries for help as she took in the sight of The Jamaican.

Karam stood over her, his hair mangled in wild black dreads. His ashen skin constricted over his beefy forearms, decorated in ridged scars. His beard swallowed up the sides of his face, bushing out on his cheeks. The bottom of his beard was twisted into tight bands, a rubber band

26

keeping each one from unraveling. His right eye, lifeless, filled with a white milky film, bore into Amber. The other eye, green and wild, didn't look at her as a human.

"Who—Who?" Amber stammered.

"Who am I?" The Jamaican mocked. "I'm Mike. We're going to have a nice swim." His yellow stained teeth split across the lower half of his face.

Amber's head pounded with the frantic beats of her heart, and she threw up. She would've passed out if the driver of the boat had not spoken.

"Well, well, what do we have here?" The Hippie approached Amber. "An Asian? Well, I have bit of an Asian fetish. What do you think, Karam? Shall we see what is under that little two-piece?" The Hippie's finger rubbed together as they crept for the bows tied on Amber's hips.

"Richard!" The Jamaican said angrily, as he pulled him back from Amber. "No touching the merchandise."

"Now, now, big guy. Take it easy. I just wanted a little peeky peek." Richard flicked his eyes from Karam to Amber.

Karam pushed Richard down into the driver's seat. "Start driving. Your stink makes me sick."

Karam pulled a needle from his pocket. Amber slid back toward the stern of the boat, her hands in front of her.

"This will hurt a little," Karam said grabbing Amber's ankles and pulling her back toward him.

Before Karam stuck her with the needle, she blacked out. He took her arm and injected her anyway. The cigarette boat sped off and headed to the boss' yacht ten miles offshore.

Chapter 8

Kaitlin

Kaitlin woke up to nothing but blackness. Her eyes were open, but the coarse cloth over them scratched her face. Specks of cloth slivered off every time she blinked, falling into her eyes and, causing them to be sucked dry. She reached up to remove the blindfold, but her hands were bound behind her back. The rope was tight on her wrists, cutting off her circulation. Her hands felt as though millions of needles were prickling into her palms. Sweat pooled on her upper lip, seeping onto the dryness of her lips, making her mouth feel glued together.

She vaguely became aware of the steady rhythmic splash of water and the sputter of a weak engine. Her mind raced to put together the pieces.

Tequila…
Fight with Sam
Walk on the beach….
OH GOD!!! PLEASE…NO!

She let out a whimper as the events of her night walk down the beach jumbled around the fog in her head. She'd tried to fight, but the hand, the arm, and the roughness of it on her mouth—it was too strong.

The engine cut off.

"She's waking up," she heard a man say in a Southern drawl.

"Don't matter," another Southern voice said. "We'll load her in the canoe, and you cover the mullet skiff with the branches and make sure it's secured good."

"Should we put her out again?"

"No, you up for carrying another one, Billy? We shouldn't have put the black girl back under. My back is killing me from carrying her. Now cut the canoe loose from the skiff and get in."

"You shut up now, girl," Kaitlin heard the man say to her, "and everything's going to be okay."

"Wa-a-ter," Kaitlin stammered through her crusted lips. "Please."

28

"Give her some, Billy. We wouldn't want Miss Little Princess dying of thirst on us now."

"Okay, Joe."

Kaitlin felt a bottle being pressed to her lips. Nearly choking on it, she gulped the water down. She could feel it flooding throughout her body.

"More, please, more," Kaitlin said, regaining moisture in her mouth. The bottle was inserted between her lips again, and Kaitlin sucked it dry. "Where—" Kaitlin managed to get out before she was cut off.

"Shut up!" the man shouted—she now recognized the voice as Joe. His voice split through Kaitlin's head. "Gag her, Billy. Blah, blah, blah. Just like every other damn woman."

Billy tied a cloth around her mouth.

"Lift her in the canoe," Joe ordered.

Kaitlin's tried to yank free when she was raised in the air, but she was clumsily flopped into the bottom of a canoe. Warm metal pressed against her ear. The water under the aluminum boat lapped against the side. The muggy air pressed on her body, soaking her clothes and quickly depleting the water she'd just gulped down. Wincing her eyes, she slowly came to the realization that what was happening to her was real, and she moaned into the gag and kicked her feet.

"Stop rocking the boat," Joe gave her a soft kick in the legs. "You tip us, and you ain't going to be able to swim."

Kaitlin's thoughts fogged. She wanted to let her mind go and slowly drift away with the remaining tranquilizer in her system. But the buzzing of mosquitoes by her ear, and then their silence when they landed on her lobe where they inserted their needle nose into her flesh, brought her back to reality. The itching, the buzzing—like an annoying alarm clock—played an off tempo symphony in her ear.

"Paddle in that small opening in between those mangroves, Billy."

"Kinda hard to see it in the dark."

"Just keep paddling straight. You're about as whiny as them women," Joe said.

Branches scraped against the sides of the boat like long fingernails going down a chalkboard as shells ground against the bottom of the hull. The paddles splashed and then made a crunching sound as the men jammed them deep into the shells to keep the canoe moving in the shallow water.

"Getting back here is a bitch in low tide," Joe said, losing his breath. "Hard left, Billy!" The canoe hit a sunken log, jolting the boat, causing the men to lurch forward.

"Damn it! Look where you're going," Joe fumed. "I about lost my damn paddle."

"I can't see a thing," Billy said. "The storm clouds are blocking out the moon. I thought that tropical storm was supposed to pass by us."

Thunder grumbled in the distance. A breeze kicked up mixing with Kaitlin's sweat, cooling her parched skin.

"And you believe a weather man? You are dumber than I thought," Joe laughed. "We better hurry and get set up. I have a feeling we may be in for some bad weather. Push off the log."

The men grunted as they tried to move the boat, but it wouldn't budge.

"We need to take some weight off the boat," Billy said, barely able to catch his breath to speak.

"You're going have to get out and pull us," Joe said.

"I ain't getting in..." Billy began to protest.

Kaitlin heard a gun cock. She bunched into as small a target as possible, petrified that a bullet would soon rip her flesh.

"Joe—now, come on, now," Billy said stuttering his plea. "We—we've been friends for a long time."

"I know, Billy," Joe calmly spoke. "That's why I'm doing this. That storm is coming. We have to get the girl secured and get our supplies safe. Because before morning this storms going to come and I ain't going to be in it. If we don't do our jobs now and make this girl safe, you're not going to have any money. And I'm not going to have no money so I can get my boat fixed and start fishing again. Now get out of the damn boat, tie a line to it, and pull us to the end of the channel."

The gunshot cracked the silence of the night. Kaitlin flinched, and she closed her eyes tight. She waited to feel pain bolt through her body. But it never came. Not until she heard Billy speak, did she realize the bullet was meant as a warning to him, not to kill her.

"Okay, okay. No problem, man, just put that .38 away." Billy couldn't hide the panic in his voice.

"Good, because the next one is going to go in your sweaty little skull." Joe put the gun back in the small of his back.

The canoe shifted as Billy moved to get out of the boat. He splashed into the water, barely keeping his balance. He jerked the boat forward resigned to his fate of being a drenched pack mule for the night.

"Not too much farther. Take the next right coming up. Be careful though. Gators like to hide and ambush in brackish water too!"

Despite her terror, Kaitlin's mind had begun to adapt to the situation. She'd heard of the flight or fight response. Until now, she thought it pertained to a physical altercation to escape bodily harm. She had never associated it with a mental process. Kaitlin could feel the fear numbing her body. She had been terrified of what these men might do to her. Every sense in her body felt she would be raped and then killed. But her brain had decided to fight. Even though her body trembled and her heart raced, her thought process would not flee from her. It could have very easily have blacked her out of her misery and spared her from the terror she felt. Her brain took notice of the noises and the conversation. It began to pick up outside stimuli. She did not know where she was, but she felt that she was still somewhere in the southern United States. There were gators and mangroves. Joe had mentioned brackish water, so she had to be near the ocean and fresh water. She knew when she was kidnapped that there were no storms in the Atlantic, but there was a tropical depression in the Gulf of Mexico that would be called Rachel if it made it to Tropical Storm status. She guessed she was somewhere in one of the states bordering the Gulf of Mexico.

Her deduction of her location and the information she was able to obtain couldn't help her, but it was proof enough that her observational prowess decided to stay with her and try to work toward survival. Her mind was working for her and not against her. It had already blocked the irritation from the dryness of her eyes and the numerous mosquito bites that welted her skin. If the right piece of information came along, her brain seemed more than willing to pick it out of a conversation and sort it out to her advantage.

The boat came to stop, and Billy panted for breath. "We're here. Whew! My heart is beating faster than a race horse."

"Pull the bow on shore a little, Billy," Joe commanded.

"What the—screw it, fine." Billy grunted, and the boat heaved forward one last time and came to rest.

"Good job! There might be hope for you yet." Joe slapped the side of the boat. "Let's get this little girl into the shack."

Kaitlin wished desperately that she could see her surroundings. But she feared looking at the faces of the two men who now controlled her. She smelled their stench and the decaying mud that Billy was covered in from his trek through the narrow channel.

"Come on, darling." Kaitlin felt Joe's grip vise around her arm. "Now, listen." He put his mouth close to her ear. Shuddering, Kaitlin cradled her ear to her shoulder. "Don't try escaping or I'll kill you. You understand? Shake your head if you do."

Kaitlin slowly shook her head.

Joe pulled her up. She became aware that her feet were bare as they rested against the bottom of the boat. "We're going for a little walk, darling. Give you a chance to stretch your legs. If you run, I'm going to shoot you in the back of the head, and your pretty little brains are going to be eat up by the raccoons and fiddler crabs. You understand?"

Kaitlin shook her head, hoping he would take his mouth away from her ear. His breath was polluted with wintergreen dip and alcohol. Joe caressed the back of her neck. Kaitlin whimpered.

"Don't cry, honey. I ain't going to hurt you if you do right," Joe said. He ran his hand through her hair and wrapped it around his finger. "I want to. You're the kind of girl who wouldn't give me the time of day. If I was to run into you on the street, you'd walk to the other side to avoid me—not even looking at me twice." Joe grabbed her hair and pulled her head back. "Well, darling, now I'm in control and you're going to do what I say." Joe kissed her cheek and yanked the gag out of her mouth. "I swear, if I could have you, I would take you right now." Joe pushed her head forward. "And keep your bitch mouth shut."

"What are you doing?" Billy asked.

"Nothing, boy. Letting her know who's boss," Joe chuckled.

"You said we can't hurt her."

"Shut your damn mouth. I'm tired of hearing you." Joe spit. "Now help me get her out of the boat and to the shack."

"I hate that ol' Hermit's shack. Gives me the damn willies," Billy said.

"Everything gives you the willies. I'm surprised you even got a willy with how scared you are all the time." Joe grabbed Kaitlin. "Come on, girl."

Kaitlin stood on the muddy bank as the men secured the canoe. She felt dirty. The dry salt water on her skin formed a thin layer of film covering her body. She knew the kidnappers must have let her dry off in her clothes after she was taken. This was a curse and a blessing. A curse in the fact that she felt grimy. Her clothes had dried on to her, using the residue salt as glue. But a blessing in the fact that the men had not stripped her naked and looked at her helpless and exposed. The thought of this happening made her feel even grimier. She decided she could deal with the dried salt. She did pray silently that it would begin to rain as she heard the thunder moving closer. Then she could stand there and let the rain fall on her, washing her. The idea of fresh water hitting her skin caused goose bumps to run along her body, and she actually felt the thin crust of salt crack on her skin.

"Bring her, Billy," Joe commanded.

"Come on, darling."

Billy snatched Kaitlin's arm and pushed her forward. Her feet had gotten sucked into the mud, and it took what little energy she had to break them free. She took a few steps and the mud gave way to a sandy shore. Joe's feet crunched the ground in front of her as he led the way. She wanted to ask where they were going. Where were they? What did they want? There were so many questions that raced through her head, but she wanted to keep her mouth free of the cloth, which tasted like it had been used to wipe up the guts of fish and bait.

"What the hell is that, Joe?"

"That's an ol' Calusa Indian shell mound. I guess they put those there to worship their gods or something." Joe paused and leaned in

33

close to Kaitlin's face. "Maybe they even used it to sacrifice virgins." Joe poked at her waist.

Kaitlin wanted to cry. She wanted to scream and to yell into the gusting wind. But all she could do was hang her head and whimper. "No, please let me go," she pleaded in labored gasps. "I won't tell anybody. I-I don't even know where I am."

"Darling, you're not going to be here forever. Few days at best. Some ol' rich man is going to have you and take care of you. At least till he gets tired of you. It doesn't matter if you know where you're at."

"What do you mean?" Kaitlin could barely get the words out.

"Shut up!" Joe grabbed her jaw and squeezed. "You want the cloth in your mouth again?" Joe chuckled, "You probably do. I put a little something special on it for you."

Kaitlin's stomach revolted against the thought. She realized what Joe had put on the cloth and vomited. Joe laughed and yanked her forward. "Let's go! Billy, do your job and push her along."

Billy took control of her again and shoved her forward. Kaitlin felt the cool sensation of damp vegetation under her feet.

"Watch out she doesn't brush up against any saw grass. The last thing we need is her slicing up her legs," she heard Joe shout from ahead.

Billy collapsed his sweaty palms on her tank top and pulled her closer. His hands stuck to her exposed shoulders. She felt repulsed by his chubby fingers touching her, his sweat mixing with hers. The stiffening in his pants pressed against her back. She whimpered at the thought of this man having any gratification from her at all. With all her strength, she pulled to separate her body from his, but she could not escape his grip.

"We're here."

"You sure that damn crazy Hermit ain't nowhere near here?" Kaitlin discerned the nervousness in Billy's voice.

"He ain't here," Joe shouted. Kaitlin heard a soft thud. Billy moaned. She had to fight to keep a small smile from forming on her face.

The blindfold around her eyes came off violently, jerking her head forward. Even in the low light, the night stung her eyes after being shrouded in complete darkness. When her eyes focused on the objects

34

around her, she saw an older, potbellied, yet muscular man standing before her.

"You won't be needing this anymore," Joe said, letting the blindfold fall to the ground. His bottom lip rounded out in the left corner from a wad of dip. His face was scorched red, splotched with pockmarks of white where the sun had bleached the pigment out of his skin from years of exposure. His teeth, discolored yellow and black from tobacco use, ripped a lurid smile across his face. He took off his soiled cap and rubbed his hand through his graying hair. Yellow stains streaked the pits of his torn, tobacco stained, white t-shirt. He moved closer to Kaitlin.

"Welcome home, darling." Joe let a black string of spit land on the ground in front of Kaitlin's feet. What spit didn't make it to the ground slipped to the corner of his mouth and disappeared into his black and white coarse beard.

Kaitlin shuddered at the sight of Joe and turned her eyes from him. A little shack stood in front of her, haphazardly made of different pieces of plywood and painted green, white, and brown. The roof was covered with tin and brown palm leaves. It stood no more than six feet high and looked the size of a small bedroom. The area around it was cleared of plant life except for stray weeds, struggling in the sand. A lightning bolt unzipped the sky illuminating the tops of tall coconut and palm trees rooted on the outskirts of the clearing.

A short stumpy man on the ground right behind Joe clutched his stomach, trying to get his breath. Billy struggled to his feet and wobbled for a moment as his legs adjusted to supporting his weight again. His black beard was full of sand. He patted the dirt off of his flannel shirt; the sleeves were rolled up over his elbows. Tucked into a pair of faded jeans buttoned below his belly, the shirt stretched over his stomach making him look like a weeble-wobble. Kaitlin thought he might topple over and be stranded on his back like a loggerhead turtle. Billy limped over to Joe.

"What did you do that for?" Billy huffed.

"Because I am tired of hearing about the damned Hermit," Joe said. "Next time I'm going to bust your damn nose."

"All right, no more talk about The Hermit." Billy turned his attention to Kaitlin. Scanning most of her body, he looked at her feet and then up to her breasts.

She felt his eyes wash over her, undressing her in his mind, thinking of other things. The wind suddenly shifted gears and begin to roar. Another bolt of lightning showed that the coconut trees were now bending in the wind as if a giant marlin had grabbed ahold and was pulling for its life. Rain barreled out of the sky.

Kaitlin lifted her head up and let the water rinse out her eyes. She opened her mouth to kill the saltiness left by the gag. The salt washed away from her body, and her clothes let loose the grip they had on her skin.

"Get her in the shack," Joe yelled over the wind.

The wind ripped across the island once more, slanting the rain, turning the drops into piercing needles on Kaitlin's exposed skin. She didn't care. The relief the rain brought to her more than compensated for the pain she felt from its sting.

Billy shoved her toward the shack. She sloshed through the sandy mud, trying to keep up with Billy's forceful push. They came to the door, which was nothing more than an old, cracked, and decaying piece of wood placed over the entrance. Joe lifted it and put it to the side, and she was pushed into utter darkness. Joe clicked on a flashlight. The beam illuminated a bed covered in dirty white sheets. A single rope ran under the bed frame. Kaitlin pushed back against Billy but could not move him. She started screaming "No! No!" But Billy's chubby hand covered her mouth and silenced her. Her mind raced in terror as she thought *No, not here! Not like this. Not these two men! Please, God!*

Joe threw her on the bed. He rolled her over on her stomach and took out his knife and cut the rope that bound her hands. Flipping Kaitlin on her back, he pinned her arms above her head with one hand. Kaitlin thrashed her legs trying to escape Joe's grip.

"Grab her legs, Billy!" A grin crept across Joe's face.

Billy wrestled her legs together and held them to the bed.

"Please—please, don't. Don't do this to me." Kaitlin searched for signs of compassion in the men's faces. Joe slithered his other hand down to Kaitlin's thigh. Kaitlin wished that she would blackout.

36

Joe leaned in on her. "If it didn't mean my life, I would." He jerked his hand from her thigh, pulled both her hands down, and tied each one to a side of the rope.

"What about her feet?"

"Don't worry about them. She ain't going nowhere. We gotta get our tent up. It's howling like a whore in church out there." Joe looked back at Kaitlin, her eyes still wild with terror. "We'll be coming to check on you through the night. Don't try anything, you hear me. Ain't nowhere for you to go anyhow, especially in a storm like this."

Joe placed the candle on a makeshift table made of pieces from a wooden pallet. A rusty old Coca-Cola chair was placed at the far end of the table. The red back cushion had faded long ago. A jagged rip in the middle spilled out yellowed foam like dried guts. On top of the table lay a picture of a man and woman with a child.

Joe fitted the door back over the opening. Kaitlin jerked her hands, causing the old metal bedsprings to creak. She stopped, afraid the noise would bring the men back. The rain pounded on the tin roof and palm leaves. The sound almost calmed her. A trail of water beaded its way down the slope of the ceiling and splashed back down in front of the door.

She looked to her right. At first Kaitlin stared as if an apparition had suddenly appeared in the shack with her. A young black woman rested on the other bed. Her hands were bound above her. The rope was attached to the rusted metal headboard. The girl's torso was covered with a sleeveless athletic shirt that had been soiled with red clay dirt. Her stomach rose up and down with shallow breaths. Kaitlin noticed that the girl's legs were powerful and strong like a thoroughbred that was born to run.

"Hey," Kaitlin whispered loudly. "Hey, wake up!"

It did cross Kaitlin's mind that it would be cruel to wake someone into this nightmare. Kaitlin rattled the bed again, trying to make as much noise as she could to wake the girl. She stopped, fearful that Joe and Billy would come back, until she realized her yelling was nothing compared to the storm rolling in outside. Besides, Kaitlin needed the girl to wake up. Her mind had already worked out their escape, and she needed the girl's help.

Chapter 9

Becker

The morning exploded into a flash of light. Becker's eyes shot open. Becker jumped out of bed and grabbed the phone and dialed Captain Harvey's number. Clutching the phone, he impatiently paced the floor of his hotel room. When he arrived the previous evening, Becker had ignored the flashes of light scattered in the horizon. They seemed too far offshore to matter. Exhausted from his trip to California and then to Marco via Atlanta, he hit the bed, and his body forced him to sleep.

"Captain, we've got to go out today," Becker said.

"You're not gonna see anything out there today. Too dangerous to go out anyway," Harvey said, yawning.

"Then I'll find somebody else."

"You can try. But I don't know anybody that stupid. This should blow over day after tomorrow. I can take you then."

"Captain, I've got to go now. Get your shit together and…"

"Let me explain something to you," Harvey interrupted. "You talk to me like that again, and I'll black ball you with every captain around here. You won't find anybody within a 100 mile radius that will let you step foot on their boat. Now, I can take you day after tomorrow. If you are still interested, meet me at the dock at eight in the morning."

The other end of the line went dead, cut off either from the storm or Harvey's anger. Becker wasn't sure which.

Becker slammed the phone down and grabbed the phone book and flung it across the room.

He walked over to the sliding glass door that led to the deck overlooking the Gulf of Mexico. Thick dark clouds swirled large droplets of rain, making the world one giant waterfall. Tropical Storm Rachel sent ten foot swells in to swallow the normally placid beach. Becker hoped that Captain Harvey was wrong about the storm. He knew the difference a couple days could make in people's lives. Becker's sister, Alexis, disappeared when he was seventeen-years-old. How Becker found her was much worse than the disappearance.

38

* * *

While attending the University of South California, Alexis Becker disappeared at a bonfire party on the beach. Her friends said that she'd decided to go for a swim. The Coast Guard and local authorities never found her body. The assumption was that one of the Great Whites in the area found her—alive or dead—before anyone else could. Becker struggled with her death and enlisted in the Marines after 9/11. For five years he blazed a trail of ruthlessness in the Afghani desert against the insurgents. His flair for destruction caught the eye of CIA Agent Kirk Dupree. Kirk recruited Becker into the CIA to destroy Afghani drug lords' opium farms that supported the Taliban. He was also tasked with collecting intelligence and delivering the drug lord alive for questioning.

Within three years Becker had become the CIA's most dependable operative. He held that honor until the night he brought down his last drug lord.

After killing the guards, Becker slinked into the drug lord's room as he slept. He tranquilized him, assuring the man wouldn't awake until he had him bound for transport. He had done this a dozen times by now. Each mission was the same, kill the guards and bring in the drug lords for interrogation. They usually had the best Intel. Becker scoured the room for intelligence. He shoved flash drives, CDs, and even old floppy disks into a rucksack. In his final sweep of the room, Becker found a black case under the drug lord's bed and popped it open. A DVD collection with women's names scribbled on them lay side by side in alphabetical order: Aimee, Alexis, Dallas, Kara, and Sasha - twenty in all. The name Alexis stood out to him. The only connection he felt was that the DVD had the same name as his sister. He slipped the DVD into the player; the picture scattered across the screen, wavy lines jumbled and contorted with voices and static. Then the lines popped into an image—an image of his sister's face, tears streaking the black mascara thickly drawn around her eyes, rivers of black dripping off her cheeks. Her hands bound together underneath her half-naked body, she rested on her knees.

"What's your name?" The man spoke from behind the camera.

Alexis sobbed and struggled to break the manacles on her wrists.

"What's your name? You'll tell me," the voice said again in an Afghani accent.

"Alex-Alex-Alexis."

The drug lord walked around from behind the camera and appeared in the shot behind her.

"I paid a lot of money for you, Alexis. American girls always cost more money, especially since the beginning of the war." He stroked the brunette hair matted against the wetness of her face and let it spill onto her shoulder. "You'll make me a happy man."

Alexis cried out. Becker could watch no more.

When the drug lord awoke, Becker knelt over him. The knife in Becker's hands trembled under the drug lord's throat. "Where is Alexis?"

"Who are you?" The drug lord said.

"CIA. Where's the girl?" Becker seethed the words in the drug lord's face. The blade cut a thin layer of flesh off the Afghani's throat. A torrent of red cascaded down to his chest.

"Stop—okay—okay. Don't cut anymore," he grimaced. "I know this girl, Alexis," he said in panting breaths. "Why is the CIA interested in one girl?"

"Tell me!" Becker's punch bent the man's nose to the side of his face. A deep crimson concoction of mucus and blood sputtered out. Trying to defend himself, the drug lord threw up his arms as a shield. "Okay," he said choking on the mixture in his mouth. "I'll take you."

Becker pulled the drug lord up and yanked him outside. The sun had already risen and had begun cooking the air. "Where is she?" Becker slugged him in the stomach.

The drug lord doubled over, gasping for air, "Outside the compound."

Becker shoved him to the edge of the camp, desperately looking for a tent he may have missed. "Where!" He brought the butt of his gun on top of the Afghani's back.

Weakly lifting his hand, the drug lord pointed to a mound in the distance. "Over there."

* * *

Alexis lay in a shallow grave. Decomposition had already begun. Her eyes sunk in and blood stained her forehead from a bullet wound. She had not been dead long. Becker cradled his sister's body and wept. All the anger, hurt, and unknowing he had held inside himself since she disappeared spilled on the dry desert sand. When he came to, he carefully wrapped his sister's body in a blanket and closed her eyes before he covered her face.

"Why!" Becker punched the drug lord, relocating the man's broken nose to the other side of his face. "How did she get here?" Becker kneed him in the stomach.

"I-I bought her."

Becker's struggled for understanding. "Bought her? Who did you buy her from?" Becker wrapped his hands around the man's throat.

"A British fellow and his son. I have files on them. I bought her from them in Cuba."

"How much?" Becker said quietly.

"How much what?"

"How much," Becker said louder, squeezing the trembling throat under his hands. "How much was Alexis' life worth?"

The drug lord's face turned purple as he forced out his words. "$300,000."

"Where are the rest of the girls on the DVDs?" Becker eased his grip on the man's throat, letting him suck in air.

"Dead. Alexis was the last."

"How long has she been dead?" Becker whispered not really wanting to know the answer.

"I had her disposed of her a few days ago." A smirk spread across the drug lord's face. "I tired of her."

"Disposed? Tired?" Becker hauled the man up to his feet. "When are you getting another girl?"

"Six months. I go in six months to Cuba. Why do you care for this girl?"

Becker studied the drug lord's face. Becker had already decided what was going to do to this man before he even realized it. "She's my sister." Becker brought his knee into the drug lord's groin before he could express his shock. "I'm going to make this painful for you."

41

"Not as painful as I made it for your sister. She…" The drug lord's words were cut off by his torment. Becker plunged the knife into the man's groin and castrated him, sending shrieks a banshee would flee from through the desert canyons.

The CIA wanted to hang Becker for killing the drug lord. But Kirk ran interference and took part of the blame himself. Becker was removed from the field. It didn't matter to Becker; he was leaving the CIA anyway. Finding the information he needed in a flash drive he collected from the drug lord, he started planning his retribution. He found Carlos in California six months later.

Chapter 10

McKlusky and Chloe

I flipped over in bed, feeling the house shudder with the thunder. Grandpa was right. Tropical Storm Rachel decided she would blast her fury along Florida's southwest coast. Phones lines were out and the electricity would soon follow. I rooted for my cell phone which was buried somewhere underneath the heap of socks and clothes by my bed. I called Chloe.

Chloe and I grew up across the street from each other before I moved to New Jersey. Shortly after I moved, her family moved to a large house on a canal. They had everything they needed until Chloe's dad died four years ago of sudden cardiac death. Chloe's mother found him face down halfway through signing a check.

The life insurance policy and selling of the restaurant secured Chloe and her mom's financial future. However, Chloe and her mom no longer had everything they needed.

When her dad died, I was down for the summer and I spent it hanging around with her and trying to keep her occupied. I even got Grandpa to let her go fishing when there weren't too many people on the boat. Chloe and I had a lot in common growing up together. She was just a year younger than me. Thinking of the great times we always had, I felt bad for not getting in touch with her sooner, but fishing is fishing.

"Hello?" Chloe said.

"Chloe, what's going on?" I said sleepily.

"You're an asshole, McKlusky. You've been on Marco for three days, and you haven't called me."

"Nice to talk to you too, Chloe," I said stunned by the tone in her voice. "I've been offshore permit fishing. Having to help Grandpa with the Yankees."

"Aren't you a Yankee now, too? You do live in New Jersey."

"Damn, Chloe. Low blow." I grimaced hating to even jokingly be called a Yankee. I was beginning to wonder if calling her was a good idea. She had never been this temperamental with me. I'd gone two weeks without calling her last summer when I first came to the island. It was no big deal then. "How did you know I was here anyway?"

"Your Facebook, stupid. You updated it before you left New Jersey. If you would bother to check it, you would see that I sent you a message, wanting to get together."

"Well, then, let's get together. We can go see a movie or something if the electricity is still on there." I waited for a response, but the other end was silent. "Listen, Chloe, I'm sorry I didn't call," I said rolling my eyes. "I just got here and have been fishing. You know I want to hang out." I tried to force an apologetic tone in my voice.

"Well, the good news is since the last time you've been here, the movie theater has installed a generator. They got tired of the summer storms knocking out the movies." Her voice suddenly changed to the Chloe I knew.

"Great, I'll get a ride to your house. See you soon." I shook my head confused by her unexpected assault for waiting to call her.

* * *

After I promised to completely clean the Flounder from top to bottom, Grandpa weathered the storm and drove me to Chloe's house. I raced to the door, leaping over rapidly growing rivers of water and knocked on the door.

Chloe stood in the doorway with her midnight hair pulled back in a ponytail. Just the right amount of Florida sun had tanned her half-Irish, half-Seminole complexion. Her cut-off shorts rounded over perfect legs. A white, spaghetti-strapped shirt fit her closely, tapering at her waist and sinking onto her curved hips. Slender, lightly muscular shoulders supported an elongated neck, and I caught the sparkle in her eyes as she watched me take her in. She blushed and gave me a smile. I suddenly regretted not calling her sooner. She was a far cry from the gawky, beanpole, brace-faced girl I'd left last summer. I tried to suppress the surprise on my face, but it might not have worked.

"I see you got your braces off," I said weakly.

"I know, right! I was so happy. Well, give me a hug, stupid. I missed you."

I'd hugged her a thousand times over the years, but this was different. I felt the changes she'd went through over the year pressing against my chest. I liked it and had to control my body. I didn't want something of mine pressing against her. I thought of cold winter days in New Jersey and the beginnings of frostbite on my face as I walked to the bus stop. These images were quickly destroyed by the scent of coconut oil and the fragrance of a palm breeze embedded in her skin. I wrapped my arms around her waist and hugged back. Feeling drunk, dizzy, I wanted to sink into her and stay.

Stop it! I thought. With any other girl, I'd let the lascivious thoughts begin. But Chloe? It wasn't right. She unwrapped her arms from around me, and I wanted to pull her back, breathe her in again. I abstained and gained control of my senses.

"You're putting on some muscle, I see," she said, playfully squeezing my bicep. I involuntarily flexed my arm and she giggled.

"You look great too. How have you been?" I fought to keep my eyes on her face.

"Great! Come say hi to Mom. She's dying to see you." Chloe led me into the living room. Her back looked as great as her front.

Their house always impressed me. The spotless white marble tile shone. Strong white pillars separated the living room from the kitchen. A large sliding glass door led to an oversized in-ground pool surrounded by a pebbled patio with a view of a canal that led to Smokehouse Bay. Their boat dock could fit an eighty-foot yacht with room to spare, but it remained empty.

Chloe's mother, Susan O'Malley, sat in the den reading *The Old Man and the Sea.* "McKlusky! It is good to see you," she said putting down the book as she stood to hug me.

"*The Old Man and The Sea,*" I said. "I read it this past year. I actually loved it."

"I've read this book a hundred times. Anytime there is a storm like this, I like to pick it up. It makes me feel as if I'm in the boat with Santiago battling the great Marlin."

At thirty-four-years-old, Mrs. O'Malley projected a beauty and grace that caused heads to turn. But the shadows of pain and loss still played in her eyes over her husband's death.

"Chloe, have you offered McKlusky something to drink?"

"No, Mom. Come on, it's McKlusky."

"Family friend or not, he is still your guest. Remember your manners."

"Yes, Mother," Chloe said endearingly. "McKlusky, what would you like?" A smirk appeared across her face.

"A Coke with ice would be great," I said. "Of course, it would be nice if the ice was crushed, too."

With her mother's back to her, Chloe mouthed, "I'm going to kick your ass." I smiled. What we were doing could be considered flirting. Even though seeing Chloe as sexy was very new, I liked the light banter we were having. She was no longer the little skinny kid who I use to pal around with and build sand castles with at the beach. *The beach with Chloe!* The first thing I needed to do was buy dark, dark sunglasses.

"So how are your grandparents?" Mrs. O'Malley asked. "I've seen them in the restaurant a few times."

"They're good." I paused. "I'm sorry, Mrs. O'Malley; I thought you sold the restaurant."

"Oh, we did, but I like to go there and eat sometimes. It reminds me so much of Charles." A pained smile grew on her face. "Anyway, what are you kids up to today?"

Chloe plopped down beside me and handed me the Coke. Her nearness made me feel warm. I fought to keep from grabbing her hand. I was dazzled at how naturally I wanted to do it, and how natural it would be to have her hand in mine.

"I think we're going to the movies, Momma."

Lightning flashed and the lights went out; thunder rattled the crystal chandelier.

"Well, I don't think I'm going to take you to the movies in this storm. However, McKlusky, if you will accompany me to the garage and help me start the generator you two are more than welcome to use the den to watch some movies." She stood up from her chair and reached for my hand to come with her.

"No problem. Do you have a flash light?" I asked.

"In the drawer by the refrigerator. Chloe, why don't you get some snacks together for you two?"

46

"Sure," Chloe said. She shot me a look that said I would pay for all this waitressing.

Chloe never played the girl role, no matter how much her mother wanted her to. Chloe always had the, *I'm tougher than a girl attitude.* She had no problem proving it, either.

When I was five, three neighborhood bullies a couple years older than me felt it would be a good idea to kick my ass. Two held me down on the road, and one hammered me in the stomach. Though it was the first time, it was not the last time, I thought I might die.

Chloe heard me screaming and looked out her bedroom window. Being the tough little girl she was, she didn't panic and cry, nor did she come out of the house screaming at the top of her lungs for them to stop. She quickly stomped out of the house, grabbed a stick from the yard, and walked up to the boy punching me. Like a mule, she kicked him in the stomach, doubling him over. The other two boys, shocked at what this little girl had done to their much bigger friend, rushed to grab her. In an instant she placed the stick squarely across one boy's face. Blood spurted from the boy's nose, splattering my shirt.

Confused by his sudden loss of authority, the last boy froze. Standing before him was a mix of proud Seminole warrior and fighting Irish spirit. A lethal combination he hesitated to confront as he ingested the screams of his friends. Her father being a big Clint Eastwood fan, Chloe's natural reaction was to look at the boy menacingly and say, "Make my day."

By this time, I'd recovered somewhat from my beating and punched him in the nuts. As he bent over, Chloe came with an overhead swing across the boy's back. The sound was sickening.

Chloe shouldered the stick and said, "You gonna cry all day, McKlusky, or you wanna go play with your Transformers?" She smiled wide and helped me off the ground.

"Okay, but I'm Megatron," I sniffed. "By the way, thanks, Chloe."

She put her arm around me. "Okay, but I'm Optimus Prime, and you're welcome."

Since then, the name Chloe and McKlusky had been tangled together on people's tongues. You saw one and the other was close by, until I had to move to New Jersey.

* * *

With the generator cranking, Chloe and I sat in the den. The drinks and food she prepared for our movie marathon littered the coffee table. Her bare feet rested on the corner of the table—knees slightly bent up, her hands lying on her lap. Between the curvaceous outline of her thighs and the movie reflecting off her eyes, I didn't notice when she shifted her attention from the movie to me.

"What are you looking at?" she asked, flirting a smile.

"Nothing," I said. Realizing I gotten busted in a dead stare, I laid my head back on the couch.

She playfully punched me in the arm. "So, I'm nothing to you now. Is that why it took you so long to call me?"

"Chloe, I didn't mean anything by it." My voice sounded weak in my head.

Chloe leaned her head back, laying it into the cushion. Her gaze turned toward me. The slight whisper of a frown played on her face. "I'm glad you called. I missed you," she hesitated, "a lot."

"I missed you too, Chloe." I reached out to grab her arm, planning to give it a quick friendly squeeze. But my hand touched her skin—feverish from the slight burn of the sun—and slowly traveled down the length of her arm to her hand. She wove her fingers into mine and gave a wicked little grin. A sizzling rush shot through my hand up my arm, punching my heart, and jamming a lump into my throat.

She bit her lower lip and looked down at our hands and back to me. I pulled her hand closer, put my other hand behind her neck, and gently brought her to me. I felt at any time I was going to feel her elbow crack me upside the head, as she demanded to know what the hell I was doing. But she didn't resist. Our mouths touched, and our breath and lips joined. Her hand tightened around mine, and she caressed my shoulder with her other. We separated for a moment to look at each other, smile, and kiss again.

48

All the conflict I felt about seeing Chloe in her new body vanished. It seemed right, now. And I couldn't believe that I'd ever seen her as a skinny little kid only to be cherished as a friend and nothing more. We kissed, and kissed again. She allowed my hands to discover the twists and turns of her waist—the ridges of her ribs under her skin. But she gently guided them back in place if I tried to explore too much of her.

After ten minutes of breathless kissing, the door opened and Chloe's mother walked in. We both quickly jumped apart with faces red. "McKlusky, it seems the roads are flooded. Your grandpa can't get here. You can stay in the guest room." She deadlocked her stare at both of us. Chloe stiffened and sat back on the couch, her eyes focused on the TV.

"Thanks, but I don't want to be an inconvenience." I wondered just how much she'd seen. Then she answered without me asking.

"It's no inconvenience as long as you BOTH go to bed in separate rooms."

"Mom!" Chloe shrieked. Her face looked as though it had been splotched with red paint.

"Sorry, honey, but when you're kissing like that, I'm well aware of the temptations.

"Mom! Stop it, please."

"McKlusky?" Mrs. O'Malley's eyes were piercing.

"Separate beds it is," I said as I shrunk into the cushions.

"Good. Goodnight, then." She left the den with a sly smile.

"I'm sorry, McKlusky. I'm so embarrassed," Chloe said, covering her face. "I can't believe she just did that."

What was the protocol for something like this? Before the kiss, I'd have told her no big deal, but it was new now. I roamed through different territory with Chloe. So I did what I thought a boyfriend would do. I grabbed her hand, squeezed it and said it was not a big deal. The answer still seemed to work.

Chloe smiled and laid her head on my chest. My fingers caressed her arm. Goosebumps budded up behind my touch. She soon fell asleep.

I woke Chloe a little after midnight. We both went to bed in our separate rooms. I'm pretty sure that if I'd tried to change that arrangement, Chloe would've cracked her elbow across my head. It might have been worth it though.

Chapter 11

Marcus

The yacht crushed the waves Tropical Storm Rachel spit its way. It raised its bow on the crest of one wave, its bulk splitting the next in half, turning the water into a foaming bubbly white mess down its hull. The stern rose out of the water, revealing the name, Albatross, out of London, England, and disappeared with the next wave. The radar on top of the beam turned with urgency, scanning the horizon for any approaching ships and detecting the most intense areas of the storm.

The Union Jack flag strained to stay attached to its mast in the sheering wind. It whipped from side to side, making loud pops as if a gun were being rapidly fired on deck.

"Sir," the aging captain behind the helm said, "we should move closer to shore to ride out the storm."

Marcus Langer scanned the helm. Waves reached out like hands on the bow trying to grapple the ship to the bottom of the Gulf of Mexico.

"I want to stay in international waters," Langer said, exhaling the smoke from his cigar.

"Yes, sir." The captain's voice was weary.

"How far?" Marcus asked.

"We're 300 nautical miles from Marco Island, sir."

"Do you think you could bloody tell me that in layman's terms?" Marcus' British accent reached an ear popping pitch.

"That would be 345 miles, sir." Dread crept through the captain. He knew when he was sitting on the docks that he shouldn't have taken this job. But he needed to compensate his loss of income after being laid off from his ferry boat position on the Mississippi River. A man with Marcus' kind of yacht wouldn't go looking for captains on a Louisiana Bayou, among the shrimpers and crabbers, unless, he was doing something illegal. The Albatross, however, had called to the captain. The yacht was snuggled up to the dock when the captain first saw her. The Albatross shimmered with her baby blue paint, colossal in size. Each of its three stories had its own walk-around deck. The fine lines of steel and wood meshed together to build a ship that could slice the heart of Poseidon himself. Even though the ship could handle the storm they were in, the captain didn't want to hurt her. He wanted to run her like a fine classic car over a newly paved backcountry road, far away from the traffic and the road debris that could scratch her paint and ding her metal.

On the day he was hired, the captain piloted the yacht right out of the Mississippi to the Florida Panhandle and anchored ten miles off Panama City. Langer ordered him to wait there until a cigarette boat approached and Karam and Richard boarded the yacht.

The captain figured Langer smuggled drugs, which suited him just fine because he needed the money. Drugs are the type of things people choose to do. So why should he care if Langer brought it aboard the ship?

Karam came up the stairs and stood by Langer. The captain turned back around to face the storm. He didn't like the looks of The Jamaican. He believed his dead eye was cursed by the devil himself.

"Father, the girl should wake soon," Karam whispered.

"Good. Let's make sure she's comfortable."

Marcus and Karam walked down the stairs to the living room. The floor, showcased with light brown stained marble, reflected the overhead lights. The walls were covered with hand crafted teak wood that complimented the custom oak furniture cushioned in tan leather. Large stretches of windows, tinted to block out the rays of the sun, surrounded the room.

"Where is the girl?" Langer asked.

"In her room," Karam said. "Richard offered to watch her."

Langer crunched up his brow and shook his head. He walked over to the bar, picked up one of the glasses secured in its holder and poured a drink. "That is like leaving the fox locked up with the hens, Karam." Taking a sip of his whiskey, Langer allowed it to drizzle its burning warmth down his throat and into his stomach, he chased it down with a long stoke of his cigar.

"He was harder to control this time," Karam said.

"One of the risks of hiring a serial killer *slash* rapist, I suppose," Marcus said. "Anyhow, we're going to have to let him have some fun soon. I'm sure we can work something out after we've made it to Marco."

"What about a spa girl? They're not as valuable to us," Karam asked.

"No, it won't be enough for him. For him it's more than the act of sex; it's about the hunt. Richard is like a beast driven by hunger. For the past two years, we've asked him to hunt and not kill. We need to let the animal loose for a while, or he will be no good to us anymore."

Karam knew Richard was getting out of control. He saw it on the mountaintop and kept a watchful eye on him while they were transporting Jada and Kaitlin to Joe on Marco. Then, when he and Richard captured Amber in Panama, he could see The Hippie was rabid for her.

"Let's go see about our girl." Langer drank down the rest of his whiskey.

* * *

Amber woke to a gentle light invading her eyes. She enjoyed the warm comfort of the sheets lying gently on her skin. Snuggling her head into the pillow, she heard the ocean roaring. It would be a great day for the surfer boys to be out. Thinking of Panama City, the sun on her skin, and sneaking peeks at the boys when her parents weren't looking woke her. She tried to curl her legs up to her stomach. Her legs only moved a few inches. She tried again, but the rope constricted around her ankles. Wide awake, she jerked her hands, but they would move down just far enough for her to see a rope knotted around her wrists connected to the wall. She yanked her legs harder. Her knees raised just enough to fling the covers to the side of the bed. Looking down she saw she had her two-piece bathing suit on, and the memories of her kidnapping pierced her mind. She burst into tears.

In a manic attempt to escape her bonds, she yanked at both of her restraints. The ropes rubbed against her ankles and wrist, making them chafe raw. Sweat, forming on her body, stung the exposed pinkish skin. She bubbled a cry. She had just wanted to meet a boy.

"Nooo... Nooo..." The plea slid out of her mouth as she caught the scent of the musk—the smell—the man with the wiry beard who just wanted to take a peek. She grabbed at the sheets with her feet to cover herself back up.

"Chicky...chicky..." came the quiet whisper from the corner of the room. Amber saw The Hippie. His eyes betrayed him, confessing the mischief in his mind. He moved out of the shadows toward her, his matted hair pulled back in a ponytail. "Why do you struggle so? You are tearing your beautiful skin."

Amber scooted to the other side of the bed, but her restraints would only let her move a few inches.

"Stay away from me," she yelled. She thought she might vomit, but nothing was in her stomach. She began hyperventilating from spasms and dry heaves.

"Darling. There's no need to work yourself up. I hate to see a pretty thing like you so out of sorts." He unconsciously reached for his knife. A flush of rage streaked across his face when he didn't find the handle there. Richard stalked closer to the bed. Every step planned, giving him the movements of a well-trained hunter, each step quieter than the next.

"What do you want?" Amber said, almost resigned to her fate of what this man really wanted. She wanted to fight, but how could she? Bound up and tied to the bed, there was little she could do. The smell of him made her want to retch. She wished that she'd vomit all over herself. Maybe that would make him leave her alone. However, no matter how hard she tried, nothing came out.

"Chicky, chicky, you know what I want." Richard sat on the bed admiring her glistening and shivering body. He stroked her black hair and curled a strand in his fingers. Amber flinched and turned her head away from him. Her stomach quivered uncontrollably, as if electric shocks were being sent through her abdominal muscles.

Richard cracked a smile, splitting his beard open. He felt himself becoming aroused. Not a physical arousal that a man feels, but an arousal that cherished the fear and suffering Amber was going through. Richard liked Amber. She reminded him of his first, a young Asian girl in San Francisco who he'd left bleeding and asphyxiated in her bed.

Richard caressed Amber's cheek, wiping her tears. The dirt on his hand smudged her face. Her lips trembled as his fingers continued down her neck, tracing the outline of her breasts, and down her stomach.

"Please, God, no! Please, God, no! No!" she screamed.

No was a word The Hippie listened to. It's a word that played a symphony in his head. With each repetition, it banged like a drum harder and harder until all else became drowned out, except for the delicate one syllable word: *NO.* He thrived on it.

One of Richard's fingers hooked under the string of her bikini bottom, stopped, and tugged at the bow. He smiled unevenly, looking her over like a butcher sizes up a piece of meat—where to cut, where to trim. Leaving the bow intact, he unhooked his finger and slid it down to her leg, relishing the touch of her soft skin. His finger stopped at her feet. "We're going to play a little game."

Amber thrashed her legs trying to kick him. The Hippie grabbed both of her ankles. The pressure from the rope forced itself into Amber's raw skin, making her cry in pain.

"Richard!" The door burst open. Karam snatched Richard by the throat and pinned him against the wall.

"I'm just having a bit of fun," Richard said. A smirk ripped his face. "I was just going to play little piggy went to market with her toes. Toes are such a nice part of the body, don't you think?"

Karam's green eye ignited a jade flame.

"Let him go," Langer said softly.

Karam reluctantly released Richard. "If you touch her again, I'll kill you."

"It's just a bit of fun." Richard's eyes darted to Amber.

"Richard, go relax a while. I'll be there shortly to talk to you," Langer said calmly, motioning his arm for Richard to leave.

Richard wiped the sweat from his face. "Bye, Bye, Amber. Nice to meet you."

"Why don't you get a shower? I'm tired of smelling that shitty patchouli you slather yourself with," Karam said. He pushed Richard the rest of the way out of the room.

Amber recognized The Jamaican from the boat, but not the older man who stood at the end of the bed. If this were any other place or time, she would mistake him for a loving grandfather.

"I'm sorry for Richard. He's a bit strange," Langer said. "Cut her loose Karam."

Karam pulled out a knife sheathed to his side and cut her wrists free. He did the same to her ankles.

Amber grabbed the sheet and scurried against the headboard. She covered herself, hugging the edge tightly under her chin.

"Please, don't rape me, please," Amber sobbed.

"I cannot speak for Karam. But I can assure you, you're not my type. You'll not be raped on this ship."

"I just want to go home! Please, just take me home!"

"You won't be going home." Langer eyes sketched Amber's body. "My son did well picking you out. You're young; you're beautiful; you'll bring top dollar."

Amber scrunched her face, confused. "What do you mean?"

"We're going to sell you to the highest bidder. To put it quite bluntly, you're going to be a sex slave," Marcus said indifferently.

Rage momentarily replaced Amber's fear. She sprang from her fetal position to attack Langer. Marcus jumped to his feet and punched Amber in the chest, slamming her onto the bed, leaving her sucking for air.

Langer patted her leg as a father would try to comfort a child. "You can deny what is happening to you or embrace it. Most of these men will provide you with a lavish lifestyle, albeit a secluded and short one."

Amber rolled over onto her side and curled up in a ball, hugging herself. Her breath heaved in and out in desperate gasps as she tried to recover from Marcus' blow.

"Karam, make sure you bandage her wrists and ankles," Langer said.

Tears mixed with fear and anger crisscrossed Amber's cheeks. Marcus could feel the increasing heat of hate in Amber's belly toward him. He respected her for attacking him. She was not afraid to conquer her fear, to give herself a chance to survive. Unlike the captain piloting the ship towering under the fierce waves of the storm, Amber would swim through the waves if it meant survival waited on the other side.

"On second thought, Karam, just leave the bandages in here with her. She can take care of herself. Bring her some food, too."

"Should I tie her up again?"

"No, padlock the door from the outside. She's free to move about the room. We'll see you soon, Amber."

The door closed, and Amber was left alone. The smell of stale cigar smoke and patchouli hung in the air. Amber lay on the bed as the boat slung up and down. Her eyes, red and puffy, would begin to close and then would shoot back open. Fresh tears filled her eyes, and she thought of her mother and father. Where were they? How long had she been gone? How she wished she'd listened to her mother about not talking to boys online.

Chapter 12

Jada and Kaitlin

The sound of the wind hammered against the plywood walls.

A heavy boom of thunder rattled the shack's tin roof like a snare drum. Jada popped up only to be catapulted back onto the mattress by the ropes wrapped around her wrist. "Help me!" Jada cried.

"You're awake."

The voice shocked Jada. A girl lay on the other bed. The rope strung under her bed frame secured her hands to her sides. The candlelight flickered with the small puffs of wind working their way through the walls, throwing a dull shadow on the girl's weak smile.

Jada's eyes darted back and forth, joining the fragmented memories of her kidnapping. "I-I was running," Jada stammered, looking at the girl. "I was running when I stopped to give some hippie directions —maybe a helicopter? Who are you? Why am I tied up?" Jada pulled her wrists down, trying to break the rope that was secured to the headboard. The bed creaked and the headboard remained pinned against the wall.

"My name is Kaitlin," she said in a quiet voice.

"I'm Jada."

"I was afraid you'd never wake up." Kaitlin smiled. She tried to speak calmly even though her heart hammered against her chest. She needed to keep Jada calm if her plan of escape was to work. In the several hours since she'd been tied up to the bed, Kaitlin had noticed that Joe and Billy would come around about every hour. Kaitlin began counting after the second time Joe walked in. She counted seconds and minutes, and then hours. Even now as she talked to Jada, her head rhythmically counted off the seconds and the minutes as if it had become as natural as breathing.

"My head," Jada said with a moan.

"They drugged us with a tranquilizer. A powerful one, from the feeling of it." Kaitlin looked toward the door. It wouldn't be long before Joe or Billy came back. It'd been Joe last time, and Kaitlin hoped Billy was next. Every time Joe came in, he'd look at her and spit on the floor.

Then he'd smile, his teeth spackled with tiny flakes of black tobacco—and undress her with his eyes and rub the growing bulge in his pants. Kaitlin felt powerless as Joe took her again and again in his head. There was nothing she could do to control his mind, so she focused on the things she could control, like escape. When Kaitlin first saw Jada, she realized escape rested with the girl next to her.

"Jada, you weren't awake when you came to the island? Were you?" Kaitlin whispered. Kaitlin knew she wasn't. She had heard Joe and Billy talk about carrying her in. But she had to be sure. Kaitlin had hoped that Jada was awake when she was brought here. Maybe Jada had been playing possum. Jada might have noticed something that she didn't, making it easier for them to escape. But apparently Jada had been running one minute and awakened in this humid hell the next.

"Island? What Island? We're on an island!" Jada yelled. "Where are we? I—I was on a mountain running when—when…" She hesitated, "I don't know what happened." Her eyes flooded.

Kaitlin wanted to comfort Jada, but she needed to get Jada to focus and listen. Joe or Billy would be coming in very soon. She tried to speak in a stern but comforting voice. "We've been kidnapped. Brought to some shack a hermit used to live in. In a few minutes there will be one of two men coming in here. They might touch you, caress you, and even touch themselves in front of you, but you need to deal with it. Wherever they touch you or whatever they say, deal with it. Touching is all they can do. For some reason, they can't actually hurt us."

"Who—Who?" Jada could barely get the words through the tangled mess of nerves in her throat.

"I need you to stay calm so they don't give you anymore tranquilizer, because you are going to free yourself, and we're going to escape."

Jada tugged at her ropes. The knot around her wrists was looped in twists and turns, each wrapped underneath the other, forming one jumbled mess. Her hands felt light and numb from the pressure of the ropes. "How can I free myself?" Jada's voice was defeated.

"Above you…"

The door to the shack moved away, letting in the roar of the rain and airing out the stagnant smell. Joe stumbled in, holding an almost-drained bottle of whiskey. He pulled out a can of dip from his back pocket and slapped it against his palm packing the tobacco inside. He wobbled, popped the lid off the can, and pinched a piece of dip into his mouth, smiled, and spit.

"Well, well, well," Joe said, walking closer to Jada. "I thought I heard me a negro woman yelling." He looked down at Jada with a perverse smile. "See, I'm all P.C. and shit. I called you a negro." Joe spit another tinted mess of saliva onto the floor and sat next to Jada.

Jada looked over at Kaitlin who mouthed the words, "Please stay calm."

"You know, darlin'," Joe said, and then tilted the whiskey bottle up to his mouth and took a big gulp. Once finished he set the bottle on the floor. "My momma said I shouldn't mess with any nigger women." Joe laughed loosely and shook his head. "Damn my manners, honey. I mean, negro woman. She said it wasn't right for our people to mix with such. It's a sin in God's eyes, she'd say. But my daddy...my daddy," a smile crept across Joe's face. "My daddy said you ain't a man until you had a little negro." Joe placed his hand by Jada's leg and rubbed his pinky along her thigh. "Is that true?"

"I—I—I don't know," Jada said.

"You don't know! Well, hell, baby, maybe we can test that theory. What...What do you think? You ever wonder about us white boys? Did your daddy tell you it's not okay to mix with white boys? That it's a sin in God's eyes? Tell you that we all just a bunch of hicks looking to keep your kind down?"

"No. No, he didn't," Jada said, concentrating on her breathing. Anger had begun to rise in her.

"He didn't," Joe said slapping her knee and laughing. "Well, he'd be the first nigger I met that didn't."

"He never said any of that," Jada said, lashing out.

"Well, then, alright," Joe said clapping his hands. "Sounds like my kinda negro. Well, what about your momma then? Did she take you aside one day when she figured you was woman enough and tell you 'Baby, you ain't no woman until you had yourself a little honkey, now?" Joe stammered drunkenly. "She—she ever tell you that? You ever laid in your bed at night and wonder what it would be like to be with a white boy? Maybe touch yourself a little?"

"Leave her alone!" Kaitlin yelled.

Joe shot up off the bed with the back of his hand raised. He swung it at Kaitlin, but stopped short of hitting her. Instead, he bawled his hand up into a fist and punched the bed violently next to her head. "Shut up, you white whore." Sweat dripped from Joe's forehead and spit pooled around the corner of his mouth.

"It bothers you, doesn't it?" Kaitlin said, trying to control the trembling in her voice. "It bothers you, that you can't have us, because you care so much about your life. Or, is it that you care so much, about what little life you have, that bothers you?"

Grabbing each side of the mattress by Kaitlin's head, Joe slammed it up and down. Kaitlin flopped at each collision with the bed frame. Her restraints jerked her shoulders and sockets, making her cry out in pain.

"Stop it! Stop it! You're hurting her," Jada cried.

Joe threw the mattress back down and Kaitlin bounced on the bed as if landing on a trampoline. Joe leapt over to Jada, grabbed her by her shirt, and pulled her to his face. "No nigger bitch talks to me that way!"

A crack of lighting hit a nearby tree, sending an electric current through the air. It stood the hair up on Joe's neck. A loud rumble of thunder followed, shaking the ground, deafening all three for a moment. Dazed, Joe held Jada up to his face. He let her go, her head flopping onto the pillow. He leaned down slowly, grunting, picking up the bottle of whiskey. Taking a deep drink, he sat at the table and set the bottle down. He pulled out his can of tobacco and replaced the dip that he'd spit and spewed out of his mouth in his rage.

Joe reached under his shirt and pulled out the .38 holstered in his pants. He flipped the cylinder open and let the bullets clatter and roll on the table. "Life, you say? What do you know about life, blondie? You ever have to work a hard day's labor in your life? I used to have a job. A damn good job." He picked a bullet off the table and placed it in the cylinder.

"I used to mullet fish, crab, made my living off the sea. I ain't educated or had a daddy like yours who could pay my way for me." Joe

61

spun the cylinder, flipped it shut, and pulled back the hammer. He delighted at the sight of the girls shoving themselves against the walls in terror.

"What about you, girl?" Joe pointed the gun at Jada. "You ever have somebody move into your home, throw up some condos, and say you can't run your mullet nets in the canals no more because you're an eyesore to them? Huh? Then they close mullet fishing everywhere. That hurt a lot of good families."

Joe pulled the trigger.

CLICK.

"No!" Jada screamed trying to hide her face.

"Well, darling, we got five more tries left before one of us dies. Not you this time."

"Stop it, Joe," Kaitlin cried.

"What? You can say my name now?" Joe fumed. He pulled back the hammer and pointed the gun at Kaitlin. "Your daddy ever have to look you in the eyes at Christmas and tell you he ain't got no presents for you this year 'cause he can't work? Can't make a living, because the Yankees who live here half the year put in a new tax for that and a new tax for this?"

CLICK.

"Please, please, stop. I'm sorry that happened to you, Joe," Kaitlin sobbed. "I'm so sorry. But you said someone would kill you if you hurt us."

"I just might kill myself, darlin'." Joe picked up the bottle and drained the last of the whiskey. Placing the gun to his head, he pulled back the hammer. "Now, here I am with two kidnapped girls," he said sadly. "I gotta make money for my family somehow. Even if I could fish, can't keep any. They won't even let a man keep enough to sell and feed his family." Joe closed his eyes tight. "Maybe three times is a charm."

CLICK!

Joe sighed. Jada twisted herself into as small a target as possible. She struggled against the rope, trying to cover her face.

"Joe, no! Shoot me," Kaitlin bellowed.

"Kaitlin, stop," Jada pleaded. "Let him shoot the negro woman," She turned her head toward Joe, shouting her disgust.

"Isn't this sweet," Joe said ridiculing the girls. "Two sluts trying to protect each other."

CLICK!

"Damn?" Joe pounded the butt of the gun on the table. "I was hoping it'd go off. There are two more left." Joe laughed and turned to Kaitlin. "It's me or you, blondie."

Kaitlin thrashed at the sheets, trying to throw up any barricade for protection. Joe cocked the hammer.

CLICK!

"Damn it! Damn it! Damn it!" Joe stamped his feet against the brittle wooden floor. "I knew I shoulda' started with me first." Joe pulled back the hammer. The gold glimmer of the bullet slipped behind the barrel. "Well, girls, I might as well make it quick. Don't worry, Billy will come a runnin'. Probably let you go because he ain't worth a damn." Joe put the barrel in his mouth and stood up and squeezed the trigger.

CLICK!

"What the..." Joe murmured, his mouth still around the barrel. He took the gun out of his mouth and scrutinized it in the candlelight. Opening the cylinder, he pulled out the bullet and turned it round and round in his fingers, holding it close to his right eye. "Why hell," he said his grin thickening, "I put in the bullet I shot while bringing the blonde whore here." Looking at Jada and Kaitlin who now cowered on their beds, Joe picked the five remaining bullets up off the table. He loaded the gun, flipped the cylinder closed and pointed it at Kaitlin. "You ever smart off to me again, blondie. We'll play this here game again, and I'll just be pullin' the trigger on you two."

Joe holstered the gun back in his pants. "I'll be seein' you in a bit." He turned his back and walked out placing the door back over the opening.

Even though she was sobbing hysterically, Kaitlin's mind started counting before she was aware of it.

"Kaitlin," Jada said, trying to keep her voice as quiet as possible.

Kaitlin wouldn't respond. She stared at the ceiling listening to the numbers rattle in her head.

"Kaitlin," Jada's whisper was almost a shout.

Kaitlin blinked. The tears that pushed out of her eyes broke her trance. She looked at Jada, her eyes burning red along with her face. "I'm sorry, Jada. I shouldn't have said that to him. I'm sorry."

"I don't care." Jada tried to smile. "We're still alive, and I'm ready to go. Before he comes back...I want to go home. You said you had a way to escape."

Kaitlin hammered through the stupor in her head. "Okay, I think you can cut yourself free."

"How?"

"Can you see your rope tied around the headboard?" She kept an eye on the door, afraid Joe would come back with his pistol drawn. "The metal has rusted out holes on the top. If you can slide the rope into one of the holes, it may fray the rope loose."

The headboard was an old metal frame. The top rung looped in an arch meeting the two sides. It was a simplistic design that would have decorated the beds of the lower class with an edge of décor in its better days. However, the constant bombardment of salt air had rusted it. Rust, made brittle over time, collapsed into the hollow tube halfway down the right side slope of the arch, leaving an open pit. Jagged metal that could possible fray the rope lined the pit's side.

Jada followed the rope from her hands to the headboard. It was looped in a tight knot around the arch. She jerked her arms from the left and right, but the knot wouldn't move. "Damn it," she muttered, just wanting to lie there and cover her face and cry. Instead, she grabbed the rope, pulled herself up toward the headboard, and grasped the knot. With her fingers, she pushed the knot to the left and right.

At first the knot held tightly in place, but with work it slowly started to grind the thin layer of rust it was wrapped around. Rust spilled onto Jada's head. With each push, the knot traveled farther down the rung.

"It's moving!" Kaitlin exclaimed quietly.

"I know! I know!" Jada kept rubbing as sweat beaded and dripped down her forehead. She slipped the knot into one of the rusted holes and twisted the rope against the toothed metal. "I hate to ask the obvious, but how the hell do we get off an island?"

Kaitlin explained how she was brought to the island and the path.

She felt sure they could find the canoe if they could find the path. "Can you run?"

"You have no idea," Jada said with a laugh. Jada felt the rope starting to give way. "How about you? Can you run?"

"I think I will be fine. I was a little wobbly getting here. But I..."

Joe kicked in the door. It crashed onto the floor, sending a heavy cloud of dust that rose slowly in the damp air. He slammed a new bottle of whiskey on the table. The gun in his other hand swung side to side as he pointed it at the girls' heads. His bloodshot eyes were glazed over. He stepped forward, steadying himself on the table.

With the gun's barrel still swinging from Jada to Kaitlin, he pointed at each girl, "Eeny meeny miny mo." Joe paused, his face blank. "My mother says to screw the best one."

The gun stopped on Kaitlin. Joe reached down and unbuttoned his pants letting them fall to the floor, exposing himself. "Time to find out if the curtains match the drapes, darlin'."

"No!" Kaitlin thrashed on the bed like an animal trapped in a snare.

Jada dug the rope deeper into the jagged hole. The rope unraveled, snapping away from the headboard. She sprang off the bed. With her shoulder lowered, she hit Joe in the chest. Joe's hands flew up pulling the trigger on the gun. The bullet pierced the roof and sent a flood of water onto the floor as Joe's head smacked the table. He dropped to the floor, unconscious.

"Joe?" Billy's scream was barely audible over the wind.

"Untie me! Untie me!" Kaitlin pulled at her restraints. Jada tried to force her fingers through the constricted knots on Kaitlin's wrists. Tugging frantically, she worked to unravel the mess that was looped and twisted with no discernible pattern. But the rope still tied around Jada's wrists limited the use of her hands.

"Please, hurry," Kaitlin begged.

"What the hell?" Billy barreled into the shack and stumbled over Joe's body.

Jada spun around in time to see Billy make a charge at her. She sprang back on her bed and jumped on the floor behind him. He turned around and took a wild round house swing that managed to graze her on the chin. Jada cried out and staggered back, but was able to regain her balance. Billy's swing carried him forward onto the bed.

"Run!" shrieked Kaitlin, drowning out the thunder that exploded outside. "Run!"

Jada looked desperately at Kaitlin, wanting to help her, but a 250-pound man was getting to his feet and stood in her way.

"Damn it, RUN!" Kaitlin cried.

Jada's legs possessed her. She ran in the gushing downpour, realizing she'd left Kaitlin. She paused. The wind injected rain into her eyes making it difficult for her to see. The coconut tree's trunk next to her head exploded little pieces of bark onto her arm before she heard the gunshot.

Billy stood outside with Joe's gun pointed at her. A flash of lightning gashed the sky, illuminating the area around the camp. Jada saw the path, and she ran for it. Her feet, shoeless, dug into ground. Fragmented shells, uncovered by the rain, caused her to wince in pain. A bullet whizzed past her head and rattled a cluster of palmettos in front of her. Her strides lengthened out, but quickly shortened as her feet hit sandspurs. The barbed hitchhikers embedded themselves on her ankles, between her toes, and stuck to the soles of her feet.

Billy crashed through the path behind her. She quickened her pace and veered off into a patch of saw grass. Each strand sliced into her legs like miniature fillet knives scaling her skin.

"Stop!" Billy huffed and fired another shot.

The sting of the bullet grazed Jada's left shoulder. She wailed. The smell of burning flesh coated her nostrils. She stumbled forward, trying to cover her wound with her hand. Blood oozed out between her fingers, quickly washed away by the rain. A glance behind showed her Billy bending over, his hands on his knees as he tried to get his breath. Jada froze, and he lifted the gun and shot again. The bullet exploded in a puddle of water in front of her feet. She ran. She didn't know how big the island was, but she knew she hadn't run far. Even in her frantic state, she could clock mileage like the odometer in a car. She figured she had a little while to go when her feet hit the water.

"No! No! No! No!" Her shrilled voice hurt her own ears. She

turned round and round, her hands rubbing over her forehead pulling back the skin on her face. The canoe wasn't there.

She wanted to run back and see if she missed the boat, but she heard Billy moving toward her. Running into the water, she started down the canal. The water rose to her waist.

She didn't notice the canoe until she was almost by it. It had floated a little ways down the channel. Not only had the tide come in, but also, Tropical Storm Rachel had pushed a storm surge onto the island, lifting the canoe from the spot Billy and Joe had placed it.

Jada tried to hoist herself into the canoe, but it kept tilting over toward her. Grabbing the boat, she clamored for the mangroves and wedged the bow in between two roots. She clutched her bound hands onto a mangrove branch and pulled herself up onto the walkway of roots, then stepped in the canoe. The water inside it came up over her ankles. Looking for a way to bail it out, she found a bleach bottle that had been cut in half for this purpose. She flung the water out trying to float the hull higher. She glanced down the canal. Sheets of water made a wall she could barely see through.

Jada grabbed a paddle. She heard a splash. Billy trudged through the water toward her. She tried to push the canoe off the mangrove roots, but slipped and smacked her chin on the canoe's seat, hitting the spot where Billy had grazed her. Blood flooded her mouth. Shaking, she pushed herself onto her knees using the paddle as a crutch. She fought to stay awake as her eyes tried to close her into blackness. Opening them wide, she looked up. Billy was there, standing by the canoe with the pistol pointed at her.

"I'm tired of this shit," Billy said. "I'm not gonna be any part of this anymore. I'm goin' and leavin' where none of them will ever be able to find me." His breath caught hoarsely in his throat. "Get out of the boat, bitch. You can deal with Joe when he wakes up."

Jada moaned. The dumpling of a man could take her life. The rain flowed down her body encasing her in a watery cocoon. She wanted to give up, but she remembered Kaitlin. The thought of her still lying there tied to the bed sent a rush of anger that streaked from the depth of Jada's gut and shot through her arms and shoulders. She clasped the paddle and swung at Billy.

He pulled the trigger. The paddle connected with his head as the gun clicked. Billy fell back into the water causing a rolling wave that sent the canoe rocking, and jarred it loose from the roots.

Jada dropped the paddle in the boat and searched her body for the bullet wound. Then she realized the gun had only clicked. She laughed. It clicked, just like when Joe played his sick game.

Billy had forgotten about the bullet Joe shot off when he forced him to pull the boat down the channel during low tide. He floated on his back, hooking onto a mangrove limb to keep from sinking to the bottom. He groaned. His forehead had been split by the edge of the paddle. Blood flowed down his face, diluted, and mixed with the rain as it rinsed away.

Jada collapsed into the seat. She'd never canoed before, but the boat slowly moved forward as she switched the paddle from side to side. The bulk of the water in the floor rushed to the back, raising the bow. Jada glanced behind her, but the rain shielded Billy from her sight. He could recover. She wanted to bail out the boat but was afraid to stop moving. Instead, she fought to control the direction of the boat. Once she squeezed between the narrow enclosure of mangroves, she threw down the paddle and tried to bail out the boat, sloshing water over the side as quickly as it poured in. She thought she heard Billy coming, but she could no longer be sure.

Bursts of lightning exposed the end of the canal in front of her and open water beyond. Grabbing the paddle, she rowed toward the Gulf. She desperately wanted to go back for Kaitlin, but she knew Billy, and probably Joe, would be waiting. She needed to find help.

The canoe scrapped past the last of the branches. The full force of Tropical Storm Rachel grabbed the tiny vessel and spun it around, pushing it east toward the Everglades. She tried to ram the paddle into the soft muck surrounding the island but the mud sucked up the paddle, ripping it from her hands. She went to grab the other paddle, but the water rose fast in the canoe. Jada fell to her knees and snatched the bleach bottle and began bailing, fighting to keep the boat from sinking. The boat nearly capsized as she worked to free it from its watery weight. Her arms grew sore as she scooped out the endless puddle of water. The thought of what Joe and Billy must be doing to Kaitlin in their rage and

68

drunkenness now twisted Jada's stomach into convulsions. She vomited the water she'd swallowed.

Kaitlin had sacrificed herself. Jada couldn't free her, but Jada's primal side told her she needed to survive. As she continued bailing, the wind blew her wherever it liked. The night was replaced gradually with a dim light haze as the storm still blocked out the rays of the sun. She kept bailing throughout the day, resting whenever her arms grew tired. The repetitive motions of the scoops became slower and slower, her head hanging down as she tried not to pass out.

The rain lessened to a light drizzle. At last the clouds broke, revealing a sun lowering its head to rest. Jada's eyelids drifted down and shot back up. Each time they stayed down a little longer until she finally collapsed, curled up on the floor of the canoe. Her mind shut down, only spending energy on the necessary functions of breathing and the beating of her heart. It wasted no energy on dreams or trying to figure out her situation in her unconsciousness. Her mind did not come too until the sweet smell of lavender seeped into her nose, her skin felt the soft caress of cotton sheets, and a cool cloth was placed on her head.

Chapter 13

Marcus and The Hippie

Marcus watched the black clouds slowly move away from the ship. A large mass of thunderheads, full of warm Gulf water, still waited to drop its payload on the mainland. It too would soon be depleted and break into individual thunderstorms. From there, it would spread around the state, bringing much needed relief from the summer heat to the farms and ranches dotted throughout Central Florida.

Langer reclined with a glass of whiskey in hand, smoking his cigar. Richard's outburst consumed his thoughts. For the past two years, he'd kept him confined to the ship, except for when girls were needed. But, just like a tiger brought from the wild and caged, he could turn on his handler. Langer knew that if he and Karam had arrived any later, Richard would have attacked Amber. It was time for Richard to be let out to play. He'd return obedient and tame for a while.

Langer rose from his chair and went to the bar. He squatted down behind it, reached in his pocket, and took out a key. Unlocking the safe door, he looked at the sheathed Bowie knife. He released the knife from its sheath, thinking of the countless women it had terrorized. Sheathing the knife again, he put it in his pants behind his coat.

Langer navigated the narrow hallways containing the suites. Passing Amber's room, he checked the padlock Karam had installed, partly to keep Amber in, but more to keep Richard out. Hearing Amber's soft muffled cries, Langer paused. In his way, he felt for the girl. He thought if he'd ever had a daughter, he'd want her to be like Amber, fierce and not afraid to fight. Of course, he would have to desire the intimacy that a woman can give. But his affections lay elsewhere.

He walked down the hall to Richard's room. The smell of incense wafted out of the crack below the door. Langer despised knocking on the doors of his own yacht. However, Richard was edgy, and the least bit of disrespect may be the weight that tipped his scale in the wrong direction. Langer tapped lightly on the door.

"What?" Richard's voice demanded through the door.

Langer tightened his fist, digging his nails into his palms. He took a moment to compose himself and steady his voice. "I was wondering if I might have a word with you."

"Sure." The disgruntled voice lost some of its malice.

Langer opened the door and incense bombarded his nostrils. He puffed on his cigar releasing long exhales of smoke, to combat the smell of The Hippie mixed with musky sandalwood.

Richard grunted on the floor in pushup position, his shirt off, rattling off numbers with each repetition. The sheets from the bed were stripped and arranged in a jumbled pallet on the floor.

For the first time, Langer noticed the tense muscles on Richard's torso. His usual baggy attire covered up what Langer thought was quite an impressive physical specimen. While skinny, Richard's entire form consisted of long, lean muscle tightened around his bones as if barely restrained from popping out of his skin. The tattoo of a dragon wrapped around a naked lady contoured the muscles on his back. The dragon constricted the woman's body, its mouth open wide over her head. The woman reached up to the dragon's face trying to push it way.

Richard flipped over and started on crunches, his chest and abs scarred with deep cuts from the fingernails of women who were his victims. The scars symbolized the women's last efforts for life and escape; Richard's trophies for each one he took.

"Working out some frustration, are we?" Langer said, taking Richard's backpack off a chair and placing it on the floor.

"You could say that." Richard continued with his exercise.

"You know," Langer paused. "There is not much I ask, but I do ask that you not touch the girls unless I give them to you. And killing is never an option."

Looking down at his stomach as if not hearing Langer's words, Richard kept counting. After quickly reaching a hundred reps, he stood up, dripping with sweat, and sat on the bed. He grabbed a towel off the floor and wiped his face and armpits. Taking a deep breath, he acknowledged Langer's concerns. "Right, then. The Asian girl. I was having a bit of fun. Feeling her out, you might say. You better sell her to a tough one, boss. She is feisty. I like that."

71

"I felt it might be a bit more than fun," Langer said through the smoke that hovered in the air. The burning of incense was such a ritual of Richard's that Langer had had to have the fire alarm disconnected in the room.

"Really, boss, it was a bit of fun," Richard said, waving away Langer's concerns.

"I understand you are, well, for lack of a better word, *frustrated.* I know you need to release some of that frustration. Am I correct?"

Richard took a deep breath, "I'm a bit tied up in knots in the inside. A little release might be great."

Langer smiled at Richard. "You know when I found you, you were digging through trash cans for food and raping and killing at will. The only thing I knew about you was that the FBI had barely any information on you. Grainy photos really. You were good. That's why I tracked you down. An elusive hunter is good in this type of business, but killing your profit is not."

Richard's thoughts drifted from Marcus' words to Amber. He recalled the feel of his fingertips fumbling across skin—the smooth feel of young fresh skin almost in his grasp.

"Richard," Langer said sharply. "I need you here with me."

"Right. Sorry." Richard focused on Langer's mouth. The Hippie flashed an embellished smile.

"We're heading back to the mainland, and I think you need to have a little fun."

"With the little Asian girl?"

"No, not with Amber. She's way too valuable. I've already sent out feelers for her at the auction. She may fund this one trip. The other two are pure profit. A pretty penny of that will go to you."

"Let me guess, another spa girl?" Richard's face gave away his disappointment at the thought.

"No, I'm talking of letting you do a full hunt, but you need to keep it clean and quick. We have a couple days." Langer reached inside his coat and brought out the knife. He held it in his hand, like a carrot for a horse.

A shudder went down Richard's body, contracting his form as if the animal within him, so long in hibernation, was now stretching its cramped muscles. A grin showed his yellowed teeth as his hand wrapped around the handle of the knife. "Where?" Richard asked, his voice quivering.

"On Marco Island. I suggest a suite on the beach. You'll see a fair share of women roaming the sand. Once we anchor offshore, take one of the boats in storage, go to Marco and dock at the marina." Langer stood up, headed for the door and turned back to Richard. "And for God's sake, take a taxi to the hotel. Most of the residents there are not too fond of anything too unlike them."

"Fine, fine, fine." Richard scratched his beard, pacing the room back and forth like a thoroughbred who knows he is about to be let loose for a race. "I'll find me a pretty, pretty one. A feisty one, better than the little Asian girl."

It had been too long since he'd felt a woman's warm flesh become cold, watching the life slip out of her eyes like he did his mother's so many years ago.

* * *

Richard's mother had just turned fourteen when she gave birth to him in the New Earth Revival Community that set itself apart from the outside world. The compound was located in the Arizona desert. Members were required to sell all they had and deposit the money into the collective bank account managed by their self-proclaimed Messiah, Jonathan Franks. In order to keep the money flowing, Jonathan sent members to local parks and malls to pass out fliers and try to recruit others to the fold.

Jonathan also opened several sandwich shops and coffee houses near colleges. Staffing his business ventures with young female converts, he used them to help prey on lost and confused youth, or those who realized Hollywood's newest religious trend was out of vogue and over-exposed.

Any male child Jonathan fathered was a possible heir to his position, the one who could lead the people and continue to show them The Way. All of Jonathan's sons slept in a small dormitory, separated from the rest of the community until they were deemed pure enough to be raised by their mother.

From an early age, Richard became aware that he needed to suppress his feelings. On some nights, Jonathan would come while they slept and ripped off the boys' covers making sure his sons controlled their bodies. One night, Richard couldn't control his. He tried to make it go away and shrink, flexing his pelvis to cut off the supply of blood.

"Control, boy." Jonathan yanked him off the bed exposing him to his brothers and violently whipped Richard's naked body with a belt. "You." *SLAP* "Must." *SLAP* "Control." *SLAP* "Your." *SLAP* "Body." The belt bruised and stung Richard's skin welting it up in shades of purple and black.

Richard soon learned control, and his father allowed him to live with his mother. His mother gave birth to Richard's brother a few years later. In Richard's mid-teens, Jonathan visited his son, touching him, telling Richard, "I must make sure you can control your body, son."

The touching progressed; Jonathan would have Richard "test" him. Richard's stomach and bottom hurt for days after, the sickening thud in his stomach hardening in him. Richard tearfully told his mother and pleaded for her to take him away from the compound. She would not.

"He knows The Way. You are his son; he is right to do what he does." She hugged Richard.

Richard fought Jonathan's assaults, kicking and punching. His screams for his mother piercing through the house. Jonathan enjoyed Richard's struggles. During one of Jonathan's more aggressive assaults, Richard's body shivered and became limp. His eyes glazed over, and he felt himself floating, drifting away, and hovering over Jonathan and himself. The sight of his father raping him dispelled his trance. Fueled with disgust, he vomited on the bed and his father. Enraged, Jonathan flipped the mattress onto the floor, spiraling Richard to the ground.

Jonathan stormed into the mother's bedroom.

"What kind of boy did you give me?" Jonathan yelled. "How dare you birth that child to me!"

Richard buried his head under a pillow, trying to drown out the sounds of Jonathan beating his mother, her screams, and cries for help.

And then her moans, her long moans filled the hallways. He buried his head deeper, but the noises still penetrated, echoing in his head.

Picking himself up off the floor, Richard dressed. He walked to the kitchen, his breath light and shallow. His matted hair clung to the perspiration on his forehead, and his hands shook as he lifted a long butcher knife from the counter.

He crept down the hallway, putting one foot in front of the other, setting his feet down, slowly and lightly, on the shag rug. His mother's moans become louder, the slapping now rhythmic. Richard grabbed the tarnished brass handle and turned the knob. The perspiration on his hand left streaks.

Richard peeked inside the room. He saw Jonathan doing to his mother what Jonathan had done to him. Two bodies twisted in rapid harsh movements. Richard let the door swing open, wide, illuminating the bedroom with light from the hallway exposing the couple's nakedness.

"You little bastard!" Jonathan hollered. "You a damn pervert, boy? You like what I'm doing to your momma? Get the hell out of here." He smirked, then looked at the boy curiously. "What are you doing with that knife, boy?" He pushed off Richard's mother and climbed off the bed. His movements were careful and slow. "Now, you didn't come to hurt your daddy, did you? Come on now, boy, give Daddy the knife and you can go back to bed. I'll leave you alone." Jonathan waved for the knife.

Richard quickly stepped back, raising the knife beside his head. His legs felt like rubber bands stretched tight, flicked by an invisible finger. His breath was rabid.

"Come on, son. Give me the knife."

Richard didn't move.

"It's okay, Richard, you passed. You have control now." Jonathan turned to Richard's mother. "I got an idea, honey. Let's celebrate our boy's control. I think I know just what he needs." Jonathan slinked toward Richard, his words raspy as he spoke. "How about I have one of the little girls come visit you tonight? We just had a new family move in with two little girls this week. Would you like that? Have your

75

first time with a girl?" Jonathan flashed his perverse grin and thrust his hips.

Richard stepped further back.

Jonathan lunged and seized Richard by the throat, pushing him against the closet door. Richard grunted and brought the knife down over his head sinking the blade into his father's shoulder. He pulled the knife back out, and Jonathan crumpled to his knees. Richard watched the blood vein out on the blade and drip onto his hands and floor. He placed his other hand on Jonathan's shoulder and rammed the knife into his father's stomach, retracted it, and stabbed him again and again.

"No!" his mother begged, standing up and pulling the covers over her.

"You…You…little bastard." Blood streamed out of the corner of Jonathan's mouth, staining his tangled beard red. "Who…the hell...hell…do…who…in the hell...hell...?" Jonathan's last words trailed off as he collapsed.

"No! No!" Richard's mother bawled and pounded her fists on the bed.

Richard knotted his hand around the knife. The warmth of Jonathan's blood squeezed out between his fingers. The stickiness gave him a better grip. "You watched." His lips trembling with rage as he moved toward her. "You let him do it to me."

"Stay away! I'm your mother!" She reached out to strangle her son.

"No, you're not!" Richard immersed the knife into her chest. Her last heartbeats pushed tiny vibrations through the blade and into his hand. He watched her eyes. Her pupils constricted and flickered, taking in the last images of this world. Then they stopped. Richard turned to see his younger brother wide-eyed, standing at the door. Richard left the knife in her chest and shoved his brother out of the way. He ran away from New Earth Revival.

Since Richard was born in the compound, his birth was never recorded. In essence, he did not exist to anyone but himself. Becoming worse than his father, he no longer suppressed his desires and terrorized women across the country until he met Marcus. By then, Richard was tired of living out of the scraps from trashcans. Marcus offered him money and even more, anonymity, sheltered away from the world. He only need give up his knife and focus on hunting women.

* * *

The Albatross anchored five miles off Marco Island. Richard stroked the knife that he'd been denied for two years. He went down to storage and stepped into a two-tone black and white twenty-two foot Pathfinder. The stern of the yacht lifted up like a garage door and hydraulic lifts launched the boat into the rattling water. They'd caught up with some of the storm on their way in, but it was nothing the boat couldn't handle. He cranked the engine sending the smell of the fuel coursing through the 250 horsepower engine into the air. Gunning it and smacking the waves, he scanned the six mile-long coast stacked with concrete fingers that reached out of the sea. A grin grew from ear to ear, and he inhaled the salt mist that splashed over the bow of the boat. He had a little fun time before he had to be at Dismal Key.

Chapter 14

McKlusky and Chloe

A light mist fell on the waves rushing over the sandbar that lay submerged by the high tide. Their white tops reached for the sky, crashing back down the length of the wave until it collapsed on itself. The wind gusted through Chloe's hair, making thin wisps dance playfully behind her head. She stood in the surf, looking at the waves that were coming in off the tail end of the tropical storm.

I couldn't help but notice her body, nearly exposed before me in her bathing suit. Her legs flexed gently as she balanced herself in the sand. They were carved in sleek curves, delicate and soft. Her chest heaving out, Chloe smelled the air that had been blown clean by the storm. The tightly woven hemp necklace wrapped around her neck enhanced her feminine nature, as she absentmindedly stroked it with her finger. Her other hand lay collapsed in mine, gently rubbing the outside of my thumb. The hair on my arms prickled, as if tiny invisible bolts of lightning simultaneously shot from the top of one hair to another.

"Living up North hasn't made you soft, has it?" she said, turning her head toward me. She flashed a sly smile that pushed away the gloom in the sky.

"Really? You're determined to make me pay for moving aren't you?" I sighed. "It's not like it was my fault."

"Well, I mean," she grasped my hand tighter, "can you still hang?" A grin parted her lips.

"I can still hang." I turned toward her with a look of mischief. "The question is can you still hang with me?"

Chloe pushed me away laughing, "As if!"

"Well, let's find out, then." I grabbed my surfboard and launched it into the surf, landing my chest on the board's waxed surface.

"Hey! You can't jump in front of me. I'm local and you're not." She scooped up her surfboard, her powerful legs pushing through the surf to catch up with me.

78

I paddled hard and lurched forward through the foaming waves. We raced out to the far side of the sandbar, beyond the break of the wind swells. The waves on Marco are mainly nonexistent when it comes to surfing, unless a good storm brews up. And really, the storm waves are not that great either. They can get three to four feet high, but they are messy and sloppy, collapsing over each other and bullying you along on your board. Regardless, they're fun to ride.

A wave rose up in front of me. I pushed the front of the board down in a mock pushup and flapped my chest back on the board. I sailed underneath the rushing wave, popping up on the other side.

"Whooo!" I heard Chloe yell as she copied my duck dive and surfaced on the backside of a wave. A wide grin consumed her drenched face. "Flex for me again."

Another wave stacked up. This time I made sure to strain and flex as I pushed the board down. I looked back at Chloe emerging from the same wave. A smile and a shake of her head told me I could stop showboating now. I dug deep in the cloudy water, one arm over the other, racing Chloe, reaching the edge of the break before she did. I popped up and straddled my board with my hands raised in mock victory. She pulled up beside me and straddled her own board.

"Whatever," she said nonchalantly, and breathless. "Not bad for a tourist."

I groaned and then gave her a light smile. Reading my face, she leaned over, kissed me on the cheek and moved her lips to my ear, sending the prickly sensation down my arms again. She whispered softly, "I don't mean anything by it. I'm just new at this. Flirting, I mean. I don't think you are a tourist. I'm just trying to figure out how to show you I like you. Us being more than friends is new for me, too." She sat back on her board, biting her lower lip. Her hands rested on her legs. The blush in her cheeks sparkled underneath the water on her face. "Okay?" she said looking back at me.

"I understand." My voice was soft, and then I laughed. "I understand I'm about to catch this wave and kick your Islander ass at surfing."

I lay back on my chest and paddled hard, catching a wave. Pushing up on the board, I tucked my feet underneath me. I about lost my balance and bailed, but then I thought of the ribbing I would get from Chloe. Steadying myself, I did a quick floater and dropped back into the face, riding the length of the wave to the shore where it fizzled out in a bubbly mess.

By the time I got to shore, Chloe had dropped in on a wave. She pumped her board to pick up speed, turned up the face, and copied my floater when the wave collapsed on her and slammed her under. Her board popped up behind the wave, her leash jerking her leg up into the air.

"Chloe!" I jettisoned back onto my board and took long hard strokes, paddling through the waves piling on one another.

By the time I reached her, she'd climbed on her board, laughing hysterically, rubbing her leg where it had been jerked by the board.

"Are you okay?"

"I'm okay," she said, still laughing. "My leg just hurts."

"You scared the piss out of me." I wiped the salt out of my eyes. "Is it okay?"

"Yeah. It just got jerked a little bit, and it cramped up on me." Her hand massaged the top of her leg as she stretched it out on her board to work the cramp loose.

"You need me to do that for you?" I said giving her my best devious grin. The waves bounced us up and down as they rolled us closer to shore.

She looked at me with a slight tilt of her head. Her brow crinkled up questioningly. "Are you hitting on me, McKlusky?"

"Whatever," I said, raising my eyebrows. "It was you who hit on me yesterday."

"Huh?" Chloe looked at me with an air of poshness. "I'm a lady, and ladies do not hit on men." She paused. "Besides, you can rub it for me when we're at the movies. Just don't think of getting too fresh during the whole ordeal."

"Are you worried about that?" My voice took on a more serious tone.

"Well, you're a boy. Your hands drifted a little bit last night, too." She looked as she may have gotten deeper into this topic than she wanted. "I'm sure you thought about it."

80

I paused and looked at the pelicans and seagulls that had come from their protective roost in the mangroves to dive bomb mullet, their stomachs shrunk and hungry from the inability to feed during the storm. I looked, not because I was interested in them, but because I had thought about sex with Chloe a thousand times since she'd opened the door in the garage yesterday. Not long drawn-out scenes, but brief clips, snapshots really, of us together. I studied her face as she shifted uncomfortably on her board. Oddly, since we were such good friends before our attraction for each other took over, I felt comfortable talking to her about this. But I couldn't think of anything romantic to say, and denying I had thought about it would've been too fake. So I told her the truth. "Listen, Chloe, I care about you. I've thought about it. Honestly, I have."

She blushed more, but fought a smile that wanted to part her lips.

"But, I want you more than I want sex. I mean, one day I'd like us to explore our options, but not now." I left it at that.

She let out a sigh of relief. "I love your answer. I've been on a couple dates." These words felt like a sledgehammer pounding away at my ribs. The images of Chloe kissing some other guy felt like nails under a hammer. "It just seems it is the first thing guys go for." She looked at me with water trickling off her eyelashes. "Just don't be like that with me, okay?"

"I promise, but you need to let me know if I cross the line. What you are and are not comfortable with." I paused. "And you definitely need to let me know when you're okay with more."

She laughed and reached out her hand for me to hold. The waves had washed us back to shore and our feet dangled off our boards into the sand.

When we paddled back out, the wind had died down, blowing the last bit of its rage in the clearing skies. The waves relaxed into their flat steady rolls that pulsed and slapped under us like the steady beat of a heart. Our boards side by side, we hooked our feet together, relaxing, and enjoying each other's touch. We watched the first sunlight in days laying low in the west, heading down to kiss the sea. I looked over at Chloe, and I could see her arms give a shake.

"You cold?" I rubbed the top of her back trying to warm her.

"No," she said nervously. "Just thinking about sharks. They like to feed at dusk."

"Now, now, big and tough Chloe is not afraid of sharks, is she?" I said, teasing her.

"No, not really. They just feed at dusk. That's all I'm saying, and it's going to be dark soon." She stiffened her shoulders in a defensive posture.

"Hey, easy now, I'm new at this whole flirting thing, too," I said, raising my hands to defend myself from the punch I knew was coming.

"Fine, I'm afraid." She shoved me, making me almost fall off my board. "Just don't make fun of me."

I reached over, grabbed her board and started rocking it, while I hummed the theme from *JAWS*.

Da Daah Da Daah Da Daah

"Stop it!" A slight shriek invaded her voice.

I slapped my hand on the water repeatedly. "You know, they're attracted to splashing."

"Then stop it!"

"Nope." My hand made a popping splash, scattering water across her face. As I brought my hand down for another smack, the surface of the water exploded in front of Chloe's board. She screamed, her eyes wide, not registering what was happening. I grabbed her by the arm to keep her from falling off. A large school of mullet had jumped over the nose of her board. I let go of her arm and lay back on my board, laughing.

"You jackass! Stop laughing." She slapped my stomach, leaving a red handprint splotched across my abs. "They—mullet," I said in between convulsions. "Mullet make great shark bait."

"You're not funny." Trying not to laugh, she hit my stomach harder.

I looked up at her. Her hair scattered over her shoulders. Tears of laughter spilled down to her smiling lips. She leaned over and kissed me. Her tongue flicked mine. I pulled her onto my board, keeping my hands from wandering too far across the warmth of her skin and breaking our spoken contract. She pulled slowly back from the kiss. Biting her lower

82

lip, she flushed, not from embarrassment, but with the warm glow of satisfaction.

My heart rapid fired every time she bit her lip. My mind at first couldn't comprehend why it had such an effect on me. I later understood her innocence and her fierceness were wrapped up in that one look, expressing her mood for better or worse.

"Let's go in." I stroked a strand of hair behind her ear wanting this moment not to end. But I didn't want her fear of sharks at night to become justified.

* * *

The sun was rapidly extinguishing itself in the distant depths of the Gulf. Tired of being trapped in their houses for almost two days, retirees walked with buckets and plastic bags, picking up shells the storm had churned from their resting place, to sling them onto the shore.

As Chloe and I collected our towels and extra clothes on the beach, two muscular figures came walking toward us.

"Chloe?" the taller and thinner of the two yelled. "What the hell is going on?" He raised his bulky arms.

The other figure I recognized as Trent Shoemaker, one of the three boys who jumped me as a kid until Chloe showed him the wrong side of a stick. His arms were a scaffold with stacks of muscles and his shaved chest rippled every time he moved.

"Let's go," Chloe said. Her head hung low. She tried to lead me the other way.

"Chloe!" the thinner boy hollered. Both boys sprinted in front of us, blocking our way off the beach.

"Well, McKlusky." Trent gave me a fake smile. "Long time, no see. How are those cold winters treating you?" He covered his arms over his chest and started to *BRRR* and shake.

"Not too bad, Trent, they're sucking my balls into my stomach. About like the steroids are doing to you," I grinned. Trent made a lunge for me, but the other guy put his hand on Trent's chest.

I looked at him warily. He was smaller than Trent, but still built; more like a quarterback than a linebacker. He was more likely to be fast and agile in a fight. Trent, on the other hand, would be more powerful, but slow and a bit clumsy.

"Brad, just go away," Chloe said.

My fists tightened when I saw him look back at Chloe and scan her from the bottom of her feet to the top of her chest, not even bothering to look her in the face.

"Chloe?" Brad said. "I thought you and I had something going? Now, I see you out surfing with this kook. What's the deal, honey?" He reached out to put his arm around her, and she pushed it away.

I jumped forward, anger burning in my gut. She caught me by the hand, her grip squeezing my fingers together.

"Please, don't," she pleaded. "Let's go, McKlusky."

"McKlusky, huh?" Brad asked. "Chloe's childhood friend, Trent told me about you."

"That's me, and you must be Brad. Chloe said Trent had a new girlfriend."

Brad's cheekbone twitched under his eye. "Listen to this guy. I like him, Trent. You said he was an asshole when he's really a dick." He turned to Chloe. "What's the deal?"

"We had one date, Brad. And you're pretty much all hands. So leave me alone." She moved closer to me.

Brad smirked. "I'm more than all hands. I could show you sometime if you like." Brad trailed his fingers down to his waist as if he were going to show Chloe then and there.

Chloe caught a laugh in her throat. "That's not what I heard in the girls' locker room. I heard, you don't have much to show at all."

Brad's face ignited like a fighter jet. His hand came up and flew to Chloe's face. She fell on her back, air exiting her lungs as she hit the compacted sand. She rolled over on her side, her hands grasping her head. Trent punched me in the head. Screaming shrieks of blackness speared my eyes. I stumbled forward into Brad, who gut checked me. I collapsed next to Chloe.

Chloe's mouth searched for air, gasping like a fish in a red tide. Tears rolled out of her eyes, over the bridge of her nose, and soaked up into the sand. Adrenaline singed my veins. My stomach stretched out, fighting the urge to collapse under the bruise of Brad's punch. Brad brought his heel down toward my head. I circled my left arm across my face, hitting his ankle before the blow shattered my nose. He leaned over to grab me. I rammed my fist into his diaphragm, spilling his liquor-laced breath into my face. Both heels of my palms connected with each of his ears at the same time. I tried to connect them by going through his skull. His hands shot from his diaphragm to his ears. They probably rang like the dinner bell on a cattle farm.

By the time I had knocked the earwax out of Brad's head, Trent was by his side. I sprang up and staggered from the sudden rush of blood to my head. Trent pulled back his arm. Even in my dizzy state, I could see a slow, bone-crunching, roundhouse punch coming my way. I ducked, and he spun around, exposing his side. I shot a quick side kick to his ribs.

"I'm going to kill you," he screamed. Trent's eyes were threaded with thin jagged red lines. He swiped at me with another punch. I dodged it, only to be quickly jabbed in the stomach by his other fist. My knees hit the sand. He flipped a roundhouse kick toward my face. Leaning back, I felt the rush of air across the bridge of my nose. I leapt up, hands raised, fingers clenched into my palms. Brad slowly lumbered toward me, still shaking his head from the percussion caused by my fists.

My breath came in quick bursts. I tried to control the rate of my breathing, to slow down the quickening race of my heart.

My eyes searched frantically for anything I might use. The shells scraped underneath my heel. I jammed the front of my foot into the sand and snap kicked a pile toward Trent's face. He shielded his eyes, giving me enough time to side kick him in the gut. He doubled over.

Brad blindsided me with a forearm to the back of my head. I had enough sense to roll forward with the blow and back on my feet giving me some distance. He charged me, kicking up the sand behind him as he ran. Right before he reached me, I fell onto my back and placed both my feet onto his chest. Looking dumfounded by the sudden change of direction, he grimaced when I squat pressed him over my head, launching him into the surf.

I couldn't keep the intensity of the fight going much longer. My head felt hollow, and my neck fought to keep it balanced. No one would help. The older couples and tourists shuffled away from the commotion.

A group of college kids on one of the hotel balconies hooted and hollered, raising cans of beer in the air. They were taking bets on who would win. According to them, the odds were not in my favor.

Trent staggered back to me, gripping his side. Pain entwined his face, crinkling it up like a discarded piece of paper. His punch was sluggish, dragging his body behind it. When my knee sunk into his stomach, his body quivered. A line of spit, fused with deep red, strung out his mouth. He lay on the sand, more concerned about breathing than fighting.

Then Brad's breath was hot on my ears. His arms shoved under my neck, locking me in a chokehold.

"I'm gonna have a little fun with Chloe once your ass goes night, night, buddy."

I clawed and scraped at his shaved arms, trying to dig into the hard muscle. My fingers glided across, frictionless on his skin. There was not a choice as to whether I breathed or not. The waves mixed with the throb in my ears.

"Let him go!"

Brad's arms released my neck and his hands went to his own. I dropped to the ground, rolling over onto my back. Brad's screams swirled up in the slow gyration in my head. A seagull above me flew circles opposite the spin, nearly making me vomit.

I struggled to prop myself up on my elbows. Chloe, her eyes silent and cold, had the leash from her surfboard wrapped around Brad's neck. He tried to slip his fingers under the leash to buffer it from his throat.

"Chloe." I choked on her name. I steadied myself on my feet.

Her eyes broke from the dead stare that had enslaved them. She shook the leash out of her hands as if the hate she felt toward Brad had ignited it. Brad sucked in air. Chloe collapsed into my arms, her shoulders shaking.

"It's okay." I said, trying to reassure her. "Let's go."

Chloe lingered in my arms before pulling away. We gathered our stuff in silence and walked down the beach.

"You okay?" I said.

She shook her head, wiped her eyes, and wrapped her arms around my waist, pulling me close. "I'm sorry," she blurted into my chest. "It's my fault."

"No, it's not," I whispered. "They're just douchebags. Come on."

We walked down the beach to the showers. Little old ladies vigorously stuffed shells in their buckets. Young children prattled with their parents on the shoreline, chasing the retreating waves and fleeing when they came charging back at them. One little girl piled buckets of sand on a doting father, who remained motionless for his daughter's sand rendition of a mermaid's tail. Chloe reached over and wrapped her hand around mine.

"You feel better?" I asked.

"Yeah...you?" A little grin came across her face. "You still got any Transformers?"

"No. But how about that movie and the leg rub," I said.

"Okay, but I get to get the leg rub."

"Okay, but I get to give the leg rub." I felt I was definitely getting the better end of the bargain.

We turned up the cobble path toward Collier Boulevard. Dragging our stuff behind us, we passed a man on a bench. Sans the beat up guitar case for alms, he reminded me of the coarsely clothed hippies that jumped up and down on their cruddy bare feet to a beat of a djembe drum. He smiled, exposing his stained yellow teeth.

"Here." Chloe smiled back. She unfurled a five dollar bill from her pocket.

The man stretched out his hands. His grimy fingers grazed hers, slowly separating, and crumpled the money into his dirty palms.

"Thanks, chicky, chicky," the man said and lowered his head to the ground.

Chapter 15

The Hippie

Richard perched himself on the balcony of the suite like a raptor on the tallest limb of a tree. His body tensed as he scanned the beach below. His hands held up the binoculars, shaping his elbows into V- like wings ready to extend and swoop down on his prey. Richard scanned the horizon, viewing the waves collapsing against the ravaged coast. The clouds slowly broke up taking routes north and south and some heading inland. He knew the storm would soon be over and hoped that it would bring out a better selection of women on the beach.

The old ladies collecting shells on the beach wore one piece bathing suits stretched across their jiggling bodies. Holding down their flimsy hats, brims flapping in the wind, they grunted and bent stiffly to pick up shells. Some needed to use plastic shovels or other aids to pick up their treasures, as their backs could not flex over the roll of their bellies.

A few surfers rode the waves effortlessly through the churning waters. One couple floated away from the others. Their boards faced the sun as it lowered in the sky. The girl's boyfriend had pulled her over to his board; she lay on top of him. At least someone was getting some affection from a woman, he thought to himself.

The lack of options on the beach nearly made Richard want to jump off the balcony and sail head first into the pool below. Geriatrics didn't appeal to him. He was quite sure the impact would snap his neck like a brittle nut, ending his misery, snuffing out the desire that burned in his hollow stomach. Instead he slung himself down into the lounge chair and rubbed his hand through his hair, jerking it through the knots and the tangles that tried to entrap his fingers. The pang of desire in his groin intensified. He visually went through all the women in the lobby, picturing their faces under his knife. He knew they would scream, but screams were not what Richard wanted. He could make any woman scream; he wanted a fighter, a girl who would struggle against the weight of his body and try to rip the hair out of his head.

It was difficult to find a woman whose spirit could take the invasion of her body and not just simply let her mind slip away. He didn't want to break the woman's spirit. Not right away, anyway. He wanted the spirit to become stronger with each passing second they were together until he decided it was time for the life to slowly glitter away from her eyes, his image being the last to burn in her retinas.

Richard heard the commotion, college kids whooping and hollering a few stories below him. He raised his binoculars to see what was going on. The young man who had floated with his girlfriend fought two bigger guys. The girl lay on the sand, her knees to her stomach. The boy fought quickly, shifting his position so as not to stay in one spot. Richard laughed when the boy kicked sand in the big guy's face. He enjoyed his new entertainment. The ebb and flow of the fight went back and forth until it looked like the blonde boy would play hero to his girlfriend and defeat their attackers.

"No, no, no!" Richard muttered. The boy walked painfully over to the girl. The leaner, more agile opponent made a full charge at the blonde haired boy and clamped his arms around the boy's neck.

Richard slapped the railing, rattling it down its length. "Their weakness," he said. "Their weakness infects man and makes him a slobbering idiot. Worthless! Only good for one thing and then their purpose is served. He would have won without her!"

Barely able to keep his arms up, the boy slipped in and out of consciousness. Richard scorned the girl lying on the ground. "See what you did? Worthless. His concern for you is worthless."

Then the girl stirred herself, shaking her head. Her eyes locked on her boyfriend, who was seconds from taking a forced nap. She hurried to her surfboard and untied the rubber leash. Stretching it taut between her hands, her elongated biceps flexed.

A shiver went up Richard's back in anticipation of what she was about to do. His thumb and fingers tightened on the binoculars as the girl stepped behind the attacker. Each beat of his heart rolled up the length of his blood-engorged muscle as the girl wrapped her leash around the attacker's neck. Richard ogled the contour of her body as she strained against her opponent. Her tanned skin exploded over her muscles as they contracted under her stance. The fire in his loins raged as the unbreakable spirit of the girl flamed like a phoenix on the sand below.

* * *

Not wanting to lose track of his obsession, The Hippie rushed through the suite and down the fire escape, bounding down stories of stairs, his breath frantic. Slamming the emergency exit door open, he sprinted through the lobby and out of the hotel. He headed to the cobbled path that led down to the beach.

He slunk down beside the path. With his head bowed low and his chin tucked into his chest, he waited for the girl to pass. The boy came first, dragging his surfboard and carrying the bulk of the baggage. The girl walked behind him, pulling her board.

Richard lifted his head and leered at the girl. The white shirt she wore—a bit wet—clung to her stomach. Her jean shorts, cut at her thigh, frayed in white strings around her legs. She stopped in front of him and forced her hand into the tight crevice of her shorts pocket, pulling out a five dollar bill. As she held it out to him, he reached for it and touched her fingers. A slight breeze blew down the path, pushing the scent of coconut oil off her skin and into his nose. A shiver like a thin piece of ice going through his veins almost made him pull his knife, slice the boy's neck, and take her there. But Richard smiled and watched them walk away.

* * *

The Hippie sat restless in the corner of the movie theater, while the movie flickered on the screen. Several rows in front of him the couple sat. The girl's head lay on the boy's shoulder while his hand gently massaged her leg. Richard examined her every movement and clocked her every breath. He needed a place to think. To the delight of those around him, Richard jerked out of his seat and left. He walked outside where the muggy night leeched the air-conditioned coolness from his body. Hunting for a place to rest and plan the kidnapping, he went down to the parking garage below the theater. The buzz of the

90

artificial lights spun through his head as he sat against a concrete pillar. His knees tucked up to his chest, he laid his face down between them closing his mind off to everything around him.

The Hippie planned through every scenario he could think of, from the couple walking home, to their getting picked up in a car. He lifted his head. A moped was chained to one of the pillars. *An easy lock to pick, easy to hotwire, perfect if they are picked up in a car*, he thought. If they walked, he could move in and out of the shadows, quietly behind houses, trees and shrubs. The plan was simple: follow them, kill the boy, and he had her.

Sweat rolled underneath Richard's baggy long-sleeved shirt. He pulled it off. The tank top underneath was smeared with sweat and dirt. He folded his shirt in his lap to hide the knife shoved in the front of his pants.

An angry, drunken voice echoed through the garage. Footsteps scraped the concrete several feet behind him and came to a stop. He reached for his knife.

"I know they're in there, Trent. That little bitch nearly choked me out. Look at my neck!"

Richard's body stiffened.

"Not here, dude. When he walks her home, we'll wait by the vacant lot behind the supermarket, by the canal," Trent said. "He'll almost have her home. The last thing they'll be thinking about is us."

"I'm going to kick his ass within an inch of his life. And then I'm going to show Chloe what the hell is in the locker room. Show the little ho under the bridge," Brad grunted. "Once I'm done with her, I'll hold her for you."

"Dude, I want to get McKlusky back as bad as you do, but I'm not doing that to Chloe. I've known her since we were kids. I'm not letting you do it, either."

"You're either with me or not," Brad fired back.

"You can't do this! It's Chloe!"

"The hell I can't. My dad's the police chief. Nobody's going to say anything." Brad's words hung in the air.

Richard peeked carefully around the pillar. The two men stood by a black Mustang convertible. He recognized them from the beach. They stood face to face, cheeks boiling with blood and fists clenched, knuckles pulsing white.

Brad moved his arm quickly, pointing to the car, and Trent flinched. "Get in the car and stop being a little bitch."

"I'm not with you on this. You're not going to do that to her. It's not right, man. Getting McKlusky back is one thing." Trent looked at the ground. "But doing that to Chloe is just wrong. How could you even think of that?"

Brad took a deep breath and let out a slow exhale turning his eyes to the ceiling. "You're right. What was I thinking? Let's just go home and chill. We'll deal with McKlusky later."

Trent smiled nervously. "Yeah, man. Come on."

In one rapid movement, Brad pulled his keys out of his pocket, clenched them inside his fist and landed a punch on Trent's jaw. A mix of blood and spit splattered across the concrete floor. Trent fell, his head whacking the ground.

After popping open the car's trunk, Brad heaved Trent's unconscious body up. Straining and fumbling to keep hold of the bulky weight, Brad shoved Trent in the trunk and slammed it shut. "You could've had a fine piece of ass tonight, buddy."

Richard's hand clenched the handle of the knife and slipped it out of the sheath. With his torso bent low, he rushed the distance between him and Brad, not giving the noise time to register in Brad's ears until he was right behind him. Brad spun around and felt the hand of The Hippie across his mouth and the blade of the knife against his neck.

Brad's eyes screamed his fear for himself at the sight of the man before him. Streams of sweat soiled with dirt streamed down Richard's thin muscular arms. The sweat dripping from his beard made Richard seem more like a rapid dog than a man.

Richard steadied his breath, ready to slice the boy's throat with a flick of his wrist. "I'm going to take my hand from your mouth. If you scream, I'll slit you like a little piggy. Do you understand?" Richard put more pressure on the knife, just enough to break the boy's skin. Blood spread down Brad's neck and onto his chest.

"Yes," came Brad's muffled reply.

"Good boy." Richard dropped his hand from Brad's mouth.

"Ple..." is all Brad said. Richard slipped the knife into Brad's mouth cutting off the rest of the word.

"I told you to keep your mouth shut. Did you think I was kidding?" He grabbed the back of Brad's hair and moved behind him, turning the blade inside Brad's mouth. The knife point peeked out of Brad's cheek. Blood spewed down the side of his face.

"While I appreciate your choice in women, Chloe is mine." Richard took the blade out of Brad's mouth, severing Brad's bottom lip. "Do you understand?" Richard pulled Brad's head back so he was looking down into his eyes. "Brad, do you understand?"

Brad nodded his head.

"Good!" Richard ripped the blade across Brad's neck. The shock the eyes displayed when his victims realized their life had actually come to an end was what Richard found fascinating. The glimmer suffocated. Here and then gone. Richard wasn't big on killing men. There was no satisfaction in it for him; it didn't excite him. It revolted his stomach and sent the pangs of reminders of what his father had done to him. He picked up the keys that Brad had dropped and popped open the trunk. He flopped Brad's body on top of Trent's unconscious one and slammed the trunk.

He quietly let the newfound name, Chloe, pass through his lips, liking the way the consonants started sharply in the back of his mouth and rounded smoothly out around his lips when he sounded the vowels.

* * *

The bugs swarmed and clung to the streetlights as the heavy mist of humidity settled down on the street. It was silent and dead. The youth had nearly been smothered out of the island by the barren old and the widows, keeping the nightlife to a minimum.

Richard watched Chloe and McKlusky from the confines of Brad's car. The couple strolled down West Elkcam Street in front of the grocery store, his arm around her shoulder, and her hand in his back pocket. The boy pulled out his cell phone and made a call. They continued their walk, whispering on their way to Joy Circle, deliberately taking slow steps to prolong their time together. The security lights flooded Chloe's driveway as they walked up to the house. McKlusky leaned in to kiss Chloe, and she in turn put one hand behind his neck and pulled him closer as he wrapped his hand around her waist. Richard fumed. He coveted what the boy possessed. He burned to cut the young fool's tongue out of his mouth, so he could never use it to kiss her again.

McKlusky and Chloe separated their bodies. Chloe put her hands in her pockets, leaned back and smiled like the devil had just possessed her. She unlocked the door and with a bend of a knee and with a sheepish wave she disappeared into her house. The boy walked down the road.

Richard slipped out of the Mustang and slinked into a row of hedges in the neighbor's yard. He pulled his knife, keeping his breath shallow and light in fear the boy would hear him. Richard knew he would have to make it quick. Reach out, grab the boy, and slit his throat. There was no time to gloat or describe in detail what he was going to do to Chloe to intensify the death for the boy. A stray car or neighbor might wander down the street and hear the commotion.

As McKlusky's footsteps moved closer, Richard crouched, tensing his calves, ready to spring. A few steps closer. The Hippie panted, shifting like a cat crouched and hidden in the weeds. A roar of an engine and headlights swept the road. Richard ducked lower, his back now shoved up against the bushes. The car squealed to a stop in front of McKlusky.

"Hey, boy," the voice from the truck said.

"Damn, Grandpa, where've you been? I called you like ten minutes ago."

"You better watch that language with me. Hop in. We gotta go check on the Flounder. I just talked to that Becker fellow. He still wants to go sightseeing."

McKlusky hopped in the truck. It sped off, leaving the acerbic taste of burnt rubber in Richard's mouth.

His heart still cranked in anticipation of the act he had been denied. He slammed his fist into the ground only to bring it back with a knuckle full of sandspurs. The spurs released thin trickles of blood between his fingers. The boy's death didn't matter. The Hippie knew McKlusky would never see Chloe again. He eyed the canals that led right behind Chloe's house, Smokehouse Bay.

Chapter 16

Chloe

Mrs. O'Malley wondered how Chloe had grown so fast. The last physical part of her husband and their love for each other now lived in the beautiful young woman who sat on the barstool. "Tell me about your date."

"What do you want to know?" Chloe asked as she sat on the stool in the kitchen.

"Well, all at once from friends to more than friends. It happened fast. How is it going?" Mrs. O'Malley set a bowl of chocolate ice cream in front of her daughter.

Chloe attacked it, talking with her mouth full. "Well, it just kind of happened. I really don't know—God! Brain freeze!" She shook her head and sucked in air to warm her mouth. "It's like it's always been there, like I have always felt this way for him, and we have been friends forever."

"Being friends is always a good thing. It makes it easier to trust each other. Do you feel comfortable around him?"

"Yes. I mean—I do, and I feel safe. He's honest with his words." Chloe jammed her spoon into the frozen clump and scooped a more genteel bite than the first.

"That's good. Just make sure you don't feel too comfortable. At least not yet, anyway," Mrs. O'Malley said with a smile.

Chloe ate her ice cream with an "mmmmm..." until the full intent of her mother's statement hit her. Her face flushed hot enough to melt the next spoonful of chocolate. "Momma!"

"I was your age too, darling. I know what girls think. Besides he has turned into a handsome young man. I'm sure having him at the beach with his shirt off was not the worst part of your day."

"Momma, stop it!" she said pleading, sitting straight up in her chair, "You're embarrassing me!"

"Okay, okay!" Mrs. O'Malley giggled. "I'll stop. I'm sorry, baby."

Chloe leaned over the bowl and snorted. "And no, Mother, it was not the worst part of my day." They laughed like friends comparing notes on a date. Chloe bounced her head on the counter, sucking in her lips. She couldn't believe she just said that to her mother.

Mrs. O'Malley patted Chloe's back with a snicker. "Honey, I'm glad you noticed. I'd think something was wrong with you if you didn't."

"He's coming over tomorrow. Don't act like this around him, please."

"I won't, but why don't we do something a little special?"

Chloe eyed her mother suspiciously. "Like what. Something that will help me be a little more domesticated?" Chloe took her bowl to the sink.

"No. Well, maybe a little. A girl can't be all grit and gristle like you. She needs a little feminine side. We could just cook something nice."

"I seem to be feminine enough for McKlusky," Chloe shot back.

"Exactly what I'm afraid of. At least if you two are here I can keep my eye on both of you." Mrs. O'Malley leaned back on the kitchen counter and drummed her fingers waiting for her daughter's answer.

Chloe considered her alternative. It was all or nothing with her mother. Either you did all she said or you got nothing. And that meant not seeing McKlusky at all if she didn't agree. "Fine," Chloe finally said, resigning herself to the fate of slaving over a stove. "What are you going to teach me to cook?"

"Snook and key lime pie." Mrs. O'Malley said the name of the dessert as if it were already in her mouth.

"Well, where are we going to get the snook? They're illegal to catch right now," Chloe said.

"Darling, we have a perfectly good dock with lights. I saw one under there a few nights ago when I couldn't sleep. I'm sure you can catch it."

"You know you're asking me to break the law," Chloe said with a hint of bewilderment.

"Honey, you're half Seminole. Our people were here long before the laws."

96

"Well, since you put it that way." There was no arguing with her mother when it came to the rights of the Seminole people, even if what she claimed was not always legal. "I need bait. Are you going to take me?"

"There are a dozen live shrimp in the bait cage tied to the dock and high tide is at 1 AM." Mrs. O'Malley's grin spread.

"You had this planned all along whether I agreed or not." Chloe raised her hands in surrender. "Okay, Momma, you win! You're sure not going to hear any objection from me."

"I didn't think I would if it concerned McKlusky."

* * *

Chloe lay back on her bed sinking into the comforter. A satisfied smile grew on her face as she replayed the day through her mind: the kisses, the silent moments looking out to sea, and the brushes of her skin against his.

She relaxed further down into the comforter, pushing her head deep into the pillow, daydreaming of what her and McKlusky's wedding would look like, the gown, the flowers, and his smile, beckoning her into his life for good. Images of white picket fences and chubby babies crawling through the house zoomed through her mind and raced to both her and McKlusky in rockers. She almost fell asleep, her thoughts becoming the continuous looping of dreams, when she turned to look at the clock. Through the blur in her eyes, she made out the fuzzy red lines that read 12:45 AM. Battling the creeping sleep that tried to pull her eyes closed, she rolled out of the comforting cocoon her sheets formed around her and slung her feet to the floor. She almost lay back down and snuggled back up with the thoughts of love being made and babies being born.

"Get with it, Chloe," she encouraged herself. She rubbed at the grit that had crept into her eyes. Fighting to keep her sandals on her feet, she clunked to the garage and flipped the light switch. The hissing fluorescents lights didn't help dispel her tiredness.

"Snook?" Exhaustion entered her voice. "What to use?" She touched each of the fishing poles that lined the garage. The lights now forced her eyes to adjust to their intrusiveness. She wasn't interested in making this a sporting expedition. The snook needed to be hooked, on the dock, and in the house before the struggling behemoth's first splash could alert the neighbors or any lurking law enforcement. *A cane pole,* she thought.

The cane pole and forty pound test line offered the quickest possible catch. As long as the pole or the line didn't break, the snook could only run as far as the pole could bend. It could be slung on the dock as quickly as Chloe could yank it out of the water.

Chloe walked her rig through the house across the cool marble floor and slid open the glass door. A wave of damp moisture hit her opening up her pores. If she wasn't fully awake before, she was now. The sounds of crickets chorused throughout the neighborhood to the left and then right in a shouting match. The moon settled low in its orange glow, taking a short rest before it began to pull the tide back out. Dew enveloped the thick sod grass and lapped over the top of Chloe's sandals, causing her feet to slip inside the rubbery soles as she walked down to the dock.

Not wanting to scare the snook away from its rest under the lights, she padded softly onto the planks. She lay her pole down and crept up to the lights, looking for her prey.

The snook rested in the middle light. Its gills huffed the water as it hovered motionless, floating effortlessly. Small crustaceans zipped past its body, avoiding the stout mouth. The light passed through the translucent yellow tinges on its tail, illuminating the slanted thick black strip that ran down each side of its body from the top of its gill down to the middle of its tail. Its eyes shifted back and forth, looking at the light above as if mesmerized by some alien aircraft entering its sphere.

Chloe surged with excitement and almost let out a string of obscenities when she saw the thickness of the silver monster. Easing to the other end of the dock, she lifted the shrimp out of the water. They popped and snapped on the bottom of the cage. Snagging a plump shrimp, its antennas whipping and clinging to her fingers, she pinched it in half. Sliding the top half of the shrimp over the hook, she set the cage in the water and quietly returned to the snook. She placed the shrimp up current of the fish and floated it down in front of its face.

The snook floated motionless as the bait approached. Chloe tightened her grip on the pole anticipating the sudden assault when the snook latched on the hook. The snook let the piece of shrimp approach and pass, not giving it a second glance.

Chloe tried again, this time letting the shrimp bounce right off the top of the snook's mouth. The fish lay there stubbornly, its mouth turned up at Chloe, refusing the dinner she offered. She ripped the shrimp off the hook and threw it into the water. Mangrove snapper, their black tattooed eyes flashing in the light, bolted from the bottom of the pylon and tore the shrimp into pieces with their elongated pointed teeth.

"Uuuughhhhh," Chloe sighed, "Can you please make this easy, Mr. Snook?" She placed a hand on her hip and released her breath, drumming it through her lips. The sweat on her face became irritating and mosquitoes honed in on the blood beneath her skin. She swatted them away. She slipped the tail of the shrimp over the hook. She bounced the shrimp in front of the snook again. Its mouth clamped stoically, ignoring the tasty piece of meat that floated in front of its eyes. A mangrove snapper, seeing another opportunity to feed, zipped from the bottom and tore the shrimp off the hook that was too big for its mouth.

Chloe crumpled on the dock, not caring whether the snook fled from the vibrations in the water. She pulled her knees under her chin, clenched her fist in a ball and punched the air in frustration. Sweat drizzled down her back, her shirt clung to her body, which added to the misery of her failure. She lightly banged her forehead on her kneecap to make herself think. "This is so not cool."

A mosquito landed on her cheek, and she whacked it so hard that her eyes began to water. Her handprint was outlined on the side of her face. Burning with anger, she stomped over to the bait cage and pulled it back up. The shrimp scattered to the left and right in the cage, popping themselves into the air to try and escape the massive hand that headed toward them.

Chloe grabbed the biggest, plumpest shrimp she could find. Its antennas wavered in the air as its little legs tried to scrape toward freedom against her palm. She glared at it menacingly. "Now, do your job and catch the freaking fish." Its little black eyes stared back at Chloe as if it were resigned to its fate. Chloe wondered if any shrimp ever met with a natural death, or if all were just eaten.

The hook went into the back of the shrimp. It snapped on the end of the line, flicking at the air. Chloe plopped the shrimp in the water. Paddling its legs one after the other, it tried to head to the bottom, but Chloe jerked the shrimp toward the snook. The shrimp froze. The snook's eyes shifted forward, curious about this new offering. But it still didn't unseal its mouth. In frustration, Chloe jerked the line and the snook inhaled the shrimp, popped the surface of the water, and tried to swim toward the bottom, setting the hook in the corner of its mouth.

Shocked, Chloe bobbled the pole, but gripped it back tight and yanked it upward to keep the fish from wrapping around the pylon and cutting itself off on the sharp ragged barnacles that grew on the pylon's surface. The snook pulled back as it shook its massive body, frothing the water. The sound of the splash hung in the air sounding far down the canal.

"Got to get him out quick." She clamped the pole underneath her armpit, planted her feet, and pulled back. The snook boiled the surface, whacking its broad tail on the water. Chloe had heard this violent thrashing sound in the canal many times before. On slow nights, law enforcement sat in the dark and listened for splashing. Then they sought out the source to write the offender a hefty fine for harvesting snook out of season.

Taking a deep breath, Chloe squatted and popped up, yanking the pole at the same time. The snook's body flew into the air, making a sucking sound as it exited the water. It flipped end over end, crashed on the dock, and tried to flap its body back to the water. The dock shook under its hammering tail. Chloe sprang between the water and the fish. She gave one powerful swipe to the fish's body with the side of her foot and sent the monster to the edge of the lawn. Pumping her fist in the air, she let out a shout louder than she should have. She rushed toward the snook, unhooked it, and picked it up by the mouth with both hands. It nearly spanned the length of her leg and would never be legal, in or out of season.

Exhausted by the day and the fish that hung by her side, she wanted nothing more now than to throw this thing in the garage's refrigerator, take a shower, and get some sleep. Cleaning the snook could wait until morning, after it had died. She heaved the snook up and dragged it to the house. Its flopping tail trailed in the wet grass.

"Hold it!" A spotlight illuminated her as a boat motored up to the dock. "What do you think you're doing, young lady?" The raspy voice waited for a reply.

Chloe's heart plummeted to the pit of her stomach. Turning around slowly, her eyes revolted against the violent light that now assaulted them.

"Where are you going with that fish?"

Chloe shielded her eyes. The snook hung heavily against her leg now caked in slime from the snook's skin. "Sir, I..." Chloe couldn't think of any words to explain.

"Bring it here," the voice commanded. "Where are your parents? Are they here?"

"My mother is asleep in the house. My father is no longer alive." Chloe felt a twinge in her chest. Even though she knew her father was dead, saying it always made it harder to accept.

"I'm sorry to hear that, Miss." The voice sounded almost apologetic. "But you need to bring me that fish now."

Chloe dragged the fish back to the dock. The snook flapped, sensing itself getting closer to the water. "Sir, I'll throw it back; I won't do it again. Please don't' wake..."

"Bring it here," the voice interrupted.

Chloe stepped onto the dock. The light grew brighter in her eyes as she drew closer to the boat. She smelled a slight stench coming from beyond the light.

"Lay the fish at the edge of the dock."

Chloe laid the snook down, holding it to keep it from flopping into the boat. The spotlight followed her.

"It looks like she is struggling to stay alive. These fish have a tremendous spirit, but there is a limit to what they can take. I like a fighting spirit." The voice hesitated. "Like the one you showed on the beach today."

"Wh-what?" The light shut off. Chloe's eyes flashed to black as her pupils opened wider trying to collect the little light that surrounded the dock. They focused on the man in the boat, his beard and smile, the dim reality of recognition. Her legs tensed to spring and run toward the house. But The Hippie's hands reacted faster. He placed one behind her head and one over her mouth. Chloe dug her fingernails into the dock to keep from being pulled in. One popped off, a stabbing pain wove its way through her body. Her head hit the dock. In one swift move, she was pulled into the boat and pinned to the deck.

Writhing underneath the coarseness of his clothes, she struggled to unlock her body from his. He placed a hand over her mouth to keep her from yelling. Chloe thrashed her legs, and he wedged his knees between them, spreading them apart. She bit his palm, but he just smiled at her. Richard pulled a sock out of his pocket and forced it into her mouth.

Chloe whaled repeatedly on his chest, sending one punch into his diaphragm causing him to gasp for breath. He leaned over pressing the weight of his body against her, closing the distance her fists could travel. The Hippie thrust his arms between their bodies, fighting for control of her hands. Grabbing one of her wrists in each of his hands, he brought them together and slammed them over her head against the fiberglass hull. Chloe breathed desperately through her nose. The sock scratched the back of her throat every time she tried to scream through it.

"Now, chicky, chicky, you need to calm down." His knees spread her legs wider, straining the muscles in her groin. Tears of anger, hate, and fear were hot on her face. "I like the struggle already." He took her wrists in one hand. With the other, he traced the hemp necklace as it tightened and loosened on her flexing neck.

Chloe felt the violence he wanted to do to her press against her body. She pushed against his hand that held her wrists. He was too strong.

"You really make me want you now, Chloe. I've never been turned on so quickly before." He rubbed harder on her. "Must be patient though." The Hippie shuddered, wincing his face.

Chloe felt the hardness slowly disappearing. To think of what he had just done sickened her. She struggled to free her legs as he pulled a piece of rope from his pocket. After he lashed her wrists together, he dragged her to the stern of the boat. She tried to hook her legs around the center console to stop her body. Richard gave a big yank, causing one of Chloe's sandals to flip onto the dock. Gaining control, he put a foot on her chest, pinned her down, and tied her wrists to one of the metal poles that supported the bench seat behind the console. He then tied her ankles to the other.

Chloe jerked against the poles. Richard looked down at her as he sat in the chair and put the boat in gear.

"We'll go have a little fun now. I will make a woman out of you soon."

Part 2

The End

Chapter 17

Dismal Key

Kaitlin tried to spring up when she heard the helicopter's blades slitting the air. The ropes were a harsh reminder that she was still a prisoner, but the thought of being rescued chased the throbbing in her wrists away. The tin roof clattered as the helicopter landed, allowing tiny drops of water stuck in the creases to shower down and wet her parched lips.

Joe still snored off his drunkenness. A small pool of blood had crisped around Joe's head and glued his hair to the floor. Earlier, Kaitlin had feared him waking every time lightning and thunder rattled the shack. Her mind devoured all other thoughts except Jada's escape. She mourned her when she convinced herself Jada was dead. She got sick when she convinced herself Billy caught Jada and had his way with her. Like a machete embedded in her head, that thought stuck in Kaitlin's mind, cancerously eating away at any hope for her survival.

Now, hope awakened in her mind. While she waited for her rescuers to storm the shack, she swore she would make them let her kick Joe awake.

The helicopter landed, and its engines shut off.

* * *

Joe woke to a kick to the gut. He doubled over, vomiting the liquor his body couldn't absorb from his binge the night before. A hand dragged him up by the scruff of his collar and shoved him outside. He fell on the drenched sand, jarring his chest. Joe felt the cool dampness spread across his exposed groin.

"Why are your pants down, Joe?"

Joe groaned and rolled on his side. The smell of a freshly lit cigar drifted down, turning his stomach, making him vomit again. He rubbed his hands over his head. The soft evening light flickering on the ground felt like a dull knife being twisted in his eyes. A boot slammed into the small of his back, contorting his torso in a backwards arch. He tried to grasp at the pain that radiated out, but he was snapped up again and slammed upright against a palm tree, a heavy hand pressed against his chest.

Several slaps across the face made Joe's eyes hang loosely open and adjust to the creeping darkness. A puff of smoke wrapped around his head as Marcus' form went from hazy to sharp. His mouth inches from Joe's nose, Marcus' tobacco-stained teeth gritted and began to move. "Three questions, Joe. One, why are your pants down? Two, where is Billy?" Marcus paused, his face turning red. "And the most important: Where the bloody hell is Jada?" Marcus' fist hammered Joe's jaw. Blood poured into Joe's mouth, mixing with the stale taste of chewing tobacco.

Marcus threw Joe to the ground. His body hit the sand with another crunch. Joe tried to congeal the hazy memories through the fog of whiskey's reality and his passed out dreams. His last memories were of Jada pouncing on him like a cornered animal, Billy yelling his name, and then blackness.

Karam placed the nozzle of the AK-47 on Joe's forehead. He leaned his shoulder on the butt of the rifle, pushing it down and twisting it in a half circle motion. Karam placed his finger inside the trigger and tapped it gently.

Joe flinched, expecting a bullet to tunnel through his skull. Karam snickered, amused as he clicked the safety off of the gun.

"Joe, ol' chap, last chance," Marcus said. "Where are they?"

"Billy," Joe stammered. "I was giving the girls a hard time. Goin' to, you know, look at them while having a little fun with myself. That's why my pants are down. Billy came in and put a gun to my head. Said he was taking the black girl. Said he always wanted one and hit me with the gun." Joe's eyes darted back and forth up into the corner of his sockets as he tried to piece his story together. Karam pushed the barrel harder into Joe's forehead, causing him to stammer even more. "He must have taken her! Marcus, I can find her. I know where Billy took her."

Marcus put his hand on Karam's hand and eased it, along with the barrel, off of Joe's head. Joe sniveled a sigh of relief.

"Joe." Marcus placed his cigar in his mouth and snatched Joe up with both hands around the collar. "When did this happen?"

"Early, early this morning before sun up. The storm was still raging. He couldn't a got far in it, Marcus I swear. He don't know this place as well as me. I can find them for you."

"What makes you think you can find them?" Karam asked.

"They couldn't have gotten far. They'd had to take the canoe because I got the key to the mullet skiff. The way the wind was blowing, they'd have no choice but to be blown east up into one of the bays. There ain't no place for them to camp up that way. It's just swamps and mangroves. Billy don't know enough to find his way out."

Figuring that Jada had escaped and Billy took off leaving him to pay the price, Joe hoped his story bought him enough time to skip town and hide from Marcus for the rest of his life.

Marcus punched Joe on the other side of the jaw, spurting a fresh gush of blood. "You'd better find her. She is very valuable to me."

Marcus stood up, brushing off his suit. "Karam, speak with me a minute." Karam followed Marcus over to the helicopter. Its skids were planted in the sand. Marcus placed his hand on his son's back. "There is a good chance we'll have to get the hell out of here if Jada is found. I need you to scan the emergency radio frequencies in the helicopter. Any mention of her being found, I want you to shoot Joe. We'll get the other girl to the boat and head to Cuba one girl short."

"What about Richard?" Karam asked.

Marcus sighed a white trail of smoke. "We'll see. The animal may be let loose on the world again."

* * *

Marcus entered the shack. His air of confidence and self-imposed suavity made Kaitlin's stomach turn sour. Scrutinizing the picture of the man, woman, and child on the desk he asked, "Someone you know, Kaitlin?" Not waiting for an answer he continued. "They look happy." Marcus picked up the chair toppled on the floor and sat down.

Kaitlin no longer felt emotions or fear. She asked, "How do you know my name?" The hope spawned from the approaching helicopter stagnated when she realized the two men who entered the shack had started violently kicking Joe, showing no interest in her whatsoever.

109

"I make it a point to know all the girls." Marcus reached inside his pocket and pulled out a license. He flipped the picture toward Kaitlin. "However, I know you from your license. My son found it on you when he kidnapped you off the beach in Hilton Head."

"Why? Why me?" Kaitlin asked.

"The *why* I can't help you with. Ask God. Wrong place, wrong time, I can help you with. We needed an attractive blonde girl. My son decided Hilton Head would be as good a place as any." Marcus sighed and looked at Kaitlin sympathetically. "And you happened to be an attractive blonde girl walking the beach at night and crossed paths with my son."

Kaitlin could no longer hold the tears she tried to hide from the presence of this smug man who sat before her. "Just because?"

"Just because we needed you or someone who looked like you. We try to be random about where we take our girls from. Taking too many at a time or even more than one from an area causes too much suspicion." Marcus stood and walked to her, pulling the chair behind him. His shoes scraped the dust on the rotting wooden floors. Kaitlin cringed from his advance.

"There's no need to fear me. I won't hurt you." He placed the chair by the bed, sat down and eyed her as if examining a prized horse. "I was actually fearful you might escape. Being pre-med and all, you're obviously smarter than Joe and Billy put together."

Kaitlin was stunned about how much this man knew about her. "How do you know I'm pre-med?"

"Your face is all over the news right now, along with stories of you accomplishments, dreams, and everything else that will strum at the hearts of Americans. The media eats this kind of shit up, until it sours in its mouth and spits it out for a new story. " Kaitlin turned her face away, her body aching with despair. Marcus leaned back in the chair and rested his hands on his head. "So Jada escaped? I'm surprised she didn't help you." Marcus clenched the cigar in his teeth.

So they had not found Jada, Kaitlin thought. The hope in her stomach shifted a little and perked up. She remained silent.

"Joe says, Billy knocked him out and took her."

Kaitlin fumed. The one thing she wouldn't do was allow Joe to get away with what he tried to do to her. "He lied. He was drunk and tried to rape me. Jada stopped him, and she did try to help me escape until that other asshole came in and took Joe's gun." Kaitlin sucked in her breath. "I hope you killed him. I don't know what happened to Billy. He ran after Jada." She considered her next words. "I hope you kill him, too."

Marcus slumped down in his chair. Kaitlin could tell from the fury that twitched the corner of his mouth he didn't like her version of the story. Marcus sucked on his cigar and exhaled the smoke with his words. "I didn't believe him either. But he is a useful idiot. He knows the area. He may still be able to find Jada. The canoe is gone. Either washed away or taken by Jada or Billy. But we both know Joe lied." Marcus' eyes looked around the room until they settled on the headboard with pieces of frayed rope snagged in the rusted hole. "Rust," Marcus said, stupefied. "Two of my men beat by a corrosive process. At least they tied you up properly."

"How fortunate for me," Kaitlin snapped.

"When's the last time you ate?" Marcus asked.

"Huh?"

"When is the last time you ate?"

"I don't know," she said bitterly. She knew Marcus was offering and didn't want to depend on him for anything, but the word "ate" automatically rumbled her stomach. The last thing she could remember eating was a lime, following a tequila shot. Her mind had been too preoccupied since she woke up to even think about food.

"We'll remedy that, then." Marcus stood to leave the shack.

"Where are you taking me?"

"Well, dinner will be here. You can call it room service if you like."

Kaitlin considered the cruelty in his words. "No, asshole, where are you taking me?"

"Cuba." Marcus walked out.

"Cuba?" Kaitlin shut her eyes and struggled to push the discomfort caused by the dampness of the mattress, her thirst, and now her hunger out of her thoughts.

* * *

The soft shadows of evening slowly crept to dark as the stars dazzled the night sky far away. Static filled Karam's ears. The local police communications coming from Marco Island and Everglades City consisted of complaints about kids throwing parties on random islands. His eyelids were heavy. They wanted to cover his good eye and hide the dullness of his bad eye. He'd slept little since he took Kaitlin from Hilton Head days ago. Moreover, he hadn't felt comfortable during Tropical Storm Rachel. He, in fact, feared it. Its tumultuous winds and towering waves reminded him of another storm. The rough ridged scars on his arms that rose and fell like a battered mountain range were the only visible trace Hurricane Gilbert left.

Karam had reached his twelfth birthday when Hurricane Gilbert sent a nineteen-foot storm surge into his village. His house, not much better than the shack that Kaitlin occupied, was washed away. Karam, his parents, and younger sister had been engulfed in the flood with the rag tag pieces of building materials left over from the construction of an all-inclusive resort on Montego Bay. Barely keeping himself on top of a makeshift plywood raft, Karam reached out for his mother. She clamored beside the raft and grasped his hand while the other desperately clutched Karam's sister. His father's body rushed by, floating face down, twisting and turning with the current like a limp fish. His mother ripped her hand from Karam's as she tried to grab her husband's body. His mother's and sister's shrieks disappeared, quickly joining the ravenous howls of the wind.

Left homeless and orphaned, Karam developed into a muscular young man. He stole to survive until his older teenage years. Then he turned to prostitution. He walked the beaches of the resorts, selling his body to rich, middle aged, white women who desired what they called, "the big bamboo." Of course, Karam savored his work as any teenage boy would.

Being caught by a jealous husband, who returned from a fishing excursion early, ended his stint at prostitution. The husband pinned Karam down on the bed and charred his eye with a cigarette. Scarred and hideous, women no longer desired him. He wore a patch for a time. But he liked the intimidation his deformed eye caused others to feel. So he used it to his advantage.

To survive, Karam embraced the slums the flood had ejected him from. He partook in back alley fights for money. Using fists, feet, knives, bottles, sticks, or any object to win, he bitterly beat the other competitors and even sent some to their death. Each battle tattooed itself across his arms and face. During one of his more gruesome fights, Karam caught Marcus' eye. As blood seeped down his face and arms, Karam killed the boy who nearly killed him, by smashing the boy's larynx. After his opponent fell, The Jamaican collapsed on the blood-soaked dust, thinking he would bleed to death.

Marcus collected Karam's broken body and cared for him on the yacht. Once the physical wounds had scarred over, Marcus made the boy his bodyguard. At first Karam feared Marcus would want to use his body. He'd witnessed Marcus around the slums of Jamaica before, calling on the young boys to visit him. However, he soon adopted Karam as his son. Marcus never showed anything toward Karam but the type of love and care that a father should lavish on his son. Marcus also lavished him with money and women provided through human trafficking.

* * *

The night relaxed its grip to allow the probing light of the sun through. Karam's head nodded and popped back up, fighting the encroaching sleep that demanded to take over his body.

Snap!

Karam sprang up, chasing the sleep away. He flipped up his AK-47 as he heard movement coming down the path. He secured a position behind the helicopter door and lined up the sights of the gun on the path. His finger slid across the trigger; his thumb clicked off the safety. Richard burst into the clearing, shoving a girl to the sand.

"You cranky little bitch," The Hippie snorted. "You kick me again and I'll slit your throat." Karam could see Richard's ritual of torture had begun. He knew The Hippie reveled in the back kick the girl tried to deliver as he pushed her along. Had Richard not been watching, she very well might have doubled him over and run back down the path to the water. But he was able to capture the blow at her ankle and flip her forward.

Karam moved from behind the door and lumbered over the girl, lifting her chin up with his boot. He observed the black tempest of anger raging in her eyes like the winds of the hurricane that destroyed his family. He knelt before her, flicking his eye over her body. His other eye, empty and cold, held its steady, useless gaze. "So you think me ugly, no?" He drew closer. "I can see it in your eyes. You despise me. It's not me you should fear, girl. But it is the man who brought you here." Karam dropped her chin. "You should fear him."

The girl choked unintelligible words through the sock. They weren't of fear or pleas for freedom but a line of obscenities and threats.

"This is Chloe, Karam. Karam, Chloe." Richard dragged Chloe up by her hair. She clasped his arm and ground her fingernails into his skin. Richard bit her on the back of the neck, sinking in his teeth, leaving an indentation. A cry of anguish escaped from underneath the sock.

"Now, now, chicky, chicky, don't go getting me all worked up just yet."

"The shack, Richard," Marcus walked toward them. "Put her in the shack for now."

"This is Chloe, boss." Richard displayed her as one would do a new toy.

Marcus examined the perfectly toned body struggling before him. The better the body the better the price: the muscular legs, Indian heritage, and raging eyes. Chloe could bring him a fortune. "Do you think one so young is wise, Richard? Even you must have some sort of a conscience."

"That died a long time ago." Richard moved in front of Chloe to halt Marcus' gaze.

114

Marcus whipped a handkerchief from his front pocket and dabbed the sweat that slowly beaded on his forehead. "Where's the boat?"

"Anchored near the passage." Richard's eyes looked to both Marcus and Karam. "How much time do I have with her?"

"Until this evening," Marcus said.

"Why so little?" Richard asked, annoyed.

"Jada escaped," Karam said. "The one you took off the mountain."

"I know it is not as much time as you wanted, but you must make do. I'm sending Joe and Karam out in the boat to find Jada," Marcus said. Karam glanced at his father, surprised at the news.

Marcus ignored the look and continued his conversation with Richard. "Take Chloe to the shack for now."

Chloe attempted to break Richard's grasp. She knew what The Hippie wanted to do to her. He coveted what was not his to take. Richard yanked her to the shack like a tethered horse to be put in the barn. Tears streaked through the sand dimpled on her cheeks.

As he watched Richard and Chloe go, Marcus lit his first cigar of the day. "Karam, I need you to go with Joe because if you find Jada, I need it to go smoothly."

What if we don't find her?" Karam picked up a shell and hurled it at Joe who slept under a tree. The shell split Joe's forehead. Joe woke with a yelp. Blood bulleted down the ridge of his nose.

Marcus chuckled, "If not, shoot Joe and then come back. I'm going to stay here and make sure nothing happens to Chloe."

"Why do you care what happens to her?" Karam questioned.

"I don't, but she can replace Jada if you don't find her."

"What about Richard?"

"We'll let Richard have his way with her, just not kill her. Either way we're covered. If we find Jada, great, Richard can kill Chloe. If not, then he can have Chloe but spare her life."

"You know killing her is what he wants." Karam slung his rifle over his shoulder. "It is all he will settle for."

"I know. All the more important you help Joe find Jada." Marcus shifted his attention to Joe, who patted his shirt on the stream of blood dribbling down his face. "You should be more careful when you sleep, Joe."

"Yes, sir." Joe struggled to form his tongue into the words that needed to spew from his mouth. He knew this was the beginning of the torture he would face for the day.

"Richard has returned with the Pathfinder. Do you know where Jada might be?" Marcus said, doubtful that any truth would come out of Joe's mouth.

"Yes." Hope loosened the words on his tongue. The Pathfinder was more than he could've hoped for. It was twenty times the boat of his mullet skiff. He'd be to his house and on the road in twenty minutes. "I'll find her."

"Good." Marcus said. "Because if you don't. I'll kill you." Marcus paused. "You're to take Karam and search for Jada."

Joe's expression changed. His drooping cheeks and jaw made him resemble a bull dog. Escape would be impossible with Karam on the boat. "I'll find her. I promise," he mumbled.

"Let's get to the boat." Karam pushed Joe forward.

* * *

Richard tossed Chloe onto the bed. Her body bounced up and down on the mattress. Chloe rocketed up to fight, only to be forced back down and have her hands tied to the side of the bed. Securing Chloe's legs, he traced the curvature of her calf and went down to her feet. He tickled the bottoms playfully. He grabbed a big toe and shook it back and forth, a giddy smile across his face. "This little piggy…"

"She told me about you," Kaitlin blurted out to Richard as he brooded like a vulture over Chloe.

Richard went over to Kaitlin.

"She told me about you. Jada told me a hippie took her. You fit the bill." Kaitlin showed no fear.

Richard looked perplexed, confused about the ease with which this girl spoke to him. "Hush, girl," he whispered.

116

Kaitlin shifted her stare to Chloe whose mouth still formed an *O* around the sock. She turned back to Richard. "Why?" Kaitlin said like a defiant child. "I know you can't touch me."

Richard ripped the knife from under his shirt and placed it below Kaitlin's chin. "I don't care what I can or can't do to you."

"Richard," Marcus entered the shack, "off limits!"

"Boss, I was just going to cut out her tongue." Richard glared at Marcus. "Through her chin."

"Not today. Not her." Marcus reached to his side as if rubbing his back, feeling for the handle of his gun. "You have her." He nodded toward Chloe. "I know your time is short to do what you want to do. Take a walk. Work out the scenario in your mind. Make it count." Marcus sat on the bed at Chloe's feet. "Make it last as long as you can."

Richard withdrew the knife from Kaitlin's throat, gazing at Marcus, and then back to Chloe. "I'll be back later to finish our game without any interruptions." Richard left the room.

"Testy today, isn't he, ladies?" Marcus loomed over Chloe and eased the sock out of her mouth. "There may be hope for you yet, Chloe. Although it may not be the kind of hope you want. But compared to what is about to happen to you."

Chloe blinked. She wanted to spit in his face, but the sock had dried the moisture from her mouth. Marcus turned to her again but remained silent. He left the shack.

"Chloe," Kaitlin said. "That's a beautiful name."

Chloe cleared her throat. "Who are you?"

"I'm Kaitlin. I was brought here a couple days ago. There was another girl, but she escaped yesterday morning during the storm. Did you see how you came in? We might be able to find out where we are." Kaitlin's voice had an edge of excitement.

Chloe closed her eyes and leaned her head back on the pillow. "We're on Dismal Key."

"How do you know where we are?"

"I'm from here—the area I mean. My parents and I would sometimes go fishing off the beach on the east side of the island. It was a great place to picnic until the crazy hermit took it over."

"Crazy hermit? Crazy or not, I wish he was here instead of these guys." Kaitlin let out a little laugh.

"Me, too," Chloe said.

* * *

Joe idled the Pathfinder into Pumpkin Bay, pretending to look for any signs of Jada. He fidgeted with the controls on the console, trying to forget that Karam stood behind him with the AK-47 slung on his shoulder. He had been waiting for Karam to move to the very back of the boat, so he could slam the engine into high gear and tumble Karam off the boat. But Karam never wandered more than a couple feet from Joe, his good eye watching Joe's every movement.

Joe turned past an island and raised the binoculars to his eyes. A little orange speck lay entrapped underneath the mangroves. "The canoe," he whispered.

"Huh?" Karam grumbled.

"There." Joe pointed. "The canoe."

Joe reached in his shirt pocket, pulled out a can of dip, and packed the tobacco in between his bottom gum and lip. And just like that, his death warrant was torn apart.

"Then who is that?" Karam asked.

A boat moved at idle speed toward the canoe. Joe focused his binoculars and grinned. "Nothing we can't handle." It had turned into Joe's day. He found Jada, and he would kill the man who had wronged him so long ago.

Chapter 18

The Flounder

The Flounder floated in its slip, left undamaged by Tropical Storm Rachel. A few pelicans roosted on the pylons, stretching their mouths open and shaking their heads as if trying to rattle the sleep out of their skulls. Seagulls circled overhead and swooped down, skimming the water, picking up small fish that tried to wiggle themselves loose from the bird's lock jawed beak. The dock creaked as the fishing guides loaded their boats and waited for their charters to show up.

Grandpa tried to tune the stereo. "You about done getting us ready?"

"Almost." I crunched some cans of Coke into the iced down cooler. "If you weren't sitting on your ass it might go faster, Captain."

"You said it." He laughed.

"Huh?" I said, puzzled. "You're agreeing with me. That's a freaking miracle."

"No, you called me Captain. I am, and you're the first mate, so shut the hell up and do your job." There was a seriousness in his tone, so I did.

"Why are you moving around so stiff today, McKlusky? That little girl of yours get the best of you?"

"I wish." I smiled. "No, just a fight. I got jumped by Trent and a friend of his named Brad at the beach yesterday. Brad pushed Chloe, and I lost it. I think I won, though."

"You think, huh?" He cranked the Flounder and the engine sent smoke bubbling out of the water. I inhaled the smoking fumes. I would get whiffs of the smell from time to time in New Jersey, and it set me daydreaming about fishing for the rest of the day. "Chloe choked the hell out of Trent's friend though."

"Good." He slapped me on the back as I walked by. Even his playful slaps could jar your body. I thought of the men who'd pissed him off in the past and felt sorry for them. It must be like coming face to face with a tornado. "Well, women are trouble, son." A hearty laugh escaped his mouth. "They're all trouble."

"Captain Harvey?" the voice boomed behind us. "I'm John Becker."

When I thought of someone wanting to go sightseeing and take pictures, the image that came to mind was a skinny pale guy with a Panama Jack hat, wearing sandals with socks. Most of the time they sported a thick northern accent and were annoying as hell. Basically the type of people I'm surrounded by nine months out of the year. Instead, John Becker stood on the dock. A black case was securely gripped in his hand, and a backpack hung over his shoulder. His crooked jaw imprisoned the smile that most give when they meet people for the first time. The grey t-shirt he wore stretched every inch of its fabric over his chest, to keep from tearing itself in two.

My grandfather's face seemed a little less surprised. "I'm Harvey."

Becker turned his gaze to me and studied me up and down. Some charters gave the feeling they didn't want me along for a ride; I usually proved my usefulness, though. But I could feel this guy despised me being here, and my presence was an inconvenience to him. Despite the fact he possibly could tear me in half, I didn't want to be nice to him, but out of necessity I put forward my best manners.

"Nice to meet you, sir. I'm McKlusky." I reached out for his bags.

"McKlusky, huh?" Becker handed me the case and slid his bag off his shoulder, though he kept hold of it. "Named after the movie, are you?"

"Yes, sir." The word "sir" had difficulty escaping my mouth. "My grandpa gave me the nickname." I placed his case in the chair.

"Gator McKlusky was an outlaw," Becker said stepping off the dock. The Flounder buckled to one side under his weight and sprung back up when he moved to the middle of the boat. "You an outlaw, boy?"

"If you call over limiting on fish and catching a few out of season an outlaw, then I guess I am."

"Ha! Funny kid, aren't you? And no, I wouldn't consider that an outlaw."

"Well, at least we have our definitions straight," I said snidely. His sarcasm had begun to annoy me, so I dropped the conversation and untied the ropes from the cleats. This was going to be a long day.

Becker showed some semblance of civility by shaking Grandpa's hand. "Good to meet you, Captain Harvey."

"So, you're wanting to do a little sightseeing, Mr. Becker." Their hands grasped each other like two bulls locking horns. Grandpa didn't like Becker right off. He discerned Becker's attitude that if he was paying for the charter, then the Flounder was his for the day. Each applied enough pressure to the handshake to let the other know he was there.

The two easily put over 450 pounds in the middle of the boat. Becker was younger and fitter. However, my grandfather did not lack in size. Even though his belly was a bit rounder, his arms and shoulders carried the weight well, and the years of hard living had made him tough and immune to the little pains of life, such as your hand being gripped too tight.

"Yes," Becker said. He released his grasp and hung his hand to his side. He moved his fingers to allow the circulation back in. "Just looking to go into the islands and look around."

"It can be done," Grandpa said. "Any particular wildlife you're looking for?" Grandpa took his seat in the captain's chair, tapped the throttle, and idled the Flounder out of her slip.

"Well, I really would like to head in as deep as we can get into the mangroves and see what's there, maybe some gators. Walk around a couple islands."

Becker took a seat in one of the two chairs on the stern. The white cushion hissed out air as his weight settled in. He grabbed his backpack and pulled it close to him. Looking directly at me with a smirk he said, "How about a Coke there, McKlusky?"

I shot an annoyed glance at Grandpa, and he just raised his eyebrows at me as if to tell me to go ahead and do it. Big or not, Becker could have his damn Coke between his eyes. Walking to the bow, I pulled a Coke out of the cooler and gave it few quick shakes. "Here you go."

He popped it open. Most of the drink erupted over the side of the can. He sucked up the froth. "Thanks a lot," he said, making no attempt to hide the disdain in his voice.

"Sorry about that, sir." I did my best to sound innocent. "Sometimes the waves shake them up a bit." I walked up to the console with Grandpa as he piloted the boat out of the marina. An osprey atop one of the channel markers scanned the shallow water for mullet and pinfish from the thicket of salvaged driftwood it used for a nest. A porpoise rolled along the side of the boat, spouting a fine mist of water in the air as it rode the small surge pushed by the bow.

"Take it easy, boy," Grandpa said, nudging me with his elbow. "It ain't no big deal... Besides, watch this." Grandpa slid open the door on the console and pushed in an old Johnny Cash tape and *Cocaine Blues* pounded its train track beat through the stereo speakers. "You like country music, Mr. Becker?"

"I gotta be honest with you, Captain. I don't." Becker leaned forward, placing his forearms on his knees, trying to menace either Grandpa or the stereo into changing the music.

"You will by the end of the day," Grandpa said.

A flash bolted across Becker's cheeks, constricting his jaw as he leaned back in his chair. Grandpa kept a half wicked grin on his grizzled face as he turned the boat toward Marco Bridge. He pushed the throttle forward, and the inboard engine rumbled. The bow rose in the air and flattened back down, gliding the Flounder over the slick greenish water, mirroring the sun's transformation from a soft subtle orange to a bright blazing yellow. The Bimini Top rounded out like a parachute.

We skimmed past Big Key and Turtle Island on our ten-minute run to Goodland. Having to slow down to idle by the docked boats, Becker ejected himself from his chair and came and stood by us. Apparently a little change of attitude during our run from Marco had occurred, and he decided to be a bit more social. The great thing about southern hospitality is that you usually get a second chance to make a first impression.

"So, what is this place?" he asked, looking at the tiny fishing village.

"This is Goodland. It's the last bit of civilization you will see for the next twenty miles until Everglades City or Chokoloskee. And some people debate if that is considered civilization or not," Grandpa said with a laugh.

Becker finally cracked a small smile. "Twenty miles? That doesn't seem too bad."

"It is when one bad turn in these mangroves can make that a three or four day trip." Grandpa shifted in his seat his hand turning the chrome steering wheel.

"Kirk Dupree told me you're pretty much the best. How did you learn all this—this area I mean?" Becker asked.

"Ol' Kirk huh? I've been fishing him for fifteen years. Kirk works for the CIA, doesn't he? As a statistician?"

A jerk of edginess ricocheted off Becker's brow before it was quickly subdued. "Yeah, and I work in research and development. Our specialties cross paths."

"Kirk's a good man. He's pretty much on the up and up with me," said Grandpa. "But to answer your question, I learned this place over time. Me and my brother used to fish for mullet with gill nets when we were young. We'd run all night and day trying to make a buck. You catch fish in the net. You learn where they're at," he reminisced. "Those were the days. The tourists stayed for a few days and left. Now they build multi-million dollar houses and change the laws so the original Islanders can't make a living anymore." Grandpa flipped off his hat and wiped the sweat off his forehead. "I guess it is what it is. But the Island will never be the same again."

Becker watched as little old men fished from the docks and dug into their coolers to pull out the first beer of the day. "Well, you seem to have fared all right with the change."

"Because I'm that damn good, Mr. Becker," Grandpa said. His boisterous laugh echoed across the pass.

Becker cracked another smile. "You must've seen some pretty odd stuff out here over the years."

"I've seen one or two things. Weird stuff happens out here from time to time." Grandpa chugged the Flounder along toward the last *No Wake Zone* sign and put her back on a plane.

"What kind of stuff do you see out here?" Becker shouted over the engine.

"Hell, what haven't I seen? I've seen barrels of drugs floating all over here. Found people lost for days. Your modern day pirates and smugglers use this place for drop offs and pick up points. This is a harsh place if you're not careful."

"So I've heard."

* * *

We turned past Turtle Key, and Grandpa pulled the throttle back. The mangrove islands seemed to shift and ebb with the tide. Each mangrove weaved together tightly to form an island that looked the same as the next. Every corner and turn replicated itself with very slight variations that eagle eyes would have trouble distinguishing. The roots of the mangroves exposed themselves at low tide, and sheltered redfish, snook, and snapper under its labyrinth of twisted and conjoined roots when the high tide came rushing back. As we motored along back toward the Everglades, past Foster Key and Dismal Key, the salt water fought to push back the onslaught of the fresh water flowing out of Pumpkin River. It turned the water brackish and then into a glistening black soup of mangrove leaves and old coconut husks.

A bald eagle perched on top of a mangrove, turning its head left and right, struggled to pierce the murk for a fish that swam too close to the surface. Sandbars lay exposed, the white sand tanned brown from years of stagnant settlement beneath the brackish water. Curlew ran along the sandbars and flew up, scanning for food, still trying to kill the hunger pangs from the storm that had cleared out only hours ago.

"Debris all over the place," Grandpa said as he steered the boat around fallen logs of cypress and large palm fronds littering the water.

Becker scanned the mangroves through his binoculars, sweeping his eyes over the shoreline. "Where are we, Captain Harvey?" He kept his eyes glued to the shoreline, not bothering to look at the ospreys and hawks that stood perched on the thick branches above.

"We're in Pumpkin Bay. You wanted to see wildlife, you can experience it all. Saltwater species meet the fresh water here. Most of the big fish we catch around the mangroves in the saltier water are born here and start to work their way out as they get bigger."

"Mr. Becker," I said pointing to one of the sandbars that humped itself out of the water, "see the gator."

"Huh?" He whisked his binoculars over to the sandbar. "Oh, yeah. She's a big one." He turned his binoculars back to the shoreline. "So, McKlusky, I take it you're still in school."

"Yeah, going into the 11th grade."

"You gotta girlfriend? Play sports? What's your deal?"

His sudden shift into my personal welfare and life was a bit shocking, considering half the Coke I'd given him looked like a map of tributaries and rivers on his jeans.

Before I could answer, my grandfather blurted out. "Yeah, he's had a girlfriend for a whole twenty-four hours and already has a fist fight to show for it. I told him they're nothing but trouble. Especially one as pretty as her." Grandpa turned a hard left to move into a deep channel that ran between two sandbars.

"Fight, huh?" Becker took a break from the binoculars. "What did she do to get you in a fight?"

"We were surfing and got jumped on the beach."

A giant smile finally defeated the scowl on Becker's face. I think the smile hurt him a bit, like a book might feel the first time you open it. "Wait—wait a minute. That little girlfriend of yours didn't happen to choke out one of those big boys after you got knocked on your ass, did she?" Becker was now genuinely interested in what I had to say.

"How did you know?"

"Well, hell, kid, everybody who didn't bail out of the resorts during the storm saw it. You decide to do a knock down drag out fight during the first sun in two days, and you don't think people aren't going to be out. I was a little farther down the beach, but I could see the action through my binoculars." He turned to Grandpa as if affirming it was now okay for me to exist. "Captain, your grandson did pretty good holding off two bigger boys until he went to help that little girl of his back up. He got blindsided. But she pulled a rubber piece off her surfboard and nearly choked one of them to death. It was a pretty impressive sight." He turned to me, acting like we had been friends for years. "What did you say that girl's name was?"

"Chloe," I said, wondering if she ached like I did from the fight.

"Chloe." Becker's eyes squinted against the rising sun. "You need to hold on to that one. Spirited women are hard to come by."

"Ain't that the truth," Grandpa said, steering the boat deeper into Pumpkin Bay.

"I thought you said they're not worth the trouble," I said.

Grandpa took his sunglasses off and looked at me. "Boy, I never said they ain't worth the trouble. I just said they're nothing but trouble. Getting your grandma got me in a whole mess of trouble. But it was worth it."

Becker had already exited the conversation. His binoculars were back up to his eyes as he resumed his search of the shoreline.

"Mr. Becker," my grandfather started.

"Please call me John or Becker, Captain. Same goes for you too, kid. I can't stand a mister in front of my name."

"Okay, Becker," Grandpa continued. "Maybe if you could tell me exactly what you're looking for I can help you find it."

"Well, wildlife, really. Just anything that moves."

"A bit of advice, Becker." Grandpa put the throttle in neutral. "Unless you're looking to see a fish crawl on its ass out of the water, the wildlife is up in the trees or in the water." Grandpa stood up out of his chair and walked to Becker's side. "Other than that, you can tell me what you are really looking for, or else we're heading back to the dock."

Grandpa had a bullshit detector implanted in his brain at birth. At least, this is how I justified the fact that he could tell when people were lying to him, even if they sounded as honest as a preacher. But it also helped that Kirk never told us he was a statistician. He'd said awhile back that he couldn't relinquish the truth of what he did in the CIA. As Grandpa said before, Kirk was on the up and up with him.

Becker let the binoculars dangle around his neck, his liquid black eyes moving slightly as he processed the type of situation he was in.

126

"Kirk said you're no pushover." He paused and rubbed the back of his neck. "I'm looking for some girls."

Grandpa looked puzzled. "Well, Becker, you're not going to find any girls out here. You want that, you should've stayed at the beach."

"No, Captain. I don't mean like that. I'm searching for abducted girls."

"Abducted?" I said.

"Yeah, your grandpa's right, kid. I bet some strange stuff does happen from time to time out here. It's remote, not easy to navigate, and not many people feel safe in it. I got it on good authority some girls have been abducted and brought out here."

"Why would anybody bring abducted girls here?" Grandpa said.

"Because they auction them off in Cuba. They collect them from around the States, hold them here until they've got them all together, and then go off to Cuba. Not a long trip from here, really, if you think about it."

"How do you know?" Grandpa said disbelievingly.

"Because my sister was one of them."

* * *

A heron landed on the stern of the Flounder, breaking our trance. It tilted its spear-like head from side to side. Its canary-colored slivered eyes snapped to each of our faces waiting for a scrap of shrimp to be thrown its way.

By the time Becker finished telling us how he found his sister, his fists were clenched and the color drained from his olive complexion.

"Let me get this straight." Grandpa broke the silence. "Not only do you drag me out here to search for human traffickers, but you drag my grandson out here too!"

"Look, I just needed help. I had no idea your grandson would come along." The color had come back to Becker's face.

"Help?" Grandpa said, moving toward Becker. "You want help? Haven't you ever heard of the damn police? You're CIA. How do you not have help?"

The tension seemed to compound the humidity, leeching the oxygen out of the air.

"I'm not CIA anymore. They don't care for me too much. They wouldn't offer me too much help. Kirk referred me to you as a friend."

"I'll take that up with Kirk later. Right now, we're heading in. You need to call the cops if what you say is true." Grandpa slammed himself into his seat and swiveled the chair around to the steering wheel.

"The cops can't help." Becker moved toward Grandpa "How many of them know these islands as well as you? How many of them are actually from here? They can't find these girls quietly."

"They can cover more ground in a helicopter than I can in my boat."

"That's the point. The first sign of law enforcement and these girls are dead. They will shoot them and stuff their bodies in the mangroves. And nothing says search party more than helicopters running search patterns over the islands." Becker grabbed his camera case and pulled out the gray stuffing. Underneath three pictures rested. "Look, I think there are three recently abducted girls somewhere out here."

I recognized two immediately. "I saw those two on the news the other night."

"Don't you start, boy. Stay out of this," Grandpa snapped.

"Kaitlin and Jada," Becker said, holding up their pictures. "Amber is the other one. They fit the profile of what these guys are looking for: young, fit, attractive. And they all fell off the face of the earth within two days of each other." Becker gently laid the pictures down on the case. "Captain?"

"No way. You sound as crazy as a son of a bitch. Take a seat and if you move, I'll throw your ass overboard." Grandpa turned the Flounder around to head out of Pumpkin Bay. "I'll have some words for Kirk the next time I see him."

* * *

None of what Becker said became reality for Grandpa or really even me, until we saw the canoe entangled underneath the overhanging mangrove branches. The mangroves wrapped around it like fingers,

128

cradling it from the outside world, nearly camouflaging it from our sight. We gaped at Jada laying on her side in the canoe—a twisted contortion of a human being. Mud and dirt from the bottom of the boat had dried on her caramel skin. Her hands were tied in front of her, clutching a bleach bottle that was cut in half. A blanket of black mosquitoes covered her body. Her face and eyelids were welted from the insects' needle noses that sucked, had their fill, and left, making room for a waiting family member. A thick black glob of blood crusted over the top of her arm, sealing up a wound. Her stomach moved in and out slightly, taking in shallow breaths of air, rippling the thin layer of water by her mouth.

"Get the girl in the boat, Becker," Grandpa said. I'd never seen him so flustered before.

Becker was over the side of the boat, slogging through the knee high water. Parting the mangrove branches aside and breaking and twisting them out of the way, he reached the bow of the canoe and pulled the snared hull free.

Becker put his hand on her forehead. "Give me some water."

I pulled a bottle out of the cooler and threw it down to him. He twisted off the lid and poured it on her face, sending the mosquitoes buzzing frantically right before the chilled liquid could cool the warm blood they held in their bellies.

Grandpa rubbed his face and ran his fingers through his peppered black hair. "Get her in the boat. We need to get her some help."

After scooping her up like he was picking up a box of feathers, Becker handed her to me. I laid her on the deck of the boat on her back. Thin flakes of skin were crusted across her lips. She was a far cry from the beautiful girl in Becker's photos.

Becker jumped back on the boat and kneeled over her. "She does need help, but we can't take her to the police or the hospital. If these guys get wind that she has been found, there's no chance of us saving the other girls. They'll kill them and bolt, if they haven't already." Becker looked at Grandpa. I think Becker and I both felt sure he was going to radio the cops, say we needed to take her to them, or take her to the hospital.

"Well, we can't take her to the marina then," Grandpa said. "We need someplace private."

"Chloe's dock," I blurted out. "It might be a little hard, explaining to her mom, but that is the safest place we can take her. We can carry her straight from the dock to the house."

"Then let's go," Becker said.

In all the confusion, we didn't hear Joe motor up beside us. Grandpa shook his head and muttered a string of expletives.

"Captain Harvey. I see you found yourself a lost little girl." Joe hocked a black stream of spit into the water.

"And I see you found yourself a new friend." Grandpa eyed the heft of the black man standing on the stern of Joe's boat. "I ain't got time for your bullshit today, Joe. Now move your stolen-ass boat so I can get out of here." Grandpa cranked the Flounder's engine. She boomed, sensing she was being restrained.

Grandpa didn't like Joe all that much. He considered him nothing more than a wife beater and town drunk. Liquor ate away his mind and desire to do anything that seemed self-respecting. Moreover, they had history, and Grandpa came out on top.

"No, Harvey, that little piece of chocolate sunshine is gonna get on my boat." Joe pulled a .45 out of the console of the Pathfinder and cocked the hammer. A smile creaked across his face. The large black man knelt down and picked up an AK-47 off the deck of the boat. Grandpa put a hand on my chest and pushed me behind the console where Becker still knelt silently over Jada. He was rummaging through his backpack.

"Joe, you're gonna be sorry you ever did that. My grandson is on this boat. I'm gonna find you." My grandfather's jawbone flexed, rounding out his hardened face.

"Boy," Joe peeked around from behind the gun, "you just help that big man kneeling over that girl put her on my boat, and we'll let your grandpa live. You hear?"

The blood pounded through my ears and my skin turned cold. Threatening my grandfather didn't sit well with me. "Hey, Joe! Go screw yourself."

"Your boy's got himself a mouth. Might ought to teach him to respect his elders," Joe said.

"I'll let him know when he says it to someone he should respect."

"Enough! Give her here," Joe screamed.

Becker patted my ankle to get my attention. The backpack was behind the console, shielded from Joe's view. Becker pulled his hand out, revealing the handle of a Model 19 Glock. He slipped it into the palm of his hand. "Alright, alright, you can have her," Becker said, the words struggling through the anger in his voice. Grandpa looked down in disbelief, about to argue. Then he saw the gun in Becker's hand.

"Bring the girl over," the black man said in a deep Jamaican accent. "We'll help her get better."

Becker had not been able to observe The Jamaican from his kneeling position, but Becker's face hardened when he heard The Jamaican speak. Every muscle in Becker's body tensed, expanding his neck and flexing his shoulders. Gripping the pistol even tighter, his knuckles turned a pale white. He muttered the word "Karam."

"Huh?" I said.

Before Becker could answer, Grandpa said, "Boy, get down and get her legs. You get down there now, boy, you understand me?"

"I understand."

Grandpa turned around. His hand covered the Flounder's throttle, gently massaging it as if waking her from a deep sleep. He rubbed the side of his face with his other hand, sanding his palm on his stubble. Glancing to the left, focusing his eyes on an island across the bay, he placed his hands on the steering wheel. The Flounder's engines rumbled, turning over, bit by bit as if taking deep breaths, inhaling her fuel-laced oxygen.

Becker looked at me giving me a slight nod of the head. "Okay, on three we're going to pick her up."

"Okay," I sucked in my lips toward my teeth, ready to hit the floor.

Becker counted, "One, Two, THREE!"

Becker's first bullet sent the scent of burnt powder and hot lead into the air. As the Flounder's bow jerked into the air under the sudden propulsion from the propeller, Becker stumbled back over Jada and me and was heading over the stern. I jumped up and grabbed him with both arms wrapped around his chest, my hands barely able to meet in the middle. I braced my legs against the stern to stop our motion.

131

The white fuzzy wake that usually followed behind the Flounder had been turned into a soupy mix of mud and plant life chopped up from the bottom. Becker regained his balance and continued firing at the Pathfinder. The Jamaican lifted his head up over the side from where he had hit the floor when the gunfire started. Joe's head popped from behind the console. A bullet chipped off a piece of fiberglass from the console, spearing the fragments against Joe's face.

The Pathfinder rocked in the wake of the Flounder. It was pushed 180 degrees around. Becker now fired at its stern. Joe was able to engage the throttle, and the boat's 250 horsepower engine dug into the water. It was not long before Joe righted the boat and headed in our direction.

Grandpa had the throttle nearly full as we raced across Pumpkin Bay straight for a line of mangrove islands. The Pathfinder quickly gained ground. The wind rushing past my ears played a high-pitched tune on the fishing line pulled tight on the rods. Becker knelt before his backpack and pulled out two more magazines. He slammed one into the gun and slipped the other into his pocket.

"Get your ass over here, McKlusky!" he screamed over the engines and rushing wind.

I knelt beside him, and he reached in the bag and handed me another Glock.

"You shoot before?" he said as he chambered the first round and handed me the gun.

"Yes," I shouted in his face.

"Then what the hell are you looking at me for? Shoot the bastards!" He raised his gun and squeezed the trigger, firing as fast as the gun would slide the next round into place.

The lead we had was being chewed up by the Pathfinder's powerful outboard. I fired off a few rounds, sending a bullet into the hull when The Jamaican stood up with the AK. Becker and I slammed onto the deck, yelling for Grandpa to duck when a covey of bullets exploded behind the stern, sending angry, sizzling water onto our heads. The Flounder seemed to find just a little more throttle as her ass end was singed by the shrapnel.

As The Jamaican reloaded his magazine, we emptied ours, making superfluous holes in the water and the Pathfinder's hull. I looked ahead, and the solid wall of mangroves Grandpa headed for grew drastically in size. The engine cranked at full force. Grandpa's eyes just stared ahead—set on his course—with his hands plastered to the steering wheel. The mangroves grew closer, the outstretched knotted branches yards away.

Joe jerked the throttle back on the Pathfinder, rearing its bow up in our wake like a horse that was pulled back suddenly from going over a cliff.

Becker and I let out screams and expletives drowned out by the engine as the mangrove's snarling teeth were only a few feet away. Right before impact, Grandpa spun the Flounder to the left, skidding her stern inches from the roots. Becker and I went rolling, colliding into each other and against the side of the boat. Water sprayed into the air, crashing into the depths of the mangrove island as the propeller whirred a scream and fought for traction in the water. As soon as the Flounder lurched forward a few feet gaining momentum, Grandpa turned to the right back toward the mangroves, sending me to the other side of the boat. Becker's tumbling body crashed into mine, knocking my head under the rail.

Maneuvering us into a narrow channel, Grandpa fitted the Flounder into a stretch of water between two mangrove islands. The Flounder had inches on each side. Branches hung low, popping at the Bimini Top. It was quickly ripped off and fell behind us making a small canvas bridge across the water. The Pathfinder roared over the top of it, chewing it into a white mess of fabric in its wake. Joe tried to navigate the passage as smoothly as Grandpa. The Flounder's wake slammed into each side of the enclosure. It ricocheted back to the middle, sloshing and rolling tumbling waves. The Pathfinder bounced in the slop. Its bow reeled back and forth as in a rabid dog's mouth. Joe pulled back the throttle to keep from veering off into the roots. We began to lengthen our lead. Grandpa stood steady at the helm, each unseen turn taken with an easy move of his hand on the wheel from left to right and left again.

The Flounder's bow plowed the water in front of her. Branches smacked the bow as roots rubbed against the hull, shaking mangrove leaves loose, and filling the bottom of the boat. I stood up only to duck and dodge whipping branches and giant insects springing in the air, trying to avoid the onslaught of Grandpa's rampage. Becker yanked me back down by the shirt and pushed me onto the deck.

Grandpa gave one more little push on the throttle, screaming the engine. The RPMs pounded through the Flounder's hull like a wild stallion's heartbeat. She shot out of the other end of the channel, skimming on skinny water, curling a twisting line of mud in our wake. Joe cleared the exit several seconds after us. Grandpa was running the Flounder on a mud flat. About an inch of water separated us from the deep soft mud. Without its trim tabs up, the outboard motor of the Pathfinder couldn't handle it. The Pathfinder's outboard engine started jumping on its jack plate and bouncing up and down, sending the propeller hissing into the air shaking the hull of the boat. Every time the engine would smack back down into the water, its intake valve would suck up the mud and weeds that quickly clogged it up, triggering the engine's emergency shut off. The Pathfinder stalled and came to a stop, stuck on the mud flat until the incoming tide.

The inboard engine of the Flounder only exposed her prop to the water. The rest of her was tucked away safely inside the hull of the boat rhythmically firing her cylinders in victory over the faster boat she left stuck in the mud. Grandpa chewed the soft mud in front of him to the safety of a deeper channel, turning our wake into a boiling white froth of water. I had heard customers tell me that my grandfather could steer his boat on a "wet blade of grass" and he just more than proved it.

The mangrove leaves we had collected swirled down the length of the deck as if caught in a vortex and shot out of the back of the boat. Several lines of blood streamed down my cheeks and forehead from the catapulting branches that sliced at my face. Jada's body had been thrashed around. The wound on the top of her arm had reopened. I poured water over it and repositioned her on her back. I cut her hands free with one of Grandpa's fillet knives. Grandpa pulled back on the throttle, but kept the boat on plane. He took off his sunglasses and wiped the front of his face with the collar of his shirt.

"What the hell was that? How in the hell did you do that?" I looked at him, astonished.

"Hell, I don't know. The last time I ran through there was fifteen years ago, and it was in a seventeen-foot mullet skiff. But we sure as hell didn't have a choice. We never would've outrun that damn boat." He yanked me to him and patted my shoulders. "You okay? You ain't hurt, are you?"

"I'm fine." I rubbed my face. My hand came back soiled with blood and dirt.

"What happened to your face?" asked Grandpa.

"I stood up. I got smacked a bit."

Grandpa smiled and shook his head, "Well, boy, if you gonna be dumb...."

"I know, I know. You gotta be tough."

Becker collected his backpack. The contents had been distributed across the deck during our hard turns. He came beside us. "That was impressive, Captain. I take it you know the guy on the other boat."

"Yeah, a local. If he is involved then I know where we need to start looking for the other girls."

"So you're going to help me?"

"Yeah, I'll help. I have no love for Joe. But first, we need to get her some help. And then I want to know who the hell these people are."

"Alright, Captain. Let's get her to safety and I'll tell you." Becker turned to me and nodded. "Good shooting, kid. I guess I get to meet that little spitfire you're dating too."

"I guess so. But this is going to be a little hard to explain."

Chapter 19

O'Malley's' House

We idled up to Smokehouse Bay, trying to seem inconspicuous to the line of police cars and boats that flashed their blue lights near an abandoned Mustang in a vacant lot.

"What the hell?" Grandpa said, as he waved at one of the police officers.

"You think you should be waving to him? We really don't want to draw attention to ourselves," Becker said.

"If I don't wave to him he's going to think something is wrong. He's one of my regular customers. I'm supposed to take him fishing next week." Grandpa put his hand back down and the officer turned back to his job.

We turned the corner to the O'Malley's dock, idled up, and tied to it. My mind was too preoccupied on how I was going to explain Jada to Mrs. O'Malley and Chloe to notice the cane pole and one of Chloe's sandals scattered on the dock. "I guess I'm up." I stepped off the Flounder and walked into the house.

Mrs. O'Malley was reclining in the living room, reading the paper. My sudden appearance startled her. "McKlusky?" She folded the paper and placed it on the coffee table. "I wasn't expecting you until tonight. Chloe is still asleep. She was up a little late last night. I'll have to get her up soon, though. She has quite the special dinner planned for you."

"That sounds great." I tried to sound enthused. "But I need to talk to you first." I sat on the couch in front of her chair.

Mrs. O'Malley leaned forward. Worry replaced the startled look on her face when she noticed the smattering of cuts and scrapes that had begun to scab over on my face. "What happened? Are you okay?"

I explained about Becker and our run-in with Joe. As soon as I finished, she insisted that Jada be brought in immediately. Mrs. O'Malley made sure Jada was comfortable by placing her in the master bedroom. Jada's face seemed to lose some of its tension as the covers spread over her. She actually moved her body for the first time since we found her and wiggled in tight against the oversized king mattress. But she still wouldn't wake. We left her in the bedroom and went back to the living room.

"All right, Becker. Who are the people doing this?" Grandpa asked.

Becker clicked open his black case and pulled out another set of files.

"This is Marcus Langer. Marcus is an English businessman. At least on the books, but he's really a flesh peddler. He is involved in human trafficking on pretty much all levels. He even owns a string of massage parlors on I-75."

"Is that where Jada was heading?" I asked.

"No, she was heading to Cuba. She would've been auctioned off there to the highest bidder like my sister." Becker paused, choking on his own words. "Marcus fills his massage parlors with women from South America and Asia. He promises them lucrative jobs in America as nannies or maids. Then he brings them over, charges them about $30,000 for freighting them here, and forces them into sexual slavery to pay off their debt, which they never do. The girls we're trying to find are for a higher class of clientele. They become sexual slaves for the rich."

Mrs. O'Malley placed her hand over her mouth. "I can't believe this is happening in our own back yard. These girls are not much older than Chloe. You need to call the police."

"If we do, these girls will die."

"Captain Harvey!" Mrs. O'Malley insisted, "You must call the police. That girl you brought me needs help."

"Becker's right. If we call the police these girls are dead. They will flee. The best way to help them is to find them," Grandpa said.

Becker reached for another file. "This is Marcus' adopted son, Karam. This was the man on the boat with Joe." His finger pressed down on the picture. One glimpse at the white pale eye gave away his identity.

"I'm hard pressed to forget anybody who's ever shot at me," Grandpa whispered almost to himself.

"You've been shot at before?" Becker asked quizzically.

Oddly, Grandpa backed off his words, something I'd never seen him do. He sputtered out a story about a hermit taking shots at him while he was fishing and quickly changed the topic. "Who's in the last file?"

"Not really sure," Becker said. "He has no identity. Higher ups in the CIA and FBI believe he is a serial rapist and murderer responsible for the death of numerous women. They call him, The Hippie Killer. The FBI had some grainy pictures of him and were trailing him, but he disappeared a couple years ago. He showed up on the Afghani's files." Becker flopped a picture of him on the desk.

"I saw him yesterday," I said.

"What!" Becker shouted, probably louder than he meant. Mrs. O'Malley jumped a bit.

"I saw him yesterday at the beach, after the fight."

"Fight? Chloe didn't tell me about a fight. You saw this guy?"

"I'm sorry, Mrs. O'Malley. I'll explain later, but Brad and Trent tried to hurt Chloe. We got in a fight." I focused my attention back on Becker. "After the fight, Chloe and I were leaving the beach. He was sitting on the side of the path, and we thought he was a homeless man, so Chloe gave him five bucks."

"Where is Chloe now?" Becker asked.

"Asleep. Why?" Mrs. O'Malley said. Concern grew in her voice.

"Go see," Becker said. "Now!"

The indentation of Chloe's body was still outlined on her comforter.

"She must've stepped out," Mrs. O'Malley said. "She probably walked to the grocery store to get a few things for dinner tonight."

I dialed Chloe's cell phone, and it rang from beside her bed.

"She must have forgot it." Mrs. O'Malley was becoming more flustered. "She'll be back in a minute."

"The dock," I said.

"What?" Mrs. O'Malley asked.

"The dock. There was a cane pole and one of her flip-flops scattered on the dock."

There was more than just a cane pole and flip-flops scattered on the dock when we rushed out to look. A stream of dried slime trailed to the edge of the dock where a fish had flopped down and back into the water. A large snook floated belly up underneath the dock. Its stomach was bloated, and the scavengers were already starting to pick it apart. Strands of Chloe's hair were stuck underneath splintering sections of the planks. Mrs. O'Malley found Chloe's fingernail. It had popped off her finger so violently that speckled pieces of dried flesh still clung to it. Mrs. O'Malley's face paled. "Oh, My God! Chloe. No-No, not my Chloe."

"He has her," Becker said, his voice dry.

"I need to call the police." Mrs. O'Malley rushed to the house.

"No." Becker bolted to intercept her. "If you do, these guys will flee, and you'll never see Chloe again."

Mrs. O'Malley pounded Becker's chest, drumming it like a musician out of synch. "You did this! You did this to her. You brought these people here!" She slapped him across his face, her fingers blistering a red outline. He didn't flinch, but allowed Mrs. O'Malley to purge the venom of her loss on him. "Take me to the man who did this!" She cried, her eyes zig-zagged with thin knotted red lines.

When her arms were too tired to deliver another blow, Becker collapsed his arms around her and pulled her close, trying to take her pain into himself. His voice was steady and soothing. "I swear I'll get Chloe back to you. This stops today."

Mrs. O'Malley's sobs muffled into his chest. Her tears drew a wet map of her pain on Becker's grey T-shirt. Her body shuddered under his arms. When she had nothing left, Mrs. O'Malley slowly pulled away. "I'll hold you to that promise." She placed her hands on his chest, gently this time, her eyes pleading, "Promise me you will. All of you, promise me you will find Chloe!"

We promised. Mrs. O'Malley slumped on the dock, hugging herself tightly.

* * *

A silence hung in the O'Malley's house like a noose before the man whose neck it was to go around. We'd convinced Mrs. O'Malley to go to my grandparents' house in case The Hippie returned to hers. My grandmother would arrive soon with the understanding that everything would be explained to her and not to call the cops.

"We're wasting time." Becker's hard edges around his face reappeared, smothering the softness he had shown to Mrs. O'Malley.

"Like I said, if Joe is involved, then I know where to begin looking," Grandpa said, meeting Becker's gaze.

"Good. Then let's go." Anger clenched my gut over the loss of Chloe. I envisioned finding The Hippie and killing him.

"You're not going." Grandpa's words deflated me like a torn hot air balloon quickly crashing.

"The HELL I'm not!" I fired back, every muscle in my body twitching.

Grandpa shook his head. "I couldn't stand it if anything happened to you. These guys are dangerous. You saw that yourself."

"I'm getting on the damn boat. Chloe needs me!"

"She does," Grandpa said. His voice calm and steady. "She needs you to take care of her momma and Jada. I can't let you go."

"Bullshit! I'm going! Just try and stop me." I started to move.

Grandpa looked at Becker. "Hold him."

Becker's arms wrapped around me, and he squeezed me toward his body. I tried to roll my arms forward to make a small gap to slide out, but he just constricted tighter, my breath being forced out of my body. My grandfather hurried to the dock and cranked up the Flounder.

"I-I," I breathed deep trying to inhale as his arms tightened. "I'm going to hurt you Bec-Becker."

"Please, don't hurt him." Mrs. O'Malley's eyes not only found room to lament Chloe's disappearance but to sympathize with me.

"I'm not." Becker's grip loosened a little.

"Listen, kid." He leaned close to my ear. I slung my head back to crack his nose, but he turned his head to the side, causing me to slam into his cheek. He didn't flinch, and if I hurt him, he didn't make a sound to show it. He only spoke. "I'd have you fight by my side any day. Seeing you on the beach and keeping your cool today, I know grown military men who can't do that, but it ain't your time. We're going to bring Chloe back. I promise."

My breath wheezed out. I had almost blacked out before he let me down on the cool marble floor. He ran and jumped on the Flounder. They were gone.

I picked myself up on my knees and took a deep breath. The betrayal I felt compounded my misery over Chloe's disappearance.

Mrs. O'Malley knelt beside me and rubbed my back. "Breathe, take deep breaths. Chloe wouldn't want you risking your life for her. She'll be back with us before you know it." The tears streaming down her face told of her doubt. I decided only an act of God could keep me away from helping Chloe.

Chapter 20

Harvey and Becker

After anchoring the Flounder off the beach in front of Becker's resort so he could grab a black duffle bag of supplies, Harvey turned the Flounder toward South Beach and headed to Goodland.

"You sure you didn't hurt him, Becker?" Harvey asked with a twinge of concern.

Becker stood beside him, his hand on the console as the Flounder skipped over the channel's chop. "Captain, I promise you. He got the breath squeezed out of him. But he'll be okay. That is one tough kid you got there. You should be proud."

"I am." Harvey cut the boat up the channel through a narrow passage of sandbars that were barely covered with water.

"Listen." Becker rubbed his mouth with the palm of his hand. "I know you had a lot of training in the Army, but your record never said you saw live action in WWII. Today you said you never forgot anybody whoever shot at you. It wasn't just a hermit who shot at you was it?"

Harvey's face hinted surprise at Becker's knowledge of his training, but it quickly settled back into its intense stare at the passage that lay ahead.

"Come on, Captain. Don't be surprised I know your past." Becker smiled. "I was CIA. I still have some connections, albeit few. It's why I called you to be my guide in the first place."

Harvey took off his Costa sunglasses and shook his head. "I guess you were honest with me about your deal. I'll tell you mine." Harvey paused, as if trying to rearrange all the memories in their chronological order. "After the bombs dropped on Hiroshima and Nagasaki, our unit was placed on a night flight and told we were going home. Our bags were packed. I was going to marry my soon-to-be wife. About the tenth hour of being on the plane, we began to mumble and wonder what was going on. The sun rose behind us and illuminated the ocean below us. We weren't the most educated group. Most of us hadn't even finished high school, but we knew enough that if we were heading

142

home, the sun should be rising in front of us, and there wasn't an ocean between Washington State and Fort Bragg. We landed in Burma. There was a renegade Japanese General named Hayoushi." Harvey paused, "General Hayoushi, I'll never forget that damn name, either. Anyway, the general didn't believe in the Japanese Emperor's decision to sign the surrender with America. He decided to attack and take small villages along the Burmese and Chinese border and recruit the villagers to his own army. He wanted his army to free his country from the white invaders. If the villagers didn't join, he introduced a new hole into their head. After getting off the plane, we were instructed to find the General."

"How did I not find this in the file?"

"There probably wasn't one. The war was over. Despite the fact that General Hayoushi didn't have a snowball's chance in hell of ever raising an army big enough to accomplish his goal, the last thing the United States Government wanted was the public thinking there was a possibility of another war popping up, or the same one continuing in any fashion. I've never told anyone this. I was ordered not to and things got really messy over there. I nearly died more than once." Harvey pulled the throttle back on the Flounder as they entered the idle zone into Goodland.

"Why are you telling me now?"

"One, you asked, and two, if we're about to get into it with these fellas you showed me in the files, we need to know what the other is capable of." Harvey piloted between the boats, heading out for a day's fishing.

"Well, what happened? With the general, I mean?" Becker asked.

"He was crazy. He raped and killed. A lot like these men you described to me. I get the same feeling about them as General Hayoushi. They won't stop until the world crumbles around them. I hunted him for months." Harvey shifted in his chair as he pulled up by a dock.

"And?"

"Don't know. Our unit killed his officers one by one. I even sniped one from 700 yards away," Harvey laughed. "Pretty good for back in those days. The General just didn't have the supplies and the support he needed. No money to keep him going. He ran off one night in the jungle, deserting his men, never heard about him again."

Becker rubbed his hand across his chest. "I hate it when they get away. It ain't happening today, though."

"No, it's not."

Becker was so enthralled by Harvey's story he hadn't noticed his surroundings until the mooring line had been cast on the dock for the bait boy. "Isn't this the place we passed, coming out this morning?" Becker saw the same old men in their chairs by their coolers, poles still in the water. A monument of beer cans around their feet represented the day's accomplishments.

"It is," Harvey said.

"What are we doing here?" Becker watched the seagulls skim the surface like precision fighter pilots on a mission.

"Answers. There is a bar I think we might be able to get a lock on where Joe's been working lately." Harvey paused for a moment, looking at Becker. "Listen, I know you're all tough and all. But this crowd is a little rough. Besides, most of them are my kin. And if they ain't my kin, then they're my wife's kin. Let's try to keep it civil, if at all possible. We have a family reunion coming up in a few months."

* * *

The music blared out of the building no bigger than a small home. It was decorated on the outside with discarded pieces of crab traps and mesh nets. Bikers tuned their Harleys to the sound of the music. One biker knelt over his bike and spewed his liquid lunch on the white gravel.

Harvey pushed open the crooked, deteriorating, pine door, and a wave of stale cigarette smoke rolled out like storm clouds into the noon air. The crowd inside sat in the dimly lit room, gathered around small tables etched with years of graffiti declaring love, hate, and phone numbers for a good time. The outside light, splitting a wedge through the room, caused the patrons to look up from their mugs of beer and food at the two men who entered. Once satisfied, they lowered their heads back down, taking sips of their beer, and inhaling another drag of their cigarettes.

A small middle-aged waitress with cutoff shorts and a black

t-shirt tied below her breasts hustled the food and beer to the customers. Her tanned leathery skin, crinkled and dark, stood out against her thin, bleached blonde hair. The customers greedily drank and ate, famished from their night of pirating in the dark recess of the Ten Thousand Islands. Most ran drugs. Others were paid by Cuban families, to run under the cover of night, to pick up family members who waited on Castro's shores. These were the children of the running tides, cradled in the treacherous arms of the mangroves that sheltered and hid them from the law.

Harvey walked toward the back of the room, slipping between the tables. Occasionally a person nodded his head and said, "Captain." Harvey would say the name, tap them on the shoulder or tip his hat, and keep walking.

Becker surveyed the room as his training had taught him. Exits, people, every threat was memorized and assessed in an instant. He stood tense and ready.

"Easy, Becker," Harvey whispered. "These are my people."

"Right, if you say so." Becker still watched.

"You old son of a bitch!" A voice shouted behind them. A large chubby man with thin rimmed glasses and a shiny bald head came barreling through the tables that were placed too tightly together. A few people grabbed their beers to keep them from sloshing over onto the table, muttering cuss words as the portly man squeezed through.

Becker tightened his fist, ready to swing, when Harvey stepped in front of him. Harvey smiled and put out his hand. "Moss, you ol' pirate, what are you doing in this place?"

Moss laughed and shook Harvey's hand. "I might ask you the same thing, but this place has got the best damn burgers on Goodland or Marco Island."

Waiting for the other to speak, the two kept shaking hands.

"Well, I'm looking for Jason." Harvey glanced around the room, "You seen him?"

Moss' warm greeting slipped from his face and turned into concern. "Harvey, you are here for no good reason, aren't you?"

"Listen, I don't have time to explain right now. I need to talk to Jason." Harvey felt bad he couldn't tell his friend everything he needed to right now. Moss and he had been best friends for some time and often teamed up to go harvest some fish out of season for fun.

"Is there something I can help you with?" Moss wiped his hand on his shirt.

"No, me and my friend here have it under control." Harvey pointed back to Becker.

"Boy!" Moss said, gawking at Becker. "Did your momma mate with an ox to spit you out?"

Harvey and Moss chuckled. Becker grunted and held his face frozen and expressionless. Harvey shook his head still grinning. "Take it easy on him. He's had a rough go at it lately." Harvey asked again, "Jason?"

"He's in the back, in his office." Moss motioned to a small hallway that contained the tiny restrooms and the office.

"Thanks, buddy," Harvey replied.

"No problem." Moss fixed his glasses, which had begun to slide down his nose on a thin stream of sweat.

Harvey and Becker headed toward the office. "Nice friend you got there, Captain." Becker didn't like to be on the back end of a joke.

"He was just funnin' you. He didn't mean nothing by it. You think having bullets shot at you would make you appreciate life a little more." Harvey approached the two guards, sitting in front of the door leading to Jason's office. They had beers in hand and were playing cards. "Besides, you might want to take that stick out of your ass and think about using it to beat these two men if talking don't work."

Guards might be too strong of a word for the two men. Willy and Glenn were no more than a couple of Jason's lackeys, common crooks with little more sense than an animal. Their dirty t-shirts were covered with burnt tobacco ash from the cigarettes they let dangle in their mouths. Glenn and Willy peeked up from behind their cards at Harvey and Becker.

"Captain." Willy, the bigger of the two, spoke, nodding his head and looking back down at the cards in his hand. "Who's your friend?"

"This is Becker. We need to see Jason."

The little one, Glenn, laid down his cards and looked up, one eye closed as if the sun glared in his face. "Ain't possible, Captain. He just came in from working. He's awful tired." Glenn snickered between the few teeth he had left in his mouth.

"Willy, Glen," Harvey said clenching his fist. "I whipped you as kids for stealing my fishing rods out of my garage. I'll do it again, but this big fella behind me is going to help this time."

Glenn and Willy stood up. "You know, Captain." Willy took a long drag of his cigarette, letting it sizzle before he spoke again. "I'm about to…"

Before Harvey could react, Becker seized both men by the collar and crashed their bodies through the brittle door that led to the office. Willy and Glen landed on their backs, the dust rising from their impact as the cigarette shot out of Willy's mouth and landed on his t-shirt, burning through to his chest. He screamed, trying to brush it off and struggled to right himself.

Jason jumped off the couch. The pretty little girl who was half naked sprang up, covered her breasts, and rushed out of the room. The patrons in the front started to hoot and holler as the girl tried with difficulty to find the neck opening to her shirt.

"Uncle Doyle!" Jason stood up, buttoning his pants. "If you'll wanted to see me, all you had to do was knock." Walking over to his makeshift desk of cinder blocks and a piece of plywood, Jason put on the shirt that lay thrown across the chair, took out a cigarette and lit it. "I was just a giving a little interview for a job," he said, taking his first drag.

Willy and Glenn struggled back up and dusted the dirt off their already grimy jeans. Becker moved toward them.

"Hey, big fella," Jason said. The cigarette hanging between his thin lips moved with his words. "They won't be bothering you anymore." Jason leaned back in his chair. His skinny arms, little more than bone, rested on his lap.

"Willy, Glenn, get the hell out of here. When my Uncle comes around, you let him in. I've been trying for years to get him to show me some of them secret places he knows in the islands."

"Yes, sir?" Willy tried to unwrinkle his shirt from where Becker had twisted it in his hand.

"Bring these two a chair, Willy. Teach you how to treat my kin."
Jason's fuzzy blonde mustache curled up under his nose as he smiled at
Harvey. "Damn, Uncle, you and that big boy sure can make you an
entrance. Who's your friend?"

"Is that the only thing anybody can ask around here, 'Who's your
friend?'" Becker asked, imitating Jason's accent.

Jason turned to Becker, his eyes narrowing. "You need a job
fella? I'm pretty sure you can keep anybody from bothering me."

"This kid is your nephew?" Becker tried to reconcile the fact that
the scrawny man with a chest the size of a thick pencil had the same
family blood running through him as Harvey.

"My sister's kid." Harvey rolled his eyes. He took the seat that
Willy brought in. Glenn set one down for Becker. Both Willy and Glenn
mumbled as they walked out.

"You fellas see what I have working for me?" Jason put his
elbows on his desk and clasped his hands. "What can I do for you,
Uncle? I guess it's a little too much to ask you if you wanna make a
run."

"Listen, you and me both know I don't like what you do, but we
are kin, and that still means something to me. Joe has done some work
for you. I need to know what island he's been working out of lately."

Jason's eyes shifted down to the floor, and he let out a big sigh.
"What are you into that you need to find Joe?"

"You mean besides the fact he nearly killed us this morning?"
Harvey said.

"Killed you? Well, he don't work for me no more. He got himself
in with some pretty bad men from what I hear. Even I won't touch the
stuff they do."

"What do you know?" Becker sat in the chair erect, his shoulders
square with his chest.

"What's your name?" Jason asked.

"John Becker."

"Becker," Jason said, "Why are you in my bar? What is you and
my uncle looking for?"

Becker shot up from his chair, ready to pull Jason over his desk and beat any information he might have out of him. Harvey held Becker back. Jason pushed his chair back to avoid the assault.

"I'll take you to a few hiding spots in the islands when this is done if you give me information," Harvey said. "Just tell us what you know."

Jason perked up. "You mean that? You will show me some places I can lay low and make my work a little easier?"

Harvey's stomach turned at the prospect of helping his drug-running nephew, but Chloe's life hung in the balance. "You help us out. You got it." Harvey spit the words out before he had time to rethink his offer. "Now, what do you know?"

Jason's smile spread from sunburnt ear to sunburnt ear. He pushed his tufted blonde hair back and put on his dirty cap. "Well, if you'll do that, I'll tell you what I know."

Jason kept quiet for a minute. His face drooped and became solemn. "Well, Uncle, rumors really. I know lots of rumors. Rumors of women being run through here and down to Cuba. Some traffickers popped in here a few months ago and started keeping women on different islands, so I hear. Joe ain't worked for me since then. I heard tell a rumor he was working with these fellas, moving the women on some boat called the Albatross. My people see and hear stuff out there. I usually just think of them as drug induced illusions or stories. At least, I thought this was rumors until two nights ago and last night."

"Go on." Harvey had straightened in his chair when he heard his nephew mention the women.

"Well, a couple nights ago, I'm doing a little work under cover of the storm, and I'm a running on the south side of Foster Key. The winds a' howling. Rain just stinging like a bunch of bees. I decides I'm gonna take a little shelter on Foster. As I'm hauling up to the beach, Billy Andrews is jumping and waving on the sand bar by Foster, yelling for help. He's a bleeding all down his face and yammering on about how they is gonna kill him for losing the cargo. I figure he is talking about drugs. But I know everybody who runs around here because I make it my business to know." Jason reached in his shirt pocket, pulled out a fresh pack of cigarettes, and lit another. "I says, '*what did you lose, Billy? I know it ain't my drugs you lost.'* I look at him and his eyes are all crazy. Apparently he'd been whacked pretty good on the head with something, and he's not thinking straight and says, *'they're gonna kill me. Joe's gonna kill me. The girl, she's gone. They're gonna kill me.'* Well, I bandaged him up best I could with a towel. We spent the night anchored to Foster and I decides I'm gonna take a look around. Nothing on the island, I just figured he was crazy from hitting his head or something."

"There was nothing on Foster?" Harvey probed.

"Nope. Notta thing."

"Okay, what about last night? You said you thought all of this was rumors until a couple nights ago and last night," Becker said.

"Easy there, big boy." Jason scratched his head through his cap. "I was heading that way with the story. Well, last night I needed to make a little delivery offshore, and I'm a thinking about ol' Billy and what he said. I passed by a big ol' yacht anchored on the Five Mile Reef. My running lights are off of course." Jason smiled like a kid who'd just been caught with a Playboy Magazine. "But her lights were bright as hell. On her stern, in that fancy lettering read, Albatross." Jason exhaled a stream of smoke from his lungs and stared at the fake cedar panel walls in his office. "I'm telling you, Uncle, I gots the chills. I know you don't agree with what I do, but them fellas has got to be sick runnin' women like that."

"Where's Joe?" Harvey asked.

"I reckon I don't know, but I know Billy does. Plus, his fat ass couldn't a been that far from Joe that night I picked him up. He had to of come from one of the surrounding islands. He'd had a heart attack if he had to go too far."

"That's still a lot of islands to cover in a few hours," Harvey said. "Where's Billy?"

"I brought him home, and he locked himself up in his trailer and ain't been out since. I tried to talk to him yesterday but all he did was babble 'bout being killed."

"Jason, thanks." Harvey stood up and headed out the frame that once held the door.

"Uncle, don't you forget about showing me those spots now," Jason yelled as they walked out.

150

* * *

The trailer was a couple of blocks from the bar on a gravel road surrounded by browning palm trees and palmettos. Dried coconut husks scattered the ground. Ants crawled over them, seeking the sweet white meat that made up the seed's core. The trailer, its foundation supported by cinder blocks, sagged in the middle. Its stained white panels hung loosely against each other, bowing out under the corroding rust. Spanish moss littered the roof, hanging over its edges. The curtains were drawn shut and the small air-conditioning wall unit struggled to change the humid air into a cool breeze.

"Is this where he lives?" Becker swatted a horsefly buzzing around his face.

"This is it." Harvey stepped on the makeshift steps haphazardly thrown together with bricks and two-by-fours. His hand pounded on the door, rattling the tin that had been placed over the mesh screen. "Billy, I know you're in there. We ain't here to hurt you. We just need to ask you a couple things." Harvey listened for an answer, but none came. He looked at Becker and nodded his head for him to walk to the other side of the trailer. Becker crept to the back.

"Billy!" Harvey knocked on the door harder. The door sounded like an out of tune snare drum. Pieces of Spanish moss tumbled off the roof and drifted to the ground.

"You leave me alone." Billy's voice came weakly through the door.

"Billy we don't have time to piss around. I need to know where Joe is. We ain't here to hurt you." Harvey tried the knob on the door. It was locked.

"You don't wanna find Joe. You don't wanna mess with him at all. Now get the hell away from here."

Becker walked back from behind the shed. "No way out back there."

Harvey punched the aluminum door, denting it in the middle. "Don't make me tear this door down. I ain't here to hurt you, but you're pissing me off. A little girl's life depends on it." Harvey was getting ready to kick in the door when the lock clicked.

Harvey peeked in the door and saw Billy, sitting shirtless on a cheap plastic chair behind a card table that was piled high with open beer bottles and old newspapers. Billy put his hands up to shade his eyes from the light invading his darkened world. Harvey moved back up the steps into the trailer with Becker close behind him.

The brown carpeted floor was littered with clothes and papers. Pin-up girls with little or no clothing lined the wall. Flies buzzed in and out of beer bottles, sucking up the stale fermented liquid that remained. The smell of urine seeped from the bathroom. Billy took a swig of his beer, looking at the two men through his glazed eyes.

"Billy." Harvey moved toward him. He stopped short, not because he was afraid of Billy, but the stench coming off of Billy made a barrier that even the flies didn't seem to cross.

"Harvey, nice enough of you to stop by." Billy leaned back in his chair, his belly rolling toward his back, nearly buckling the rear two legs of the plastic lawn chair. Billy reached behind him and opened the mini refrigerator door. A stream of cool condensation swirled out. "Want a beer?" Billy said, his words slurring over one another.

"No," Harvey replied in a short voice.

Billy twisted the cap off his bottle and took a long hard drink. "Joe, huh?" Billy's eyes rested on Miss March 2010 in a slinky red see-through nightgown on the wall; her eyes peered back at Billy's. "Those girls are done for. Who's your friend?" Billy opened a pouch of Redman, put a chunk in his mouth, and took another drink of his beer.

"I was wondering how long it would take for him to ask that," Becker said.

"This is Becker. Those guys you and Joe worked for killed his sister," Harvey said coolly. "We need to keep them from killing more."

Becker felt no pity for Billy and wanted to rip his heart out of his fat chest. Had Billy seen Alexis, tied her up, touched her? His heart thudded and if it hadn't been for the lives of the other girls, he'd have cut Billy's throat on the spot.

"I don't know nothing about them murdering anyone. Joe came to me a month ago and says I can make good money. Said we'd just have to hold a couple girls here for a few hours before we moved them to the mangroves." Billy's eyes watered up. "I got a daughter myself. I just wanted to be able to buy for her and see her. Ever since her momma up and left to Oklahoma a couple years ago, I ain't been able to see her." The tears flowed out of Billy's eyes and disappeared into the edges of his beard.

"Then do something right and tell us where Joe and the girls are." Becker moved behind Billy. Billy flinched his shoulders in toward his chest and ducked his head like a dog that's been beat too much. "I'm not going to hurt you, Billy. Not yet, anyway." Becker crossed his arms. "Not if you tell us where they're at."

"It could be your daughter out there. There's a girl I care about that hippie fella took last night. We need to know where they're at." Harvey moved through the putrid barrier that surrounded Billy and had to swallow hard to keep from losing his breakfast. "Now tell us, or else it is about to get real nasty in here."

"It don't matter if I do. There ain't much you can do for them, especially the one taken by The Hippie. I met him a couple weeks ago and he ain't right in the head. He'll kill that little girl before…"

Harvey flung the table, scattering the papers into the air. The beer bottles crashed and rolled onto the floor. He grabbed Billy by the throat and pushed him back, snapping the chair's plastic legs. Becker side stepped out of the way, caught off guard by Harvey's sudden rush of anger. Billy's body hitting the linoleum kitchen floor shook the little trailer, sending rats living in the walls scurrying and scratching. "Not before we get to her!" Harvey screamed in Billy's face. He squeezed Billy's neck. The blow against the floor jarred the scab on Billy's head, spilling blood down his face. Billy gasped for air and squirmed to get out from underneath Harvey's grip. Harvey released some pressure to allow air to pass into Billy's lungs. "Now you pissed me off, boy. Where the hell are they?"

Billy took a few deep breaths "No! They'll kill me!"

"If you don't tell me, I'll kill you." Harvey reached out a hand to Becker. Becker pulled the pistol secured to his back and placed it in Harvey's hand. Harvey squeezed tighter on Billy's neck and rammed the barrel down Billy's throat. Billy gagged, trying to force the muzzle out of his mouth. "I'm going to kill you, Billy. I ain't going to shoot you. I'm going to make you puke up all that beer and hold you on your back and watch you drown in it. You'll never see that little girl of yours again, which might be a good thing for her."

Billy fought to keep from throwing up and ending his own life. He tried to mumble but couldn't enunciate with his tongue against the barrel of the gun.

Becker moved over to the door and locked it.

"Here's the deal. I'm going to take this gun out of your mouth just once. I'm going to ask you just once. If you don't answer, the gun goes back in and doesn't come out until your dead. Nod if you understand me."

His pupils wide like thick black pools of mud, Billy nodded his head frantically. Harvey yanked the pistol out. The front sight chipped one of Billy's teeth on its exit. Billy's hand covered his mouth as he screamed and coughed in pain.

"Where are they?" Harvey squeezed a little tighter on Billy's throat. "I ain't asking again."

"Dis-Dis-Dismal!" Billy screamed. "Just leave me alone, please. Leave me alone!" Harvey pounded his fist on the floor, causing the rats to scatter again.

Becker leaned over Billy. "Yep, Billy, things look pretty damn dismal for you now."

"No." Harvey stood up, letting go of Billy, who rolled over to his side to let the dip juice and blood flow out of his mouth. "He means Dismal Key." Harvey handed the gun back to Becker to keep from putting a bullet in Billy's head. "We were right by Dismal this morning." Harvey tossed the broken lawn chair across the trailer. "We went right by it to go into Pumpkin Bay. The son of a bitches were under our nose the whole damn time."

"Let's go. We can still save those girls." Becker unlocked the door.

Harvey headed for the door, stopped, and stormed back over to Billy. He rolled Billy onto his back, grabbed his neck, and pulled his head off the ground. Billy tried to push back, but Harvey dropped his knee into Billy's groin. Billy's face turned white.

"Get packed and get the hell off my island. I'm coming back here after we're done with your friends. If you are here, I'm going to kill you." Harvey slammed Billy's head back on the floor. Billy erupted into tears and rolled back on his side.

"We were right there," Harvey said, his steps crunched on the gravel.

"Just get me on an island near Dismal to do some surveillance, and we can get them." Becker quickened his pace to keep up with Harvey.

"Piss on surveillance. We're going to go in there and beat the piss out of these guys and get Chloe back and those other girls."

Becker jumped in front of Harvey. "Listen, you know better than this. You're thinking with your emotions, not your training. These guys are no joke. They're going to be heavily armed and ready to roll. We've got to take the time to set this up right, or else we have no chance of saving Chloe and the others."

Harvey took a deep breath and as much as he hated to admit it, he knew Becker was right. He had experienced what acting purely on emotions could do to a well-trained soldier. More often than not, it put him in a body bag and those around him, too. "You're right. I'll get you on Foster Key. The same one Jason found Billy on. It is right across from Dismal Key."

* * *

Harvey knew it would have been easier to beach the Flounder on the south side of Foster Key, but they would have been in full view of Dismal Key and anyone who might have been on lookout. Harvey let out the anchor and jumped out in the knee high water. He pulled the Flounder close, trying to butt it up against the roots. He worked branches over the bow and the stern, concealing her as much as possible. The tide flowed in fast; it would not be too long before Joe and Karam could escape the mudflat if they hadn't completely clogged the engine with mud.

His duffle bag slung over his shoulder, Becker jumped off the bow into the water.

"I hope you got a lot of good stuff in there," Harvey said.

"I might have a thing or two we can use." Becker heaved the bag higher onto his shoulder and stepped on the roots.

From tip to tip, Foster Key was just a little larger than a football field. Its thick roots and branches took time to navigate through, however, before they reached the other end. Harvey and Becker bent and broke their way through the snarled vines and brush. They concealed themselves just behind the tree line on the North West side of Foster's beach. Becker unzipped his bag and pulled out two Beretta REC7 assault rifles, eight loaded magazines, one set of night vision binoculars, and one set of regular binoculars.

"What else you got?" Harvey said.

"Captain, this is all I need because I'm that damn good." Becker pulled out some magazines for the Glocks.

"You're alright, Becker. So, what's your plan?" Harvey picked up the binoculars and surveyed Dismal Key. A place that had always held fond memories of shore lunches and camping trips with his brother had now been replaced with the harassing memory of The Hermit taking shots at him, and now the terror of losing a girl who he'd always felt was part of his family.

"Well, Captain, any ideas of what's on that island?"

"Yep." Harvey continued to scan, focusing the binoculars on the sandy beach on the south end of Dismal Key. "I know there's a shack on the northwest side. I imagine that is where the girls would be, unless they set up some other camp."

"Okay, then we'll gamble on that's where they're at. However, I say we approach from the east to cover our tracks and work our way across the island. We can move in at night." Becker checked the batteries in the night vision binoculars.

"And if they leave before dark?"

"We know where the ship is at. The Five Mile Reef, right? You know how to get there?"

"Yeah, I know it. But we won't catch them in that Pathfinder if it's still working."

"Well, I hope you got some more tricks up your sleeve with your boat."

Harvey was hesitant. "We'll see. The Flounder is built to bully this backwater, not speed through it. If we can take them on the island, then we need to."

"Then that's what we're going do." Becker slapped the back of his neck, trying to annihilate the hoard of mosquitoes that pricked at his skin. "Why aren't they bothering you?"

"I put on mosquito repellent before I jumped off the boat." Harvey slipped a magazine into the assault rifle and chambered a round.

"Thanks for offering." Becker almost looked hurt as he swiped at the buzzing mass.

"You said you had everything you needed in that bag." Harvey reached in his side pocket, slipped out a small bottle of repellent, and tossed it to Becker. "I'm just funnin' you, Becker. Stop looking so miserable."

"Thanks." Becker sprayed the repellent on his neck, sending the black swarm in multiple directions. "What time is it?"

Harvey looked at his watch, "Two-forty. We've got a while until dusk. We should…Hold it—look what we got here." Harvey lifted the binoculars up to his eyes. Joe brought the Pathfinder around to the island. "Looks like our friends got off the mud flat."

Joe rammed the bow into the soft sand of Dismal Key's beach and tilted the engine out of the water.

"At least he learned how to raise his engine." Harvey chuckled.

Karam stormed off the beach and into the island's tree line while Joe inspected the propeller. Once satisfied, he went off after Karam.

"Your call, Becker."

"We wait."

A few hours later Joe idled back around the island, but this time in a little skiff.

"Where is he going?" Becker muttered under his breath, now holding the binoculars.

"That's Joe in the boat. Do you see anyone with him?" Harvey asked.

"No." Becker focused the binoculars. "Nobody is with him. Where could he be going?"

"Don't know," Harvey said quietly. "Hopefully to hell."

Harvey and Becker watched the Pathfinder for a few hours and saw no signs of anyone else. The tide was high as dusk began to settle, bringing relief from the sun. Becker was getting ready to suggest they sneak over to Dismal Key when another small mullet skiff motored around to Dismal's southwest side.

Becker snapped up the binoculars, trying to focus them through the grainy dusk. "Uh ohh," he said alarmed. A figure eased the boat's anchor into the water, slid in after it, and started swimming toward a little passage between the mangroves. "Captain, you're not going to believe this."

"What, Becker. Who is it? Joe come back?" Harvey said impatiently.

"Afraid not, Harvey. Have a look," Becker said, his face knit with concern.

Harvey adjusted the binoculars on the head, bobbing on the placid surface of the water. His hands tightened on the binoculars, anger convulsing through his body. Harvey shook his head in disbelief. "That bastard!" He slammed his fist on a root. "I'm going to kill him."

Chapter 21

McKlusky

Despite her gentle soul and frail appearance, my grandmother could be as ornery as an alligator when anybody wronged her loved ones. She'd raised three daughters, me, and most of the neighborhood kids at one time or another. We'd all experienced her skill of flicking one of Grandpa's belts or the sting of her hand across our backsides. We thought we could outrun her when we got in trouble, but she could move like a rattlesnake, striking at prey. And I loved her all the more for it, too, because it was that precious lady's love and discipline that kept our immediate family in line, including my grandfather.

Grandma loved Grandpa the most, though. She never admitted it, but everyone observed it in the way she cooked his dinner, made his coffee, and stole glances at him when he wasn't looking. Everything she did for him was just a little bit better than the rest, prepared with just a little more care, and cherished just a little bit longer.

They'd grown up together on the island, constant childhood friends. He left for the Army, and she became engaged to another man. Two weeks before her wedding, Grandpa wrote an impassioned letter, declaring his love for her. She dumped her fiancé and married Grandpa when he returned from the Army. He was twenty-one and she was seventeen, soon to be an old maid by her standards.

Now she shuffled about the house doing what she did best, caring for those who needed a gentle, loving hand to mend their wounds. I felt her soft, frail touch and smelled the lavender soap she used earlier in the morning as she patted my arm. It was her signature scent that I've associated with love and protection since I was a little boy. It didn't matter how old I got. I could always give her a hug, and I felt like I was a child, seeking comfort from a skinned knee or nightmare.

Jada now rested in my grandparents' bed, her head propped up on the pillows. I had the honor of moving her. For such a petite girl, she was heavy, a solid piece of muscle carved out into the girl whose breath was becoming deep and steady. With the cool breeze from the overhead fan pushing down on her, she seemed to sleep peacefully under the quilt blanket my grandmother had knitted years ago.

"McKlusky?" Grandma waited for my response. "Honey?"

"Yeah?" I broke from my trance. My mind rebelled against the images of Chloe being tortured by The Hippie.

Putting her arm around my shoulder, Grandma furrowed her brow with concern. "Honey, you know your grandpa is gonna find her. If anyone can find her out there, it's him."

My words struggled to find a path through my throat. "I know." My grandfather, leaving me crumpled on the floor, was another source of contention for me. "He shouldn't have left me. I'm pissed off."

Considering the circumstances, she didn't pop me across my mouth. "You know as well as I do I would've killed him if he took you. I know the good Lord in heaven isn't going to let nothing happen to that little girl. It isn't right." She rubbed my head, and then picked up a washcloth, soaking in a bin of cool water by the bed. She wiped the dirt and mud off Jada's face to reveal a beautiful girl with light chocolate skin who couldn't be much older than me. "Her fever is coming down." Grandma tossed the soiled cloth into the hamper and placed another clean one on Jada's forehead. "I'm going to check on Mrs. O'Malley. Watch Jada for me, and if she wakes up let me know. We need to make her drink some water."

"Okay," I said dryly. I felt the failure of not being able to help Chloe sink into my gut. It sat there like a pool of acid, burning up my throat. So I sat in a chair watching Jada, waiting, determined to find Chloe and kill the man who took her.

Jada moved her hand underneath the sheets and her head turned to the ceiling. Her voice cracked a low moan, and I moved my chair up beside the bed. I wanted to talk to her privately when she woke. Her eyes sprang open, focusing on the ceiling fan. Then they settled on me. She flung herself back against the wall on the corner of the bed. She took the sheets with her, glancing around the room. Her breathing was hectic and guttural, like a cat trying to dispel a hairball. Curling up in a ball, she glowered at me. I tossed a bottle of water to her, and it landed in front of her feet.

"It'll help break up the junk in your throat so we can talk," I said.

160

Suspicious of my intent, she let the bottle lay there. I knew her problem. I knew it the second she retreated from me. I was a male. No telling what she had been put through: raped, tormented, abused. I had no clue. Honestly, as much as I hated to admit it, I didn't care. I focused on one thing and one thing only, trying to find out where Chloe was. So I spoke first.

"My name is McKlusky. My grandfather, me, and another guy named Becker found you, floating in a canoe. You're safe." I paused to see if she would respond. "Please drink some water." She just stared at the bottle afraid to pick it up. Tiny shivers worked their way up her arms.

"Look," I said. She flinched and hugged into the corner a little tighter as I reached for the bottle. I screwed off the cap and took a swig and swallowed. "I'm not here to hurt you." I tossed the bottle back, and she slowly inched off the wall and grabbed it. Trying to steady it in her trembling hands, she brought it to her lips. Her eyes kept their gaze on me as she drank. She wiped the water running down her chin and relaxed her feet back under the covers. "What's your name again?"

"McKlusky."

"I'm Jada." She drained the bottle and cleared her throat. "Where am I?"

"At my grandparents' house."

"No, I mean what state?" Jada rubbed her eyes to help break some of the dirt that had crusted in her eyelids from her night in the canoe.

I realized just how lost she was. She had disappeared from outside of Chattanooga, and now she was hundreds of miles away. "You're in Florida. On Marco Island to be exact."

Closing her eyes, she shook her head as if trying to clear my words out of her ears. "Florida? How? How?"

"I don't know how you got here, but I need your help. The same guys that took you took my girlfriend last night. Can you tell me where they took you?" Tears pushed the rest of the dirt in her eyelids down her cheeks. "Kaitlin…" her voice trailed off. Jada pulled the pillow up to her mouth to muffle her anguish.

"You saw Kaitlin. She was there with you, then?" I glanced behind me to make sure that my grandmother was not lurking around.

"Where did they keep you? Can you tell me anything at all?" I had to keep myself calm. It was obvious that any little movement could send her off in fits of fright, and my one chance of helping Chloe would be sunk in Jada's despair.

"I left her," Jada cried, burying her head in the pillow further. "I couldn't save her." She looked up at me suspiciously. "How do you know who Kaitlin is?"

"The news. I saw you and Kaitlin on the news."

"The news?"

"Yes." I was growing impatient. "I'll help her if I can find her. But I need you to give me some idea where you were. Did you hear the name of the island, did Joe..." Jada shuddered at the mention of Joe's name. "We rescued you from him this morning. You're safe. Please, if you can remember anything at all. Help me, so I can go get Chloe and Kaitlin."

Jada considered my words for a moment. "I-I don't know where we were," she said. The hope of saving Chloe plummeted.

"We were held in a shack on an island. Kaitlin said it was some hermit shack."

"Did you say hermit shack?" I asked in a hushed voice.

"Yes."

"Don't tell my grandmother what you told me. I think I know where I can find them." I stood up from the chair and started to hurry out of the room, nearly barreling over Grandma.

She glanced at Jada huddled on the bed. "How long has she been awake?" She gave me a disapproving stare. "Not long. She's really scared, Grandma. I was coming to get you." Lying to Grandma just compounded my misery

"Of course she is. After all she's been through with men, she wakes up to see one staring at her." She turned to Jada, concern spread across her face. "Poor baby." Grandma went to the side of the bed, as if approaching a wounded animal. "I'm Delores Harvey. I'm going to take care of you, honey."

At the sweet, smooth sound of Grandma's voice, Jada broke and let all the horror and frustration out. Grandma sat on the edge of the bed and Jada scooted close and buried her head into my grandmother's arms.

Jada had finally realized she was okay. "I've got you, baby. I promise nobody is going to hurt you as long as I got something to say about it." Grandma rocked Jada back and forth. I used the distraction to exit the room. I decided to trade my flip-flops and shorts for jeans and work boots. I knew where I needed to start my search.

* * *

The midday sun lit up the weather-worn brown boards that made up Jason's Bar. Harleys, lined up like dominos, sat on their kick stands, supported by the white gravel road. Jason's Bar was my cousin's bar in Goodland. He used it as a cover to account for the cash he brought in from smuggling drugs and illegals from Cuba. He distributed drugs out across Florida, running barrels of weed and kilos of coke across Alligator Alley to Miami. But mostly he met boats in the Gulf to pick up or deliver shipments.

Jason and I grew up together when I lived on Marco. We're six years apart, but we were like brothers back then and fought like it, too. We always tried to outdo each other, jumping ramps on our bikes. I hadn't seen Jason since he started running drugs at sixteen years old for his daddy. I wasn't allowed to be around him. But I'd already run away to help Chloe. Why not add associating with a known drug smuggler to that list?

As I pushed open the door, my lungs revolted against the cigarette smoke laced with hints of pot. My eyes strained to focus through the fog that encompassed the room, and its ragged brood of men and women that sat in their chairs blurry eyed, sucking down their beers. I didn't see Jason. A shudder of excitement went through me as I thought of the lifestyle these people lived. Some of them stared at me, a hint of familiarity in their faces as they tried to place where they'd seen me before. Some I recognized from family photos, but most of them hadn't seen me since I was a kid; my grandmother saw to that.

Others shook their heads and looked back at their card game or beer. Some whispered to the person next to them as they slowly solved the riddle of the mysterious person who'd walked into the bar, "That's

Captain Harvey's boy," or "That is my Aunt Delores' grandson." I walked up to the bar and motioned for the bartender.

The bartender put his forearms on the bar, his face a sickly wan from days and nights of serving drinks. His black t-shirt, the sleeves ripped off, hung loosely on his chest and tightened as it slid over the hump of his belly.

"Listen, kid." The words had to fight through the muck that accumulates in one's throat over decades of smoking. "I don't care if you drink or not, but you gotta at least have a fake ID and a baby bottle to put your beer in." The bartender laughed and the whole bar joined in.

"Funny fat fuck, aren't you?" I said. The whole bar stifled their chatter except for a couple of snickers that lingered into it. "I ain't here to drink. I need to see Jason."

His face turned crimson as he reached across the bar and shoved me in the forehead, snapping back my neck, knocking me off balance. "Piss off, kid. Jason don't wanna see you."

The laughter and the smoke seemed to swirl around me, compacting me into a tiny tight funnel, a tornado of images spinning into my head. Chloe's face, the fight with Trent and Brad, The Hippie sitting on the sidewalk leering at Chloe, Becker crushing my ribs, Grandpa driving away in the Flounder, my step-dad's abuse, the loneliness at school, having to live in that toxic waste of a state, who the hell is my father anyway? They all ripped through my mind like shrapnel, severing the few strained pieces of thread that connected me with reality. I lunged toward the bartender. Grabbing the back of his head, I bashed it against the bar, making the glasses and beer bottles jump. I snatched an empty bottle and broke it against the edge of the bar and held the fragmented top against the bottom of his jaw, letting it prick into his skin. A stream of blood worked its way down his neck, dripping on the greasy floor. The people at the tables jumped up and pushed out their chairs, scraping the floor. Torn between kinship and money, they didn't know if they should help or not.

"I said, I want to see Jason." My voice was calm, almost resigned, but my hand shook, wanting to plunge the bottle into the double chin quivering under the shard of glass. Someone needed to pay for all that had happened to me. "Where is he?" My voice sounded foreign in my head. No longer a boy pleading, but a man demanding.

"McKlusky! What the hell?"

I turned and saw Jason, staring at me from across the room. His mouth opened. His face was perplexed, but he immediately assessed the gravity of the situation

Jason laughed. "I swear to God, if another member of my family busts up my place today I'm gonna lose it." Jason threw up his hands and walked over. "Let my bartender go and come talk to your cousin." He clutched my hand that held the bottle and tried to pull it away, letting go when he realized he no longer had the strength to outdo me. We weren't kids anymore. I think it shocked him more than me.

"Think about your grandma. You'd break her heart if you killed this man." He rubbed the back of my shoulder trying to get me to relax.

I liked the feeling of the bartender's neck pulsating under my hand, of his blood quickly pumping through the veins I so badly wanted to open up. I moved the bottle away from his neck. The bartender jumped back on his feet and scrambled far behind the bar, putting a dirty towel to his neck.

"Go bandage that shit up and get back to pouring beer," Jason yelled. All eyes were trained on him, waiting for the word on what they should do. "Son of a bitch, our family gets pissed easy." Jason laughed, rubbing the back of his neck. Most of the people chuckled, sat back down, and resumed playing cards and drinking as if nothing happened.

"What are you doing?" He pulled me by the arm and led me to the back. "You're getting some muscles from the last time I seen you. How long has it been now? Five years? Six years?" He shook his head. "Barely even recognized you. I bet Aunt Delores don't know your here."

"She doesn't know I am here. I'd like to keep it that way too."

I walked past some of the people in the bar. Some stood up and slapped my back saying, "You're growing up good, boy. You're doing the family proud."

I nodded my head and tried to remember faces and names.

"I know you don't remember all of them. Your grandma wouldn't let you near any of them once my daddy brought them into the business." Jason led me into his office, sat behind his chair, and lit a cigarette. "Course, she probably is right to keep you away. You got options in life." He looked me over and smiled. "Cousin, you got big! I remember when you was just a skinny little turd like I still am."

"It's good to see you. We had us some good times when you weren't beating me up." I sat down in a chair in front of his desk.

"Well, it must have did you some good with what you did to my bartender and all." Jason pointed toward the missing door. "Your grandpa and some big fella handled Willy and Glenn at the door there pretty well a couple hours ago."

"They were here? Where did they go?"

"Well, I don't know. They was lookin' for Joe, so I sent them to see Billy. Billy up and left. He left town about an hour ago. Came in here, grabbed him a beer and said he was never coming back. Told me to let Uncle Doyle know." Jason smirked. "Whatever he did to Billy, he put the fear of God in him." Jason took a drag of his cigarette, letting the silence smother the air. He exhaled the smoke. "And here you come tearing up my place too. What is it you need, McKlusky?"

Getting Jason's help wouldn't be easy, nor would it be free. I had nothing to bargain with except for the fact that Jason didn't want any unneeded attention in the Ten Thousand Islands.

"I need to know where The Hermit is."

Jason nearly choked on his smoke, mocking me. "I ain't telling you where The Hermit is. He's my boy."

"I need to know where he is. I'm not looking to mess up your business."

"Listen, cousin, The Hermit is my eyes in them islands. He lets me know where the law's hanging and if anybody's trying to move in on my territory. All that info for taking him some gas, liquor, and food. I couldn't do half of what I do if it weren't for him." Jason stood up to show me the way out.

"Chloe's life depends on it." I used my last civil bargaining chip.

Jason sat back down. "Chloe?" He rubbed his forehead and shrunk back in his chair. "That little girl you run with?"

I thought this would be enough to get him to help me, but he leaned forward, "Cousin, I would love to help you…I'm sorry, bro, but it's business."

166

I pounded my fist on the desk, causing Jason to jump in his chair. My pulse pushed against my neck. "Here's how this is going to play out, Jason. You're going to tell me where The Hermit is and you're going to give me a boat to get to him or..."

"Well, ain't you a cocky little son of a bitch!" Jason sprung out of his chair. "Or what, boy! What do you think you can *or* me with? Just 'cause you grew up a bit you think you can take me?"

We stared each other down like when we were kids, waiting for the other to act. I wanted to reach across the desk and beat the information out of him. But I hit him where it would hurt him the most. "*Or* I'm walking out of here and calling the police and telling them we found one of the missing girls in Pumpkin Bay." Jason's face lost its color. I continued. "We haven't called the police yet because we're afraid if the guys who took her see the law around, they'll bail and then we'll never find Chloe."

Jason studied my face for a bluff. "You found a girl out there? Your grandpa didn't say anything of the kind."

"Yeah, Joe tried to kill us over her."

"So I heard."

"I'm going turn her into the authorities if you don't give up The Hermit and give me a boat."

"You want a boat now, too?" Jason snuffed out his cigarette.

I locked my eyes onto his. "Those islands will be crawling with FBI, Coast Guard, and local authorities for weeks, searching for the rest of the girls. You'll be shut down, cousin. You wouldn't be able to smuggle a pot leaf up your ass without getting caught."

Jason clenched his hands into fists. "Damn it!" He smashed his fists on the table. Then he took his hat off and scratched his head. "My own kin."

"Just business. Don't take it personal."

"Cousin, you win." He reached down and opened his drawer and threw me a set of boat keys. "There is an old mullet skiff at the end of the dock. It ain't fast, but it'll get you where you need to go. It's all I can spare right now."

"Thanks, and The Hermit?" I said, putting the keys in my pocket.

Jason scowled, "You're shrewd. You might not like what you find when you get to him, but the last time I heard from him he was on Brush Island across from Coon Key." Jason smiled. "You know where that's at, Yankee boy?"

"Screw you. I know where it's at." I put out my hand to shake his. "No hard feelings, cousin?"

"McKlusky," Jason said as he put out his hand, "you're just doing what you need to. We're always gonna be family."

"Thanks for your help." I turned to walk out.

"McKlusky," Jason hollered. He reached in his desk drawer again. "You be careful and take this." He tossed me a knife in a battered, cracked leather sheath. I took it out and inspected it. "It's my daddy's old KA-BAR knife from his Marine days. I ain't ever needed it. Besides this bar and a smuggler's life, it's the only other thing he ever left me when he died."

I balanced the knife in my hands and inspected the blade. I flipped it, turning it in my hands.

"Where the hell did you learn to do that?" Jason looked at the knife twist in my hand.

"Just little tricks I picked up from some Filipino guys I know." I sheathed the knife and stuck it in the small of my back. "Thanks."

My boots weighed heavily on the dock's wooden planks as I walked to the skiff. The boat had seen better days. Its fiberglass hull was webbed with cracks jetting out of the seams. The plywood console had long ago lost its paint, showing the decaying grain of the wood. I stepped onto the skiff. It was small, twelve feet long and maybe four feet wide. I cranked the little twenty-five horsepower motor. The hull shook like a wet dog. Black smoke sputtered out of the two stroke dinosaur as I pushed the throttle forward. The gear caught with crunches and clicks. The engine labored to turn the prop and move the boat forward. Brush Island was about a quarter of the way to Pumpkin Bay.

I'd never seen The Hermit before, but it was well known that Jason used him to scout out the area for signs of the law. Jason kept in touch with him with a marine band radio. The Hermit moved from island to island in his little Boston Whaler, rarely staying in the same spot for more than a week. Jason contacted him to find out where he was and what he saw. Sometimes Jason would ask The Hermit to move to a particular area, and The Hermit would go. Jason in return provided him with booze, food, and gas for the boat.

The Hermit set up shacks on his favorite islands. He'd become sort of a legend in the area. Any island he was on he considered his, and the fish around it too. If The Hippie had taken Chloe to one of The Hermit's shacks, The Hermit may be able to tell me where, or at least narrow down the options.

As I approached Brush Island, I gunned the skiff's engine, and it sputtered back that I was demanding way too much from it. However, it still managed to put the bow onto the sand. With the tide still incoming, I wouldn't have to worry about being left dry. I just needed to secure the boat with an anchor in the sand so the tide didn't carry the skiff away.

Grabbing the anchor, I jumped over the side. My boots sunk a little, imprinting my soles into the compacted sand. I walked the anchor several feet in front of the boat and embedded its forks deep into the beach. I searched for any signs of The Hermit. The sand was littered with debris and small twigs, outlining the shape of the waves that pushed them up on the beach. The only prints in the sand were mine. The wind blew off the Gulf, rustling the trees and swaying them in the wind, waving to me to invite me into their canopied jungle. Sweat dripped down my legs under my jeans, down to my socks, and into my boots. While jeans and boots were not a staple for me in such weather, I knew they'd do a great job of protecting against the bugs and ankle-twisting roots.

I breathed deep, surveying the fortress of green in front of me, knowing I would have to penetrate its thick branches and underbrush to search the island for The Hermit. I pushed the first branches aside. Their snapping spooked a raccoon out of its hiding spot. It rustled the underbrush, causing me to jump, my KA-BAR knife in hand, slashing through the air in front of me.

Despite my nerves, the knife felt good in my hands. Its round black rubber handle helped me grip it securely in my sweaty palms. I'd never actually been in a knife fight, but I'd trained using knives in simulated combat in my dojo. The first thing taught to me about a knife fight was you are going to get cut, period. End of question. It wasn't like the movies where the hero blocks and dodges every attack, coming away unscathed. The best offense and defense of a knife fight is to control when and where the cut happens. Instead of blocking an attack and being cut on the inside of the arm where a person's wrists can be severed and they bleed out, I knew to block with the outside of the arms. While cuts may be deep and painful, no major arteries or veins are on the outside of the arms.

Taking a deep breath and closing my eyes, I forced myself to push the sound of my heart out of my ears and take in the sounds and scents of the island. I thought about my situation and how unprepared I actually was. My grandfather had tons of knives and guns. I hadn't thought to bring one with me. How long had it taken Jason to realize I was not armed? He'd really done me three favors instead of two by giving me a knife. I'd find a way to repay him. Right now, I needed to concentrate and figure out any other mistakes I might have made in preparing for my own covert operation.

The sounds of the island filtered into my ears. The raccoon chattered about fifty feet in front of me. Pelicans and curlew swooshed in and roosted in the tree tops, finished with their afternoon snack. The wind jittered the leaves like light tambourines jingling in the air. The trunks of the trees swayed back and forth like hands raised up in praise to God. My heartbeat slowed.

Hearing The Hermit coming wasn't hard. Screaming, he crashed through the bushes with a machete raised over his head into the clearing where I stood. "My island!" he screeched. His eyes were bloodshot, crazed—burning with the rum dilating his pupils. His white hair, kinked and wavy, bushed out over his ears.

The machete swung down over his head toward my shoulder. For a fraction of a second my body felt frozen solid, as if trying to turn itself to stone to protect me from the impact of the blade. My left hand moved first, popping his wrist and the machete away from me. The machete broke free from his hand and fell to the ground. My right hand brought the KA-BAR's blade up, slicing from the outside of his rib cage to the bottom of his pectoral muscle. Sinking the heel of my foot into the back of his knee crippled him into a kneeling position. I glided behind him, knife out, waiting for him to get back up.

The Hermit moaned, looking down at the cut that had sliced through his ragged Calcutta shirt. The skull on the back of the shirt looked back at me. The Hermit's ragged breaths moved the skull up and down as if it were nodding in approval.

Blood soaked up in his t-shirt, flowing down to his blue jeans, turning them a blackish red. He turned around on his knees to face me, his hand trying to stop the flow of blood. Stretching his legs in front of him, he collapsed back on a palm tree. His face was wrinkled and old, his beard as white as the Florida sand that had been bleached under centuries of sun.

I sheathed the knife and came to the realization I'd cut and beat up a crazy old man. Even when I rationalized that he was coming after me with a machete that could have cleaved my head cleanly off my shoulders, the sense of courage and bravery I'd felt sunk into a pool of shame and guilt. The old man bled in front of me.

He reached in his side pocket, pulled out a small silver flask, and took a drink. "Okay," he breathed, "do it! Your island now. Do it." He took one more drink and closed his eyes.

I sputtered, my tongue trying to force the words out of my mouth, "I-I-I'm sorry."

The Hermit cracked a raspy laugh and gripped his side. "Sorry for what?" He took another swig of his flask. "I would've done the same thing." He pushed himself up against the bark of the palm tree, grunting in pain. "Let an old man die standing up at least. Come on now, kill me. You must be the other one they were talking about."

"I don't want to kill you, and I don't want your island," I said.

His potbelly rounded, pushing out his shirt, which was way too big for him. His disintegrating blue jeans were frayed, worn at the ankles, ending just above his boat shoes with a hole that revealed toes and the top of his foot.

"You don't want my island? What the hell are you here for, then?" The Hermit straightened a little against the tree.

"You; I need your help," I said taken aback by his sudden change of mood.

The Hermit squealed in delight, revealing the gummed toothless line in his mouth. "Me, help someone? I ain't no help to anybody but

171

looking out for the law for drug smugglers. And from the looks of you, you ain't no smuggler."

"No I'm not. But..."

"What, darling? I should trust him?" The Hermit's eyes looked up, scanning the tops of the trees, speaking to a figment, an apparition that lived in his mind. One that made me doubt how effective he would be in helping me. "Okay, darling. If you say so." The Hermit's eyes settled back on me. "My wife says I should help you. So you help me back to my hut, and we'll see if I can." He reached out his hand, waving for me to come to him. "Come on. She says it's okay."

Lingering for a second, still wary, I eased toward The Hermit, letting him wrap his arm around my shoulder. I supported his weight as he took a step forward. "Your wife?" I asked.

"My wife, God rest her soul," he said tenderly. "She still talks to me."

He reeked of the rum that provided the voice of his wife.

"Where is your hut Mr. I don't know what to call you," I said.

His steps were slow but steady. He took an occasionally drink from his flask. "Ain't got a name any more," he said. "My shack ain't far. Just through those bushes twenty yards over." He pointed to the east. We headed that way.

The shack was camouflaged by the branches overhead and the trunks that surrounded it. Even a trained eye could miss it if it didn't know exactly what it was looking for. The shack's green tin roof blended with the natural elements as did the bare plywood walls. One could walk a few feet from it and never know it was there.

I moved an old wooden door to the side and helped The Hermit through the opening. The room was rather neat, considering the haphazard construction. A mattress lay in the far corner covered with coarse, moth-eaten blankets. To the side of us was a wooden chair that The Hermit shuffled over to, sitting down on it with a grunt. On the wall was a shelf made from old planks loosely nailed together. They were lined with unopened rum and whiskey bottles. No doubt, Jason kept The Hermit well supplied with his favorite drinks. A small chest sat in the opposite corner of the bed.

"Open that chest," The Hermit huffed. "Hand me that milk jug on the far right on the shelf too."

I opened the chest to find a small supply of bandages and medical tape that were stained from years of dust. By the bandages was a slingshot made of hard oak wood that I held up and admired. "Man, I used to play with one of these all the time as a little kid."

The Hermit grunted in pain as he removed his shirt. "I use it to kill the occasional bird to eat. Don't worry about it. Bring the bandages to me with the milk jug on the shelf." The Hermit slapped his knee for me to hurry or from another stab of pain up his side.

I put the sling-shot back and grabbed the tape, bandages, and the jug. The jug was nearly filled to the top with water. "Mind if I have drink?" I was dying of thirst and realized water was yet another thing I hadn't brought along.

"Help yourself to whatever you want."

I twisted off the cap and took a big gulp. The liquid burned. It felt like the bacteria in my mouth popped and died under the heat. My lips felt raw, as if a layer of skin had been peeled off. I coughed out what remained in my mouth, spraying it across the hut as the rest funneled down to my stomach and turned it into a comforting furnace of warmth.

The Hermit sputtered with laughter. "That's some mighty fine fire water there, huh?" He straightened back up in the chair, both hands gripping his side, and talked to the voice in his head again. "Hush up, baby. I was just having a little fun."

I continued coughing and struggled to put the lid back on the jug. "That's moonshine. I thought it was..."

"Water?" The Hermit laughed. "I can't tell you the last time I had a sip of water on these lips. Give it here." He motioned for the jug. He flipped off the cap and took a giant gulp, sending an air bubble up through the jug, sinking in its sides with a pop. He let out a big sigh of satisfaction and poured some down his side along the cut. He cussed and took another gulp and said, "If I don't kill the infection from the outside, I'll kill it from the inside." He sat the jug down by his feet. "Hand me the bandages."

When I went to hand him the bandages, the moonshine sloshing in my stomach forced out a belch. "You need some help, old man?"

How about tearing me off some strips of tape."

The tape was brittle. I ripped off some strips and tried to keep them from tearing into short useless pieces.

"Now, how is it you think I can help you?" The Hermit asked as he tried to arrange the bandages across the cut.

"My girlfriend was kidnapped." The knot in my throat bunched up again, and I wanted to take another swig of the moonshine to straighten it out. "Taken by some hippie."

"Huh?" said The Hermit. He took the strips of tape I handed him and placed them over the bandages. "Sorry to hear that, but I don't know how I can help you there. Sounds like a job for the law."

"That's not all, me and my grandpa found a girl this morning in a canoe in Pumpkin Bay. She'd been kidnapped. She said she was held in one of your shacks. Some Jamaican guy and a local tried to kill us over her."

The Hermit stiffened in his chair and screamed, "MY ISLAND!" I darted back. Craziness possessed him again. He stood and paced back and forth across the hut. "A Jamaican took my island a few weeks ago. I watched them from the woods as they went into my shack. He and another fellow, fine looking and distinguished, said in his funny accent that my island would be a perfect spot. I heard them talk about a fellow named Richard was ready. But they said some fellow named Carlos was ready too." He shook his fist at me. "I thought you was Richard or Carlos come to take my island again." Settling back down into the chair and picking up the moonshine, he took a drink. "I watched them for an hour. They went into my shack and came out. I moved ever so slightly and the Jamaican bloke tensed up and rushed me. I screamed, 'MY ISLAND!' and he grabbed me and beat me in the head until I was bloody in the mouth. He dragged me off to the middle of my island and kicked me in the gut until I puked. He said, 'Crazy old hermit, if you come back I'm going to kill you.'" Tears spilled out of The Hermit's eyes. "My only picture of my wife and kid was in that hut." He made the sign of the Trinity across his chest. "God rest their souls."

"What island, old man?" I moved close to him. "What is the name of the island they kicked you off of?"

174

"They died on me fifteen years ago. I want my picture back." His toothless face mourned. "I don't wanna forget what they look like. Their faces are becoming fuzzy."

"If it's still there, I'll get it back. I promise. Tell me the island."

"Dismal Key. They took Dismal Key. You know where that is? You would've had to pass it to get to Pumpkin Bay this morning."

"I know, old man." I rushed for the door and out into the thick branches.

"Boy!" The Hermit yelled after me.

"Yeah," I said, turning around, not stopping my movement toward the beach.

"My wife says it's best you kill the man that took your girl. Ain't no place in this world for the likes of him." He took a swig of the bottle. "Ain't no place at all."

* * *

The sky pushed down on the sun in the west, squeezing out shades of pink and crimson. I chugged past Foster Key and was going to run up on Dismal's beach, but I saw the Pathfinder. My heart nearly crawled out my mouth as I felt the isolation surrounding me. Honestly, I'd thought I would have run into the Flounder by then and found safety in numbers. But it hadn't happened. I knew Chloe had to be on the island if she was still alive. The thought, *still alive,* twisted my insides. I turned the skiff around the south side of Dismal, hoping the clanking of the engine wouldn't alert anyone to my presence. I stopped short of a small passage I knew canoers took into the island. The skiff was too big to make it through.

I slid the anchor into the water and slipped in after it. The water immediately filled my shoes and weighted down my pants. Another mistake, no change of clothes. Luckily, the water only reached to my waist, but I crouched down, keeping a low profile, and moved into the narrow passage between the mangroves.

The crickets filled the night air, soothing the atmosphere around me as the first stars burned through the fading light. I sloshed around the curve and plummeted several feet under the water. I struggled toward the top and broke the surface as my feet kicked to stay afloat in the big hole I'd stepped in. A couple strokes of my arms and I was able to set my foot in the muck. I stood up, knee high in water. The hair on my neck struck up like tiny spears as Chloe's screams echoed down the path. "Noooooooooo…Don't…Please! It hurts!"

Chapter 22

Chicky, Chicky

Richard inspected the shell mound left by the Calusa Indians. The Calusas used shells to build foundations for their houses that stood on stilts, and some say mounds for human sacrifice. The mound Richard looked at was jagged with shells caked in mud that had loosened over time from breaking the brittle clay that encased them. Richard trailed his hand around the mound, the place he would take Chloe, offering her up as a sacrifice to himself. He knew if he stripped her down and pressed her back against the shells it would cut into her back, their ragged edges slowly slicing her skin. Her imaginary screams reverberated up his spine, forcing him to run his tongue over his teeth.

Richard's stomach was consumed with anticipation like a fire consumes the oxygen in a closed room, leaving it void and hollow. He gingerly kicked the bottom of the mound. Mud and shells rolled to the ground. Pulling his knife out, he scraped into the mound and imagined the blood the Calusas might have spilled on it before. He plunged the blade deep into the mound. The shells ground along the steel. When he withdrew the knife, he half expected to see a deluge of blood wind its way down to the ground.

Richard sheathed the knife. He began to walk back to the camp to bring Chloe to the spirits of the Calusa Indians by joining them through a sacrificial bond. He walked the path and stopped short of the clearing. Karam and Joe stood across the clearing, talking to Marcus. Richard stepped to the side behind a row of high shrubs to listen.

"I know who's got her," Joe said. "He's a local. We grew up together. I got no love for him. I know where they're gonna take her if they ain't called the police."

"It doesn't matter," Marcus said, turning his attention to Karam. "I'm afraid Richard may not have as much fun as he thinks. We can't allow him to kill the girl. She's heading to Cuba."

Richard nearly charged out of the bushes ready to plunge his knife into Marcus' pale face. But he stayed hidden, his belly becoming

177

an inferno of rage. He knew if he attacked now, he would not be able to take all three. Quietly, he slipped back down the path to think, to kill.

* * *

"So, Jada is out, then," Karam asked.

"No, we can still sell her or kill her. She saw Richard and this idiot." Marcus stared at Joe. "I don't want her linked to us. I want the people who helped her dead. All of them." Marcus turned his attention to Joe. "You failed me again by letting them get away. Now, you find a way to be useful to me again. I find it frustrating that I can't kill you. But if you manage to kill those helping Jada, then I'll forget about you. Keep Jada alive and bring her to the Albatross."

"Those three will be dead by morning, Marcus. I swear to it," replied Joe.

"Joe, I want the whole family dead. I want them all dead. Is that a problem?"

Joe didn't want to do what he was about to do. He bit the inside of his lip so hard that blood spurted out from the puncture. He tried not to think about how it would be to kill Delores as he made his way to his skiff and freed it from its camouflage. He would spare her if he could, but then she would know. She would know it was him if she didn't already, and he couldn't live with her knowing. But she owed him for her betrayal. He turned the key, starting the engine. Turning the boat toward Goodland, he headed to the marina to drive over and pay the Harvey house a visit.

* * *

Richard paced back and forth, wearing a path in the unspoiled vegetation. His hand clutched the handle of his knife as he muttered to himself that Chloe was his. Ripping off his shirt, revealing his scarred body, he gently pulled the knife out of the sheath and rested it in his hand, cradling it as one does a fragile object that is an emblem of many precious memories. A twisted and knotted piece of driftwood about five feet long, weighted on one end, lay in front of his feet. He snagged it up and moved to the clearing.

Karam and Marcus were huddled close together, light whispers escaping their mouths. Marcus saw Richard first.

"Richard!" Marcus greeted him. "Good to see you." Marcus stopped short of Richard when he saw the blade pointed in his direction. Karam came close to his father.

"I'm afraid I can't wait anymore. I need to have her now." Richard lowered the knife and began to move toward the shack.

"Richard," Marcus said.

"You know," Richard said, turning to the men, "I want to thank you for letting me out for a little R&R. I think Chloe is just what I need to set me right. It should set my cravings aside for a while."

"That's good, but there has been a change of plans I'm afraid. First you must hear me out," Marcus replied.

"Has there?"

"Somewhat." Marcus' voice showed a rare sign of nervousness. Richard's behavior was still unpredictable. Marcus could never guess how he might react, nor could Karam, who had clicked the safety off the gun. "You can still have the girl, but she must live. She is going to replace Jada."

Richard drew a circle in the dirt with the stick. "Well, that is some news." Stopping the circle, he tapped the stick in the middle of it. He put the knife back in its sheath. "I can still have her, just not kill her?"

"I'll make it up to you. I promise. You're far too valuable to me. I hate doing this to you." Marcus turned to Karam, "See I told you he would understand. He is a reasonable fellow."

Karam grunted.

"Okay then, I guess I should get to it then." Richard's wiry frame was quicker than Karam's bulk. The end of the staff nearly cracked The Jamaican's skull by the time the gun was half way up. He fell to the ground. A pool of blood oozed through the sand like a stream of lava.

Marcus jumped back and reached for the gun under his jacket. The staff connected with Marcus' hand, sending a paralyzing jab of pain up his arm. Marcus' fingers flexed out like a trap, frozen and broken.

Richard bludgeoned the Englishman's temple, turning Marcus's peppery white beard into a red sponge. Marcus tried to keep his eyelids open, but their weight dropped down over his eyes sending him to the ground.

"Hey, chicky, chicky," Richard sang.

* * *

Chloe heard Richard's voice. Kaitlin closed her eyes, squinting like a child, trying to make the boogey man go away. Tears poured out of them as she shook the bed, trying to free herself to help Chloe. Chloe pulled the single rope that was looped under the bed and tied to both of her wrists, attempting one last time to escape.

Richard appeared in the doorway and leaned against the frame. "I see you." Richard's eyes devoured Chloe.

"No—No!" Chloe hoped she would wake up in bed, a snook in the refrigerator, and her mother busily getting ready for tonight's dinner.

"Take me damn it! Take me!" Kaitlin cried.

"Ssshhhhh, you need to be quiet now." Richard stepped inside the shack.

Chloe pushed herself up against the headboard like she wanted to try and ram it through the wall. "You stupid son of a bitch! You can't have me!"

"Son of a bitch?" Richard said. "That is true, but I'm going to have you, too." Richard's eyes followed the path Chloe's tears took as they fell down her cheeks to her neck, and as they twisted and wound down in between her breasts. "Don't cry, Chloe. I will dry the tears soon."

"Leave her alone, you…" Richard brought the staff across Kaitlin's face. Chloe nearly vomited from the sound of the crack. A tidal wave of blood exploded out of Kaitlin's mouth. She fluttered her eyes, and then they snapped shut.

"Kait—Kaitlin?" Chloe whispered, as if trying to wake a sleeping baby. "Kaitlin, come back. Wake up."

"Now, we're alone." Richard moved closer to Chloe, hammering the staff down in front of him with each step he took.

180

Chloe jerked her arms together, ripping the skin off her wrists as the rope twisted around them. "No!" Her chest heaved in and she breathed out sobs. "I—I'm going to kill you. I will kill you if you touch me!"

Richard let the stick fall to the floor and moved toward Chloe. "Now, that's my girl." He pulled his knife out. Standing over her, he grabbed her legs and pulled her violently off the headboard into a lying position on the bed. He raised his knife, placed the point on Chloe's neck, and traced it down her chest, in between her breasts, over her clothes, and down her stomach. The tip of the blade flicked the skin off her body leaving a white trail. He stopped the knife at the top of her shorts and smiled at her. "Save that for later."

Chloe kicked her leg up at his face, but Richard moved to the side. He jumped on the bed, straddling her legs to keep them under control and leaned into her face. Reaching behind her, he slipped the knife up the small of her back, forcing her body to press against his as she arched to avoid the blade. He felt her heart beating against his chest.

"Get off me," Chloe cried. The sweat and dirt on his chest stained her shirt. He brought the knife from under her and cut the rope on each of her wrists. She tried to come around with a swing, but Richard pinned her arms on the bed as he moved up and straddled her stomach.

"Don't worry. I'll get off." Richard flipped her on her chest, twisted her arms behind her back, pulled the rope from under the bed, and bound her hands behind her. Once he had her tied, he got off her and pulled up the chair by the bed.

"You don't disappoint, Chloe." Richard breathed deeply. "When I saw you on the beach choking out that boy, I said to myself, there is a girl who can satisfy me."

Chloe turned her face to look at Richard. "With that thing it's a wonder you can be satisfied. I felt it against me. You're a damn joke!" Chloe bristled. She pulled on the rope trying to slip her hands free.

"We'll see. We're not here for you. We're here for me." Richard got on his knees by the bed. His finger started at her ankle and slowly traveled up over her calf muscle. Chloe visibly shuddered at his touch. She tried to think of other things, such as the beach and her father, but his finger continued up to her thigh, to the bottom of her shorts where his

181

finger paused. Richard let his whole hand wrap around her leg as he massaged it. His hand, rough and calloused, sanded her skin. Chloe whimpered. Letting go of her thigh, Richard walked his fingers up to the small of her back, slipped his hand under her shirt, and unsnapped her bra.

"NO!" Chloe screamed, and Richard yanked her up off the bed and threw her to the floor. Her face burned with anger. She spat at him. He slapped her across the face, swinging her head to the side. Richard grabbed her hair, forcing her to her feet, and dragged her out of the shack.

Chloe lifted her head. Through the blur of her tears she could see The Jamaican and Marcus lying on the ground, blood coming from their heads. Richard tugged her harder and forced her to walk in front of him. Karam groaned as they walked by.

Richard muttered under his breath, "Not much time."

Chloe dug her feet into the sand and pushed back against The Hippie. He grabbed her bound hands and slung her to the ground, knocking the breath out of her. Thoughts ricocheted in her mind like streaks of lightening flashing here and there: her childhood, her mother's face, her father's death, the sweetness of her first kiss only a couple days ago, and the magic of it that played on her lips until she was taken early this morning. The sand scraped her face and stuck to her cheek as she turned to look up at her attacker.

Smugness outlined his face as it might do a lion looking over its prey. Richard pulled her off the ground by her arms, her shoulder sockets feeling as if they would pop.

"Now, let's walk like a good girl, Chloe." He wrapped his free hand around her waist and pulled her body close to his, enjoying the friction the bouncing created. With her feet off the ground, Chloe kicked the ball of her heel into his shin. Richard cussed in agony and dropped her. Chloe sprinted toward the path, easily treading the rough ground, not feeling the pointy sticks and sandspurs. Her soles were tough from years of walking with no shoes on the beach's shell walkway and hot summer asphalt boiled under the Florida sun.

Richard thrashed through the path after her, yelling for her to stop.

As she cranked her legs faster, a searing pain exploded through her right calf and sent a spasm up her leg collapsing her to the ground. Chloe looked down at her leg for the source of the pain. Richard's knife handle protruded out of her calf. The pain burned up her body like a slow trickle of acid. Chloe tried to pull her wounded leg under her to get up, but Richard put his hand around the handle, his smile curling up his beard. He slowly pulled the knife out of her leg, the blade slicing through the muscle fiber as it dissected itself out.

"Noooooooo…Don't…Please…It hurts!"

Richard grabbed the back of Chloe's neck and jerked her up, her head snapping back against his hand. Adrenaline gushed into her veins like morphine, numbing the shock and pain. She felt like her body was electrified, the tiny hairs on her arms prickling up. "You coward," she yelled, the anger rising over her fear. "You don't even have the guts to let my hands free."

"Now, there you are. The girl I saw on the beach." Richard sheathed his knife, putting one hand around her waist feeling the curvature of her hip bone under her shirt, the way it slid down to her pelvis.

"Untie me, freak, and I'll show you what I can do," Chloe said.

Richard spun her around and stood face to face with her, his eyes staring into hers, studying her mood. He pulled her close and kissed her forehead. It was as if death itself had grown cold and died where his lips touched her. Her skin chilled over her bones.

"This is not about what you can do, Chloe, but about what I can do to you. You seem to forget that." Richard scooped Chloe up in his arms, carrying her down the path, eerily resembling a groom carrying his bride across the threshold of a new house. Chloe fought to wiggle free, but Richard pulled her tighter to him. He placed Chloe on her feet, reigniting the pain in her leg. "We're here." Richard wringed her shirt by the collar, nearly ripping it off of her and pulled her to him. "This is it, Chloe."

Chloe looked at the shell mound. "If this is it, then this is it." She wrenched herself from Richard's grasp and turned toward the mound. Richard caught her by the shoulder to keep her from going any farther.

"Let me go, hippie!" Chloe pulled her shoulder away from his grasp and limped to the shell mound. When she reached the mound, she leaned against it, feeling the shells scrape through her thin shirt scratching her skin. Richard unbuttoned his pants. "So you've accepted it."

Chloe watched as he came close, his body tensed and aroused. Looking up at him with her dark eyes flashing in the dying rays of the sun, she bit her lower lip. "Well. Come on! Get it over with, you bastard!"

Richard looked puzzled. He took the knife out of his sheath, threw it to the ground, and leaned in close to Chloe. "Maybe more than once before I need that."

Chloe slid her leg up next to his as his hand pushed up underneath her shirt. His other hand worked at the button on her shorts. Richard felt a warm sensation growing in him, igniting his body in a sensual lust he'd not felt before. He kissed her neck. The taste of her lingering perfume and sweat exploded in his mouth, the sweet saltiness rumbling his stomach for more. He wanted to sink his teeth into her skin, beginning the bleeding. But the intense pleasure made him lean harder on her, wanting more.

Chloe nearly screamed when The Hippie thrust his hand under her shirt, but she was almost free. Frantically, she scraped the rope on the jagged shells in the mound, as Richard pushed harder on her body. The shells torturously tried to break the barrier of her skin. The rope began to break, its strands weakening with every stroke across the shells. She focused her mind on her mother and McKlusky, as The Hippie explored parts of her body she'd not intended any man to touch any time soon. A tiny sound between a whimper and a cry escaped her mouth as one of his hands trailed down to the button on her shorts. Richard's thumb and forefinger worked to slip the button out of its clasp. The rope popped free. Richard heard the snap. His mouth pulled off her neck, and he stepped back to pin her arms down.

Chloe's fist slammed into the front of his windpipe using his Adam's apple as a punching bag. Raking her fingernails across his face, she felt The Hippie's skin peel off underneath them. Richard's eyes went red. He gasped for breath as he staggered back and went on one knee.

"I said, you can't have me, you bastard!" Chloe spun around, limping, to the trail. Trying to put as much weight on her wounded leg as possible, she barreled down the path toward the mangrove waterway. Unsteady on her feet, she tried to piece together what to do next when a pair of arms reached out from the brush and snagged her, bringing her to the ground. She screamed and tried to pull away, but the weight of the man fell on top of her.

Chapter 23

The Gangs all Here

Disbelief kept her from recognizing me right away. But her eyes constricted and relaxed, bringing me into focus. Chloe clutched my back, pulling herself up to me, clinging to me, letting a mix of whimpers and sighs escape her mouth, her heavy warm breathing on my neck.

"You're here." Her arms wrapped tighter around me as if I might vanish and leave her there alone. I put one arm under her back and pulled her up. We both knelt, staring at each other. She buried her face back into my neck. Rubbing her back, I tried to calm her. I saw the blood coming from her calf.

"Chloe, your leg." I pried her off of me to take off my shirt. "We've gotta move." I cut it in strips to use as bandages. I moved around her to bandage her wound. She flinched, as I tightened the two strips over the puncture. Stuffing the rest of the strips in my pocket, I came back around facing her and pulled her to me again. "Where is he?"

"He-he-he tried," she cried in my arms.

"I know what he tried to do." I looked up the path. "Where is he?"

"By the shell mound. We need to go. Please!"

"A girl named Kaitlin is here. I need to get her." I found a stick Chloe could use for a crutch and picked it up.

"How do you know about her?" she asked bewildered.

I realized just how little Chloe knew about her situation. Even though this time yesterday we were in the movies, I felt that I had a whole other life she knew nothing about, Becker, Jada, and the truth about the men who took her. Although, she had figured the last part out on her own.

"I'll explain later, Chloe. But you need to go before The Hippie finds us. Head down the channel. You'll find a mullet skiff anchored a few yards from the opening."

"No. I'm going with you. I know where she is."

"No, you're heading back to the boat. I've got to go fast and your leg will slow me down."

"I'm going," she said resolutely. Chloe hopped up on one leg and moved toward me. I covered the distance before she could take another step and wrapped her in my arms again.

"Chloe, no. I'll be right behind you with Kaitlin," I said, trying to turn her around toward the water. I checked her calf one more time to make sure the blood was slowing and handed her the make shift crutch. "Stay along the roots for support and to avoid a big hole. Go home."

Chloe grabbed my arm. "You take me home," she said, looking up at me, her eyes pleading. "Use the radio to call for help. It won't take them long to get here. Just don't leave me."

Chloe's words made sense. She was safe. There was no reason the authorities couldn't come in, clean house, and rescue Kaitlin. Billy probably sent Grandpa and Becker on a wild goose chase. Being here alone with Chloe hurt wasn't good for her, and the sooner I could stop Mrs. O'Malley's suffering the better. Her eyes kept pleading.

"Okay. Then let's go fast."

"I think we're even now." She said, sniffing and trying to smile. "I owe you."

"Touching, boy, but she's mine."

The voice came from behind me, striking like an arrow in my ear. Chloe shuddered. I turned around to see The Hippie standing on the path, his knife in his hand. His hair hung over his shoulder, making him look like a male version of Medusa.

My eyes narrowed in on his knife. I imagined it sticking in Chloe's' leg, and my body shook, igniting hatred and revenge in my gut that burned out into my chest, arms, and legs. The sweat on my palms evaporated, making them feel cool. I reached for the KA-BAR and slid it out of the leather sheath, balancing it in my hand. I wanted The Hippie's neck underneath it, just like the bartender. Only this time, no one could stop me. Maybe The Hermit did talk to his dead wife. Maybe there was no place on earth for him.

"Please, don't," Chloe pleaded. "Take me home."

I dropped her hand and pushed her behind me. "Head out now, Chloe. There is a mullet skiff. Take it."

187

"No! I'm not!"

"Shut up!" I turned on her, my words angry. They burned coming out of my lips, and I could see they burned her too. Her eyes jerked away from me like I'd turned into a monster right in front of her. Maybe I had. The one that always lay inside me, hibernating, waiting to stretch and stalk its own prey. I didn't want her here to see what I wanted to become.

"Leave!"

Chloe tried to move her mouth, her chin quivering, but nothing came out. I turned, ignored her and waved her away. I know she wanted to protest.

"Go! Now!"

Chloe turned to the water and dragged herself along. Richard and I stared at each other, menacing the other to make the first move.

"Boy, I'm not a couple high school kids on the beach now." He shook his knife loosely in his hand. His voice cracked when he spoke as if he was having trouble breathing.

"Seems a lot of people saw that fight. I'm not some pretty little girl you can throw around. You hurt her."

"Not as much as I would've wanted." Richard rubbed his mouth with his armed hand. "But that will change soon."

He took a step closer. I took a step too, our circle becoming tighter. My heart raced under my chest, pounding like the pistons in the Flounder.

The tension in the air coiled around us, suffocating us more than the humidity that dampened us.

Richard broke the silence. "Her tits feel firm."

Rage made me lunge at him with a weak attack. He swiped his blade across my back as he dodged my thrust. The blood spread down my back before I felt the stinging of the cut. Richard quickly kicked me in the back, driving me to the ground on my side. His boot nearly landed on my ribs. Instead, it imprinted itself on the soft side of my obliques, forcing the last of my oxygen out.

"I expected a little more. I guess tits really do make teenage boys crazy." Richard laughed. "Especially ones like Chloe's."

Trying not to give the pain time enough to settle in, I moved to get up, but Richard pounced on me. With each of his knees on one side of my chest, he brought the knife over his head and plunged it toward my throat. Blocking his wrist with my forearm, I stopped the knife's descent. He put all his weight onto me, trying to stick the blade into my neck. The tip floated over the middle of my throat like a pendulum, inching closer. Wrapping my free hand around my forearm, I pushed up. The point of the knife began to move away from my neck. Once far enough away, I snagged his wrist with my hand and secured my elbow against the ground to support his weight. My other arm now free, I placed my hand on the side of the blade and pushed, turning the point of the knife away from my neck and up toward him.

"Chloe fought harder," he said. His breath came in short gasps as he tried to reverse the direction of the blade.

I hated Chloe's name coming out of his lips. It was too familiar for him to say. I pushed harder. The sweat dripping off the tip of his nose landed on my face and in my eyes. He started to reverse the point of the knife back toward my neck.

My arm shook and felt like rubber under his weight. The blade tip turned to the halfway point, heading back in my direction. I stopped resisting with my arm holding his wrist and gave the blade a quick push toward him. Without my resistance stopping him, he collapsed on me. The knife gashed into his collar bone. He jumped up off me, squealing. I struggled to my feet.

Every movement I made felt as if the skin would rip down my back and peel off my bones. I pushed the pain out of my mind and gathered my feet underneath me. Enraged, The Hippie came at me with an overhead attack. This time, I caught his arm. I slipped my knife around the inside of his bicep and cut to his tricep. He leapt back, placing his other hand over the fresh cut.

"I got something for you, hippie," I said, relieved as I saw the blood, flowing freely down his shoulder and arm.

Richard bellowed, his rage fueled by his lust for Chloe. He flipped his knife in his hand. I took a step forward, and we were locked in the fight. With short jabs and thrusts we deflected each other's blows, trying to land a fatal cut. Richard slipped the blade past my block and swung his knife toward my throat. I placed my free hand over my neck in time for the knife to slice deeply between my pointer and middle finger. He pushed down on the blade, trying to cut through my hand. The pain was blinding, sending sparks through my eyes. Blackness began creeping into me.

Richard's smile spread across his face. "I'm going to catch her, you know. He struggled to push the blade through. "She can't walk fast enough to get away. I'm going to bring her here to see you." I cut him from his stomach up to his chest.

I wobbled back and reached for one of the strips of cloth I was saving for Chloe's leg. I bound my hand quickly and then cupped my other hand underneath it while still holding the knife. Blood filled my good hand, and I cradled it close to me.

The stinging in my back and the throbbing in my hand became one with the drone in my head. We'd only been fighting for a little over a minute and both of us were bleeding from multiple cuts. Richard wiped the blood off of his chest and watched it splatter to the ground.

"If you were a girl, I'd be having the time of my life." He lunged toward me and I threw my handful of blood into his eyes, blinding him. I followed with a slice across his forehead. A red waterfall cascaded down over his eyes. He wiped frantically so he could see me, but his blood wouldn't stop pouring over them.

"You little shit!" He placed a hand over the cut and charged at me. I cracked a spinning kick to his head. He toppled to the ground. Slowly, my body aching out its pain, I landed my knee on his chest.

"What now, boy?" he sputtered through blood and spit.

My knife went to his throat before I could think. It twitched in my hand, itching to sever its way into his jugular.

"Do it. It's the only way I'll ever stop coming after Chloe."

I tried to make my arm move to slice his throat, but I couldn't. My hand wouldn't move. I couldn't do it. Something in his eyes was familiar. Something I couldn't figure out. I screamed and slammed the knife into the ground by his head. I punched him in the face and flipped him over. Taking another strip of my shirt, I tied his hands behind him.

"I should kill you," I said, as I tightened the strips around his wrist, constricting the strips until I saw him wince in pain.

Richard spit the mess of blood out of his mouth, "Taking...taking the moral victory are you?"

The butt of my knife cracked the side of his head. He fell silent, unconscious. I decided to go for Kaitlin.

* * *

"He damaged you!" The man hurled a chair out of the shack. The accent was strange, sounding like one of the offbeat British comedies my grandfather watched on late night cable. I slunk through the shadows on the edge of the clearing; I recognized Marcus from Becker's files.

"I'll kill him!" Marcus punched the side of the wall, his fist exploding through the thin plywood. "When Karam comes back with him, I'll kill him." When he moved, I saw a girl tied to the bed. *Kaitlin,* I thought. She pulled weakly at her ropes.

"Just kill me, too. Just kill me."

Marcus leaned against the door frame with his back to me, rubbing his temples as if considering his options. As he reached into his jacket pocket, I ran. The sound of my boots scraping the sand hit him just before I did. Turning around with his gun drawn, he saw me at the point of impact. With my shoulder lowered, I barreled into Marcus, hitting him in the gut. I lifted him into the air, his breath bellowing out of his mouth, and slammed him against the back wall, nearly toppling the shack. He slumped down, resembling a wino sleeping in a back alley. I pulled out my knife. If she was scared, Kaitlin didn't show it as I came toward her. Once I cut her ropes loose, she stared at me blankly, not believing she was finally free. A throbbing blue and black lump bowed up on the side of her jaw.

"I'm a friend of Chloe's and Jada's."

She clutched her head as she sat up on the bed. A long moan reverberated out of her mouth. "They're okay?" she asked feebly.

"Yeah," I answered. "Come on. I need to get you out of here. You don't look so good." I gently lifted her off the bed. She wrapped her arms around me as she leaned her weight onto me.

"Oh my God! Your back. You're bleeding."

"I'll be okay," I said insistently, wanting to hurry out.

"Let me see first. I'm pre-med. I might be able to help." She pushed on my shoulder. "Turn around for me." I turned around with a

191

sigh. "We gotta go before he…" I said, motioning to Marcus on the floor.

"He's not getting up soon. With that cut on his head and the way he just slammed into the wall, it should be a while." I could feel her prodding at the cut trying to figure her first move.

'How'd you get past The Jamaican?"

"I didn't. That's why we need to go."

"The Jamaican? You didn't—oh, God, let's get out of here." Her voice carried a sense of urgency now. She moved forward pulling me out of the shack, making me stumble. Suddenly, she came to a stop, as still as a statue expect for the quivering of her lips. I heard it too.

The grass on the path was being slapped by rushing feet. I guided Kaitlin behind me. I yanked out my knife and flipped the blade behind the back of my lower arm, concealing it by my side. Grandpa broke into the clearing followed by Becker and then Chloe, limping, trying to keep up.

"McKlusky!" Grandpa shouted. But the relief on his face quickly changed to despair as he came to a skidding halt. "No!"

Karam appeared behind me like a lurking shadow and wrapped one arm around my neck. The barrel of his gun lightly tapped the side of my head. Kaitlin dropped to the ground, her hands covering her face.

"You're gonna get me out of here. Drop your knife." His voice was hot in my ear.

"No!" Chloe's voice was low, consumed by fear.

Karam tensed his arm, pushing his bicep into my throat. "Drop your guns. Your knife. I won't tell you again." His voice was calm and calculating. I dropped my knife. Becker and Grandpa's jittered movements told me they were without a plan. They glanced at each other, each apparently hoping the other had the answer. They both lowered their guns onto the ground and stood back up.

"Bring them to me," Karam said to Kaitlin.

Kaitlin inhaled a sob.

"Bring them to me now, or I'll kill him!" He jammed the barrel into my temple pushing my head to the side.

Kaitlin struggled to her feet, picked up the guns, and put them in front of Karam.

"Go," he said to Kaitlin and motioned with his head for her to stand with the other three. Kaitlin inched her way to Chloe.

"Easy, Karam," Becker said. "Let us have him."

"No. You and your friends cause too much trouble." Karam moved back away from Becker. Chloe went to take a step forward to follow, but Kaitlin grabbed her by the arm to hold her back. She broke free and lunged toward me. Becker quickly had her in the same ironclad grip he'd put me in only hours ago—but this time he withheld the squeezing out of breath and bruised ribs.

"I'm sorry, Chloe. I didn't mean to speak to you the way I did," I said.

"I don't care," she sobbed. "Let him go!" Her pleas scared an owl that had been watching our situation unfold.

"You got a little girlfriend." Karam took another step back.

"Come on. We can make a deal." Becker moved closer.

"How do you know my name?" Karam said, indignant.

"My last name is Becker."

"Becker...Becker?" Karam said the name slowly in his mouth. Recognition and shock came across his face. "Alexis Becker. Sold to an Afghani Drug lord." Karam bellowed like a base drum. "Tell me, Becker. You wouldn't happen to know what happened to Carlos, would you?"

"Before, or after he shit his pants?" Becker said caustically.

"Ha! Good for you. I never liked him anyway." His smile evaporated. "Now get my father out of the shack."

"Let my boy go." Grandpa's voice wasn't pleading. It relayed a warning. "I'll find you, Karam. And I'm gonna find you hard if you don't let him go."

Karam paused. "Get my father. Maybe I'll be nice today."

Grandpa walked to the shack and drug Marcus out. Marcus moved with moans and muttered words that tried to form themselves on his tongue.

"In the helicopter," Karam ordered.

Dragging Marcus to the 'copter, Grandpa helped him step up to the passenger seat and sit down. Marcus' head rolled back, his neck unable to support it.

"Now, let him go." Grandpa moved to get me. But Karam turned the gun on him.

"I'll let you find him, fisherman," Karam said. "You run your boat so good. I know you'll find him in the ocean somewhere." Karam grinned at Chloe. "Besides, I think Richard has something for you first." The Hippie stood behind Chloe at the entrance of the clearing, his eyes pawing at her body. The strip of shirt I'd used to bind him was wrapped over his forehead.

Chloe and Kaitlin shrieked at the same time, clasping onto each other as he took a step closer. Becker stood in front of the girls, ready to finish my job. I elbowed Karam in his stomach, but the blow bounced off as if hitting a brick wall.

"Richard, I call a truce." Karam waited to see if he would reply. Richard's eyes remained fixed on Chloe. "Come and get a gun. Kill the men. Take the girl. We'll forget what you did earlier. You can go back to living out of trash cans."

"Chloe," I yelled, trying to break The Jamaican's grasp.

She turned to me and froze, and then looked back at Richard. I could tell she was torn by her two fears: Richard and losing me.

Richard walked a wide circle around the group, distancing himself from Karam. Fixated on me now, he held up his free hands. "Your girlfriend taught me how well shells cut," Richard said, as he leaned down for the assault rifle.

Karam dragged me to the helicopter, the gun still glued to the side of my head.

"Wait," Richard said. "McKlusky, I have her. I won. You should've killed me. Think of her screams while you die."

I tried to break free from Karam's grip. But he slammed his elbow into my back, buckling me to my knees. He flipped me into the back seat of the helicopter without a grunt or a sigh. I lunged toward him and he slammed the butt of the gun into my head. I didn't wake until I hit the water.

Chapter 24

Amber

Amber looked at the bandages wound tight around her knuckles and up to her wrists, like a boxer stepping into the ring. There was nothing in the room for her to wrap inside the bandages, to weight them, to give her punches more impact. But, that was not the problem. The problem was the door. It stood in her way of escaping.

She had spent most of her time curled up on the bed like a pale, wilted flower after Marcus and Karam left the room. Finally, after she decided she had to wash the smell of The Hippie and the cigar smoke off of her, she showered. Rummaging through the closet, she found an assortment of clothes, ranging from the obscene to the innocent. Her only guess was that she would have to try on different clothing for potential buyers. She slipped into a pair of jean capris and a black spaghetti strap shirt. Then, she ate the food left for her and tried to figure out a way to escape.

Standing in front of the door, clenching her taped hands, she started with a punch. The door outlined the impact of her knuckles in splintered shards, shuddering its resistance. The door was porous and hollow, not like the solid oak doors they were made to resemble. She backed up a little from the door, her hands at her side, her head low. Taking a deep breath, she tensed her legs. She heel-kicked the door, the impact landing over the lock. The wood let out a light crunch, and the lock slipped out of its hole, popping the door free of its frame.

Amber rattled the door. The padlock on the other side kept it from opening. She slammed her fist into the door again. It rattled back at her. Furious, she backed up to the opposite wall. She lunged for the door. Colliding into it, her body sheared the hinges off the door with a fibrous rip. She flew through the hallway and came to a sudden jolting stop against the much stouter hallway wall. She quickly gathered herself, despite the stinging in her shoulder and trouble catching her breath.

When she turned toward the stairs, the captain stood on the bottom step looking perplexed. She sized up the aged man and ran for the steps with her shoulder lowered. But the startled captain leaned his back against the stairwell wall, avoiding Amber's assault. Her feet snagged the bottom step tumbling her onto her chest.

The captain jumped on her. "Who are you? What are you doing here?" His voice squeaked. He had to use all the weight on his frail frame to keep Amber from turning around and attacking him. He struggled to wrench her hands behind her back. "Calm down, girl. Who are you?"

"Get off me," Amber yelled, trying to work her way out from underneath him and up the steps.

"Who are you? I promise." His voice pleaded to be heard. "I'm not going to hurt you."

"Liar!" Amber said.

"I'm going to let you go." The captain brought his weight off her and stepped back toward the bottom of the steps, out of Amber's reach.

Amber pushed herself up. She was caught off guard by the captain's weatherworn face. His sad and defeated eyes hung low.

"Who are you?" Amber asked, taking a step up the steps to distance herself.

The old man sighed and pulled out a handkerchief from his pocket. "Don't' really know any more, girl. Why are you here?"

"I was kidnapped to be sold, douchebag. I'd think you'd know that." The poison in her words hissed out of her mouth.

"Kid-kidnapped? No, Marcus ships drugs."

"It's not drugs. It's human trafficking." Amber's voice lost its intensity on the last part of her statement. She feared the captain would keep her from escaping. Though she was out of the room, she felt enslavement encroach upon her. The hallway seemed narrower than it had.

The captain wiped his eyes with his handkerchief and blew his nose. "I'm not a bad person. I'll call the Coast Guard right now on the radio. I'll call them now. I swear, I thought it was drugs."

"You'll call? And help me?"

"Yes."

"Okay, let's go." Amber moved to head up the steps when the beat of the helicopter reverberated through the halls of the ship. She looked up to the ceiling as if she'd be able to pierce it to see the aircraft.

That's him coming back now," the captain said. "We've gotta hurry."

The captain grabbed Amber's wrist and hurried her up the stairs. They ran through the living room. Amber could see the lights of the buildings on the coast stacked vertically in rows through the windows; a row of lighthouses to lead her to shore. She knew she could swim the distance to the coast if she had to.

As they bounded into the helm, the captain stopped dead in his tracks. The helicopter hovered over the pad. The helicopter slammed onto the landing pad. Its blades slowed. Karam swung open the door and pulled out Marcus who moved unsteadily on his feet.

"Get out of here. Hide down below. I'll come help you when I can," the captain said.

"But."

"Go. He'll kill us both if he sees you here."

Amber sprinted down the stairs right before Karam opened the door to the helm, gripping Marcus in his arm. He sat Marcus in a chair. Marcus had gained some control of his head again. He placed his hand on Karam's shoulder, pulling his son to him.

"The boy," Marcus muttered. "Drown him."

Karam went to the helicopter and slung the unconscious boy over his shoulder. He carried the boy to the edge of the pad. As he looked over the edge, Karam saw a shadow moving below, the tip of its fin slicing through the water. Karam ripped the bandage off of McKlusky's hand and squeezed the wound. A fresh flow of blood broke through the caked scab. Karam hurled the bandage into the water. When the bandage hit the water, the shark's body tensed as if a lethal current of electricity surged through it. The shark's fin rose higher. Like a torpedo locked on its target, the shark darted to the bandage, nosed at it, and then devoured it with a quick extension of its jaws. Karam threw the boy over the railing. McKlusky sprang to life, gasping and choking, his eyes wide as he looked at the stern of the ship in front of him. The shark's fin broke the water again.

* * *

Marcus' fought to steady his body in the chair, his eyes slits as they watched Karam carry out his order.

The captain grabbed the marine radio and clicked the button and screamed into the static. "Mayday! Mayday! This is the Albatross."

Marcus reeled around in the chair. "What the hell are you doing?"

"Putting an end to what you're doing."

Marcus grasped the chair and pushed himself up, pulling his gun out from underneath his jacket. "It never ends, Captain." Marcus' hands waved the gun from side to side, unable to steady the pistol's weight.

"You don't scare me anymore, Marcus. You've got a concussion. You couldn't shoot the broad side of a skyscraper with the way you're moving." The captain felt a confidence in his voice that had been smothered out many years ago. It was a great feeling to die with. The captain collapsed on the floor, parts of his brain splattered on the windshield and control panel.

The radio squelched. "This is the Coast Guard, Albatross. What is your Mayday?"

Marcus stumbled back into the chair, the kick from the pistol stunning him in his fragile condition. The thick smoke from the gunshot swirled in the air. His head hung low.

Part 3

A New Beginning

Chapter 25

Tiger Shark

It's true. They're all dead, and I'd soon be too.

I should've killed the son of a bitch when I had the chance.

Now The Hippie had them all because my balls were the size of walnuts when it came to killing him, not the brazen brass balls I thought I had this time yesterday.

Treading water was becoming harder. The trail of blood from my hand strung out in front of me like the Nile River during the plagues. I was sure that the small fish had already begun to pick the skin from my wounded hand. It was too numb to feel. I moved my good hand to try to swim, but my body was becoming cold and weak. The reopening of the wound made me feel faint.

A gun blast exploded from the helm. Karam ran off the helicopter pad. The tiger shark became more erratic, flinching, heading to the stern of the ship and circling back to me as if it were having difficulty choosing which way it should swim. Something was confusing it. It vanished. Then I saw the surge out of the corner of my eye. The water rose like a moving submarine breaking the surface, making a direct line for me. I braced for the impact of the shark's jaws.

My body was hit hard, but lighter than I imagined it should have been. The jaws were painless. Oddly, I remembered reading that some people didn't even know they were bit because the rows of razor teeth cut so cleanly. The actual pain didn't start until the shark started shaking its head, sawing into their sinews and bones.

"I got you." Her voice was breathless in my ear. I didn't know sharks could talk.

* * *

Amber stumbled down the stairs from the helm and out onto the back deck. She stripped down to the black bathing suit she wore underneath her clothes. The shadow moving in the water halted her dive. A gasp barbed itself in her throat. Visions of *Shark Week* froze Amber as she tried to make herself dive. She tried to decide where she could jump off the boat without coming near the shark. She decided.

Her bare feet slapped the deck as she sprinted to the bow of the ship. Stepping over the railing, she poised herself on the bottom rung, her hands holding onto the top rail behind her. She looked down into the black water, a consuming ink that she didn't fear, until she saw the shark. Being eaten alive hadn't even entered her mind until she saw the girth of the shadow move behind the boat.

Hesitating, she tried to force her legs to push off the rail, but they froze like latches that had been rusted shut, afraid another shark might lurk below. She silently encouraged herself, trying to will herself to jump. But the gunshot from the helm was more convincing. Not thinking this time, she plummeted off the deck and was sucked several feet below the blackness of the Gulf. Instead of panic, her body found itself in a familiar and comfortable environment for the first time since she had been kidnapped.

She rocketed to the surface, nearly launching herself out of the water like a dolphin. Gathering her bearings, she saw the lights on the shore. With one kick of her legs and stroke of her arms, her body propelled toward the stern of the ship.

The shark had been forced to the back of her mind until she saw the boy bobbing up and down in the water behind the stern. He hadn't been there a moment ago. Then she saw the shark again. The light illuminating the water behind the boat gave the shark's shape an even more sinister look. The shark looked liquid, dissolving in and out of the shadows as if disappearing and appearing from one place to another.

The boy's head struggled to stay on the surface, his one arm flailing to keep him afloat every time he slipped underwater. She couldn't leave him. Shark or not, she knew she'd be no better than the men who took her if she abandoned him to die.

She studied the shark's movements. There was no option but to go for it. Sucking in a giant breath, she flung the top half of her body forward, her arms outstretched in front of her, fingers pressed tightly together to form artificial webs on her hands. The top half of her body submerged into the water and her legs joined in with rapid powerful kicks. She cut the distance so quickly, she rammed into him, grabbing him with one arm. Amber found herself wishing she could have this type of adrenaline rush for her meets. She headed to the yacht's dive platform.

The shark fin broke the surface behind them, following the thrashing in the water. Panicking, Amber kicked and pulled her weight and the boy's. Her hand banged the platform. The shark charged forward and Amber's heel kicked it in the nose, sanding the skin off the bottom of her foot. The shark shot down into the depths and resurfaced yards away, acquiring the trail of blood in its nose again.

Amber pulled herself onto the platform as the shark neared again. She reached down and grabbed the boy. With the help of a perfectly timed wave and his frail effort, she rolled him up and out of the water as the shark slipped underneath the boat, denied its meal again.

The boy's body was shaking. She pulled him close to her to warm him. He opened his eyes briefly and muttered, "Chloe." Amber didn't know who Chloe was, but she considered her lucky. His blonde hair and blue eyes were what she took notice of first. She patted his chest and leaned back against the hull of the boat, gasping. Looking at the condo lights, she wondered how she was going to reach them now. A lifeboat had to be stashed on the ship somewhere. The thought of sneaking on the yacht made her body feel like Jell-O. She looked at the buildings again thinking of other possibilities. One of the lights on the horizon displaced itself. It broke out of the pattern, heading toward her. The sound of a boat engine rolled over the waves in the distance.

Chapter 26

The Sacrifice

"Just take me. Let the rest go," Chloe said softly as the helicopter faded in the distance.

"We'll get to that soon enough." Richard jumped up and down, bouncing like a child with a new toy. "Decisions, decisions. Do I kill them first while you watch, Chloe? Do I do what I want to you, let them watch, then kill them while you watch, or rape you, kill you, and they watch the whole thing?"

"Shut the hell up." Harvey's face was bleeding red. "You took my grandson. You're not taking her."

Richard seemed amused with the outburst. "Old man, what are you going to do about it?" Richard held the gun as if to display it.

"Why don't you and I settle this like men?" Becker said. He reached for the knife in his boot.

Richard zeroed the gun in on Becker. "Really, settle this like men? So cliché, don't you think?" Keeping his eye on Becker, Richard moved closer to Chloe. Kaitlin drew Chloe into her, trying to protect her.

"Wanting to get in on the action are we, Kaitlin?" The Hippie grinned, his eyes slit like a tiger's as he considered the idea.

Harvey moved in between the two girls and Richard. "It'll be over my dead body." Harvey's voice twisted with hate.

"Everybody is so anxious to die," Richard shouted. "Well, I decide who dies when." Richard swung the gun back over on Becker who was trying to move behind him. "If I had some punch and cyanide, I could make everybody happy couldn't I? We could all go out together."

Richard sat on a log, keeping the gun on the men. He let out a big sigh and briefly looked at the sky. "What to do?" he said more to himself.

"Just let him have me." Chloe choked on her words "Maybe you can escape while he is—while he is …" she couldn't finish her sentence. Her body tried to revolt against her mouth for offering it up as sacrifice to save the others, but she forced herself to finish. "While he is raping me."

Harvey put his hands on her shoulder, squeezing it to reassure her. "That's not how it's going to be, Chloe."

"Besides," Becker said, "I promised your momma I was going to get you home safe, and that is what I'm going to do. She doesn't seem like the type who likes promises broken."

Chloe gave a paper thin smile. "She's not." The smile dissolved. "How though?"

"A friend. At least I think," Harvey said looking into the bushes beyond Richard.

"I saw it too," Becker said. "A friend or foe, Harvey?"

"I don't know," Harvey replied in a hushed voice.

"What are you two talking abou—" Kaitlin words trailed off as she followed their gaze. Her eyes latched onto a figured that sulked in the palmettos, watching and listening.

"I have decided." Richard jumped up with a shout, raising his hands in the air in victory over his difficult decision. "I'm going to take Chloe and—"

THRRRRRRP! The sound bulleted from the palmettos. Richard barked in pain, his hand jumping to his face to cover where he'd been hit. Before Becker could tackle Richard, another shot to the side of the head brought The Hippie to his knees, disoriented, teetering back and forth. He dropped his gun.

"MY ISLAND!" The Hermit charged into the clearing. His slingshot was in his hand. Bypassing the others, he headed toward his shack. "The mess, the mess!" The screaming stopped. A moment later he stepped back out of the shack, cradling his picture as gently as a newborn.

"Thanks, old man," Harvey yelled over to The Hermit.

The Hermit put a hand over his eyes as if trying to bring each face in the group into focus. "Where's the boy? McKlusky?"

"How do you know him?" Harvey said, taken aback.

"I told him where to find his girl." He looked at Chloe. "Well, I can see why he wanted to save you." He showed Chloe his picture. "I had one just as beautiful once. She's my wife." He took Chloe's hand and traced her finger on his wife's face.

"She—she is beautiful," Chloe's face streamed tears. "But McKlusky is gone."

"Don't cry, pretty girl," The Hermit said, letting the picture hang to his side. "He ain't gone. My wife would've told me if a nice boy like that joined her in heaven." Chloe smiled.

"We gotta go get him. They're not taking my grandson."

"Old man," Becker said, handing The Hermit the assault rifle. "You know how to use this?"

"Yeah, boy! I was in Nam." He made a disgusted face. "I hated them hippie fellows like him, protesting me. I'll watch him. You go get the boy."

"Watch the girls too," Harvey said.

"No!" Chloe shouted, "I'm going. Don't argue with me. We're just going to waste time if you do."

Harvey only hesitated for a second. "Fine. Let's go."

The group headed down the trail to the Flounder.

The Hermit admired his new gun in one hand and cradled the picture in the other. He glanced at The Hippie lying on the ground holding his head, and then back at his wife and child. Afraid the picture might get damaged, he scuttled back to the shack and placed it gently on the table. He stared at it, letting their images brand themselves back into his brain.

"Oh, hell, honey, you're right." The Hermit ran back into the clearing. Richard was gone. The Hermit followed his tracks heading west to end at the beach. The Pathfinder's engine screamed after the Flounder.

* * *

"Five Mile Reef?" Becker asked as he readied more magazines for his guns.

"Yep," Harvey said. The bow of the Flounder settled into its plane.

"Shit!" Chloe saw the Pathfinder cut into the wake of the Flounder.

206

"How the?" Harvey already had the Flounder at full throttle.

"I got him." Becker raised the Glock and fired.

Richard snaked the Pathfinder back and forth, avoiding the shots. Becker slammed another magazine into the gun. Richard pushed the throttle and brought his bow across the stern of the Flounder, causing her rear to skid to the left.

"Get your big butt back over, baby," Harvey said. The Flounder righted herself and plowed forward.

Becker raised his gun to fire again.

"Hold it, Becker." Harvey turned the Flounder to the right.

"What? Why? What are you doing?" Becker protested. "I can kill him."

"So can I," Harvey grinned.

The Pathfinder lined up for another hit. The boats cut through the darkness, their engines echoing across the water, dispelling the silence of the night.

"Whatever you're going to do, you better do it fast," Becker shouted. The Pathfinder inched closer, its bow only feet from the stern of the Flounder. "I'm going to take him out!"

"I'll drown you if you do," Harvey threatened.

"Do something, Mr. Harvey!" Chloe shouted, the fear in her voice rising. Kaitlin drew up in the chair and shielded her eyes, grabbing onto Chloe's arm.

"Hold on, girls!" Harvey ordered, his grin latching onto each ear. He jerked the Flounder hard to the left. Her propellers chipped the slightest bit of shell from the oyster bar. But Richard stabbed the bow of the Pathfinder into it, scattering the oysters into an explosion of shells, snatching the boat to a stop. The stern flipped out of the water, catapulting Richard from his seat, sending him sliding over the razor sharp oysters. Each shell filleted deep into his chest and legs, reopening the jagged scars left by the fingernails of his victims. As his body slid, the trail of blood soiled the oysters, reflecting a sickish deathly grey in the moonlight. When the oysters had their fill, they brought his body to a stop, and supported it as it twitched and finally stopped moving.

* * *

Harvey forced the Flounder to strain her engines until he saw the lights of the Albatross. He reached down and switched off his running lights.

"See what you can see, Becker." Harvey shut the engine off.

"What are we doing?" Chloe asked. "Why are we stopping? We have to go get him!"

"We've got to scout it out," Harvey said. "If we go storming in there, things could go wrong. Not that they haven't already."

Chloe's brow dipped, trying to dam the tears that clung to the corner of her eyes. Death's shadow had waylaid her life as of late: her father, her own close brush with death, and now the reality that it stalked her best friend and first love.

Becker looked through the night vision binoculars. "There he is. And Amber too. The other girl."

"Another girl?" Kaitlin asked. "How many are there?"

"You're the last four of many," Becker said hopefully. "They're on the dive platform, Captain."

"Let me see." Harvey took the binoculars. McKlusky and Amber rested against the stern. The green outline of a fin cut the water. "Tiger shark between us and them. About twelve feet long by the looks of it."

"I hate sharks," Becker grumbled. Becker patted Harvey on the back. "Going in, hoss."

"What?" Harvey said.

"I'm going in, swimming to the dive platform and then going to raise a little hell. When you hear me shooting, get to the Albatross, pick them up and get out of here," Becker said as he stood on the side of the boat.

Harvey disregarded Becker's last part of the plan. "We aren't leaving you."

Becker turned on Harvey. "Your grandson needs medical attention and so do these girls. It's been a pleasure, Captain. Take care." Becker holstered his Glock and jumped into the water.

"Stupid asshole," Harvey said under his breath.

Becker slipped through the water like a stealth plane. Amber didn't hear him until his silhouette appeared in the light.

She gasped. "Who are you?"

"Rescue," Becker said, a little out of breath.

Gaping wide, the tiger shark's mouth tore open the surface of the water. Becker paddled his hands back out of the way of the shark and punched the tiger's gills. He grabbed onto the dorsal fin and was dragged deep into the murk. Becker struggled to pop his ears as the water rushed by, echoing the pops and clicks of the tiny crustaceans that littered the water. The shark thrashed under its new weight. Becker pulled his knife and repeatedly rammed the handle on the shark's nose. Disoriented, the shark swam in erratic circles around a pile of concrete blocks.

Having spent years thinking his sister was dismembered by a Great White, Becker had no love for sharks. He would have bled this shark out, but he knew it would only attract more.

His lungs sent the contractions to his mouth to open up and breathe deep. The spasms were becoming raw in his throat as he swam up. He broke into the air a few feet behind the platform, his mouth filling the empty vacuum of his lungs. Pulling himself onto the platform, he leaned back on the hull of the ship, gasping.

"Amber Lee?" He breathed deep. He slipped two fingers onto McKlusky's neck. "He's still alive." He waved to the Flounder, knowing Harvey would be looking through the binoculars and gave a thumbs up. He slid the knife back into his boot.

"Who are you?" Amber asked puzzled.

"John Becker. Are you okay?"

Amber nodded her head, knocking the last bit of water clinging to her eyelashes off.

"Listen, there is a boat out there." Becker pointed past the circle of light. "When my gunfire starts, it's going to pick you two up and get you out of here. Hold on to McKlusky until then. Start talking to him. Talk to him about his grandpa and Chloe. Let him know they're still alive."

"Becker?" McKlusky mumbled.

"Hey, kid. You're going to be okay," Becker said, patting his arm.

"Chloe? Grandpa?" His eyes struggled to stay open.

"They're alive."

"I should've killed him."

"It's already been done. You take care of that little girlfriend of yours now. She's a tough one."

McKlusky's eyes drifted back down. The concussion from Karam's rifle butt and the blood loss were taking their toll.

"Take care, kid." Becker stood up and started to climb the ladder to head topside. "Nice to have met you, Amber."

Amber watched Becker climb the ladder. She stroked the boy's hair and whispered to him about his grandfather and Chloe. A slight twinge of jealousy brewing in her gut made her smile. "I finally meet a surfer boy, and he is spoken for."

* * *

Becker crept onto the deck of the Albatross, his feet gently treading across the teak. Squatting behind a set of steel white steps leading up to the helicopter pad, he listened for any sounds, but the ship rocked tranquilly in the night, the air lightly blowing across the deck. A pair of Capri jeans and a spaghetti strap shirt lay scattered on the deck, nothing else. He slipped out from behind the steps and through the open glass door into the living room. The helm cast down a shadow of hurried movement onto the steps leading to it. Becker heard Karam curse and slam his hands on the console. The Albatross' large propellers turned, jolting the boat forward. Amber screamed. Becker flipped around to head out to her. The chambering of a gun halted him.

"Why are you leaving?" Karam said.

* * *

A scream grappled through the fog behind my eyes. They fluttered up focusing in on a tiny speck of light, which was quickly cutting through the waves toward us. *Running lights*, I thought, the static still in my head. The Albatross' propellers boiled the water through the bars of the dive platform. The boat lurched forward, rearing itself up into a plane, nearly slipping me off into the propellers. An arm tightened around my chest. I weakly latched onto it.

210

"Shark," I muttered.

"No, just me, surfer boy," a girl yelled over the drone of the engine.

"Who are you?" I said wearily.

"Amber." She pulled on the rung of the ladder, slipping us back against the stern. "We're about to die. Can we dispense with the pleasantries until later?"

The dire circumstances of our situation dawned on me like a distant sunrise peeking over the horizon. The Albatross was on a full plane. Only Amber's grasp on the ladder kept us from tumbling into water and becoming a pureed chum for the fish.

"You have to help me get you up," she said, panicking. "I can't hold on to you much longer. You need to help me push you up." Her voice had a menacing insistency that made my body forget the ragged state it was in. I dug my heels into the space between the steel rungs on the platform; she did the same. Her legs strained, pushing us back up. My effort was half of hers, but we managed to fight ourselves against the hull into a standing position. She jammed one arm behind the ladder and with her other hand guided me behind her, pinning me against the stern. I pushed my arm behind the ladder too, grabbing on to her hand. I wrapped my other arm around her waist. The slight awkwardness of our wet, half-naked bodies being pressed against each other was interrupted by the Flounder breaking into the Albatross' flood lights.

From the front, the Flounder looked like a wild eyed Moby Dick ready to ram the Albatross and sink her to the depths of the ocean. But Grandpa looked more dangerous. As he brought the Flounder's bow near the dive platform, he didn't pull back on the throttle. Instead, he slid the bow onto the dive platform, nosing the tip of the bow against the Albatross' hull, scraping the black "T" off the yacht with every bounce.

"She's yours, Chloe." Grandpa released his grip of the wheel. Chloe grabbed on, white knuckled, determined not to move the wheel to the right or the left.

Grandpa walked across the bow, reaching out his hands to Amber. "Give me your hand."

Amber slid her arm from behind the ladder and grabbed onto a rung. Without hesitation, she dove for Grandpa's hand. He snagged her up and over the bow before her feet even had time to slip.

"Get your ass over here, boy," Grandpa said, reaching his hand out to me.

I let go of the ladder and was beginning to move when a large swell rolled under the two boats, sending the Flounder's bow crashing up and down onto the dive platform. Grandpa's chest slammed onto the bow, his knees and hands flying out from underneath him. Chloe screamed, panicking, not sure what to do as she was rattled in the chair. I was toppled back toward the edge of the dive platform, about to go in, when I was thrust in the back and slammed against the hull. I was sure the Flounder had speared me with her bow. I waited for pain to engulf my body.

"I got you." Grandpa lay sprawled out on the bow. His hands were stretched out and pressed firmly on my back. The edge of the Flounder's bow rubbed on my side. With Grandpa's help, I stumbled onto the bow and collapsed on the deck.

Chloe pulled off the throttle and the Flounder slid off the platform and came to an idle. She ran to me, knelt, and clutched me, looking at my wounded hand. "I need towels," she demanded.

"You okay, McKlusky?" Grandpa asked.

"Yeah, if you're gonna be dumb." I waited for him to finish his saying.

"You ain't gotta be that tough, boy," he smiled. "Just wait until your grandma gets a hold of you. We'll see how tough you are."

Kaitlin brought a towel up and started wrapping my hand. Amber hobbled around the deck and sat down on the cooler, bringing her knees up to her chin, breathing heavily.

Chloe's fingers wrapped around my shoulder. I reached up for her hand. She scooted around beside me, putting her hand on my cheek. "Thank you for coming for me, thank you for saving me." She leaned in and kissed me deep. I relished the softness of her lips against mine. Her breath inside my mouth felt like a warm blanket, safe, secure, scorching throughout my limbs, combating the coolness from the blood loss.

"Knock it off, will you," Grandpa griped.

Way to ruin it, I thought.

Kaitlin was bandaging Amber's heel by the time I got to thank Amber. Her wet black hair scattered in chunks clung to her face and neck.

"Not a problem, surfer boy." She smiled and looked at Chloe. Amber quickly shot her glance back to Kaitlin.

Chloe's hand wrapped a little tighter around my shoulders, more a jealous grasp than a tender caress. I winced as her nails dug in a little.

"Where's Becker?" I'd noticed he wasn't one of the ones brooding around me.

"We're about to find out." Grandpa put the Flounder in gear to intercept the Albatross. Gunfire flashed out of the Albatross' living room.

* * *

Becker's body became rigid. Karam moved to Becker's side and put a pistol against his head. Reaching into the back of Becker's shirt, Karam jerked the Glock from the small of his back and tossed it across the room.

Amber screamed. Karam shot his gaze toward the back of the stern. "Who's that?"

"Really a women screaming on this boat surprises you?" Becker said.

"Is the Asian out?"

"Apparently," Becker mused, shrugging his shoulders.

"It doesn't matter." Karam's eye returned to Becker right before the Flounder fell behind the wake of the Albatross. Becker tensed up, waiting for Karam to react, but he stayed still. His one good eye fixated on Becker's movements. His other eye, drooping in its socket, gave him no peripheral vision to see Harvey approaching.

Becker turned around to face Karam, letting the barrel of his gun drag across his forehead until it pointed directly at the middle of his skull.

Karam laughed, "You killed Carlos and now Richard. If you weren't trying to kill me, I could like you."

"Well, Karam, I'm not like your father. I don't like boys."

"Funny?" Karam sneered, pressing the gun harder against Becker's head.

BANG!

Karam swung his head toward the back of the boat, searching for the sound. The Flounder's bow was rammed up near the back of the Albatross. Harvey was sprawled out on the bow.

Becker popped the gun away from his head, sending it flying out of Karam's hand to the floor. Becker slung his elbow across the bridge of Karam's nose. The Jamaican's nose exploded, wrapping Karam's beard in a cocoon of red. Clutching his hand around Karam's throat, Becker saw the Flounder pull back from the Albatross with both McKlusky and Amber on board. *Safe*, Becker thought.

Karam hit Becker's jaw. Becker countered with a punch to Karam's gut. His fist felt like it hit a brick wall, but Karam staggered back, his breath taken. Lunging forward, his fist drawn back, Becker pummeled The Jamaican across the face, splitting his lip. Becker rammed him against the wall by the stairs leading to the helm.

"Karam?" Marcus' voice came groggily from the helm. He stumbled down the steps.

Becker leaned his forearm into Karam's throat and grabbed Marcus by the collar with his other hand. Pulling Marcus off the last step, Becker slung him to the back of the room as Karam struggled to push Becker's elbow away. Marcus backpedaled toward the bar, his body shattering the bottles on top. Becker head-butted Karam, knocking him to the floor.

Weakly pushing off the bar, Marcus reeled on his feet, trying to steady his gun on Becker. He fired, putting a hole into the wall far left of where Becker stood. Becker ripped the knife from the sheath strapped on his ankle and rushed toward Marcus. Becker disarmed Marcus and rammed the Englishman's back up against the bar. His hand curled up in Marcus' jacket, his knife at Marcus' throat. "You did this: Kaitlin, Jada, Amber, Chloe, ALEXIS!" Becker spit his sister's name into Marcus' face.

Marcus looked at him, his Adams apple sliding up and down under the blade. "I'm just one of many and so was your sister." His head rolled limply as he spoke. "My boss has…"

Becker didn't even realize he'd cut Marcus' throat until the warmth of Marcus' blood washed over his hand and down his arm. Karam's screams startled him out of his trance. The Jamaican knelt on the floor. His father's body, slumped against the bar, stared at him, hollowed of life.

Wild eyed and crazy, The Jamaican resembled The Hippie more than himself as he charged Becker. Lifting Becker off of his feet, Karam slammed him on the marble floor. Streaks of red and white slivered through Becker's eyes. Karam grabbed Becker by the neck, punching him in the face. Becker's nose broke and the blood rolled into the back of his throat. He had to spit it out to breathe. Grabbing Karam's wrist, Becker punched the inside of Karam's arm at the elbow, collapsing Karam on him. Becker clamped his teeth down on The Jamaican's nose. Karam squealed like a shocked dog, and Becker threw him off him. Gaining his feet, Becker spit out his and Karam's blood that pooled in his mouth. Limping for his gun, and then taking it in his hands, Becker wearily moved over to The Jamaican who pushed himself to his knees.

Becker saw the Flounder, racing toward them. "Harvey, you get out of here," he shouted, waving the Flounder off. He placed the gun to Karam's head.

The Jamaican swayed on his knees. "You may kill me, but Joe is gonna pay Jada a visit."

Becker's face dropped, as if all its muscles had been sucked out of them. "No. Jada is with Harvey's wife?"

Karam snorted, "If—if Jada's with his wife. Then his wife dies too."

"Becker, get off the boat!" Harvey's voice crackled through the radio in the helm. "Get off the boat! You're going to ram a reef!"

Becker could see Harvey yelling into the radio behind the wheel of the Flounder.

"Now!" came the frantic call as the Flounder skidded to a halt, reeling in the wake of the Albatross.

"Harvey's wife!" Becker screamed. "You can drown, you son of a bitch." Becker ran for the deck. The vengeance of wanting to kill Karam himself almost drove him back. But he wouldn't let another woman die at the hands of these men, especially Harvey's wife. He dove off into the water.

The Albatross hit the reef with its engines on full throttle. She shuddered down the middle, splitting the hull. Her stern slung herself to the right, landing on the reef, and rolling her on her side. The reef splintered through the yacht. Karam rolled down to the wall as the yacht flipped. All the furniture in the living room followed after Karam. The granite top flipped off the top of the bar and pinned him down. Water rushed into the boat through shattered windows and walls, submerging The Jamaican. The screams of his mother and sister filled his ears.

Chapter 27

Grandma

Joe sat on a stool in Jason's Bar. His hand shook with every shot he brought to his mouth. The bar was emptier than it had been earlier in the day. Most of the customers had melted into the night to work under the inky blanket that shrouded their illegal activity.

Joe had motored his boat up to the dock after leaving Dismal Key to find Jada. Finding Jada was not the hard part. He knew where to go. What he was going to have to do when he got there was a different story. He needed all the liquor in him he could stand to submerge the memories of the upcoming night into a blur, so he wouldn't have to remember her face.

Joe fiddled with the lid on his dip can and pulled out a pinch of wintergreen. He shoved it in his lip quickly to keep his unsteady hands from dropping it. He popped the lid back on and slapped the bar for another shot. The girl who Jason had shirtless in his room earlier worked the bar. She filled the whiskey glass and Joe slammed it back, letting the drink burn the back of his throat and breathing out the fumes in a sigh.

"Well, look what the cat drug in tonight." Jason sat on the barstool next to Joe. "How 'bout a beer, darling," Jason said, eyeing the girl.

"Jason," Joe said, acknowledging him.

"Buddy, you got all sorts of my kin in a tizzy over you." Jason grabbed the beer the girl sat in front of him.

"What's your kin got to do with me?" Joe spit a slug of tobacco juice onto the floor.

"Well, when I hear you're taking shots at them with a gun and kidnapping." Jason lit a cigarette and took another sip of his beer.

"Who's saying?" Joe muttered.

"My uncle and cousin." Jason tapped his boney finger on the bar.

Joe stood up from his chair, pushing the barstool out from under him. "Piss on your uncle. He's always lying about me." He flung the stool across the room where it landed on a table and bounced off onto the floor. "You know what the hell he did to me."

Jason laughed, "It wasn't all him unless you forgot."

"Your family's all the same," Joe fumed, pointing in Jason's face. "All you damn Harveys, whether you be crooked or straight, you act like you're better than the rest of us. Well, I got news for you, Jason, you ain't. No matter what I've been doing, you're still a low level drug runner, and your uncle's still a damn fishing guide."

Jason backhanded Joe across the face. Joe put his hand to his cheek and stared down Jason.

Jason breathed hard, his temper rising. "We may be what we are, Joe. But we're still family, and there ain't no arrogant son of a bitch gonna come in here and talk about them."

Joe took a couple of hundreds out of his pocket and tossed them on the bar. "For your trouble, honey."

"Joe," Jason said, "don't you come back in here no more."

"You won't be able to find me any place near here after tonight." Joe slammed the door on his way out.

Joe drunkenly climbed into his old '79 Chevy truck. His face still stung from Jason's slap. He turned the key, and the engine choked to life. He slammed the accelerator and slung gravel onto the building as he skidded onto the paved road.

As he turned left onto 92 to head to Marco Island, Joe banged his hand on the steering wheel and tears trailed down his eyes. He reached under the seat of the truck to pull out a half drunk bottle of vodka. Turning it up, he took several long swallows and set the bottle between his legs and wiped his eyes. He turned on the radio, and the sounds of old twangy country music filled the silence of the truck. He reached back under the seat and pulled out a .38 with duct tape wrapped around the handle. He drove into the Marco Highlands and up to Captain Harvey's house. The lights filtered through the blinds.

* * *

Delores sat crocheting, the needle slipping in and out of the yarn like a timed machine as she worked on the quilt laid across her lap. She

218

worried about her husband and McKlusky. She swore to herself, McKlusky was not too old, and she not too small to strap a belt across his backside for up and leaving. *Stubborn and pigheaded*, she thought. *Just like his grandfather.*

Delores rocked hard in her chair, trying to pound her nervousness and anxiety into the floor. To a casual observer it would seem the rocking chair would sling her out of its seat. She kept herself busy after McKlusky disappeared, tending to the girls under her care, but both of them now slept in their beds, exhaustion finally beating down their cares and worry.

Joe kicked in the door, the wood splintering around the lock. The knob embedded itself into the wall behind it. Delores jumped and squealed. The needle fell from her grasp as she shoved her hand under the quilt. Delores prayed that Doyle would hurry home as Joe staggered into the room, the gun hanging loosely in his hand.

"Hello, Delores." Joe took a step toward her.

"Stay away, Joe." Delores quaked.

"Can't reckon I can. I got to have the girl," he said, slobbering his words.

Delores glanced to the door, hoping a rescue would come bounding through at any second. No one appeared. She took a deep breath. "You can't have her."

"No, no, no, Delores." Joe shook his head. "You denied me once. You won't do it again."

Delores shuddered, not out of fear, but at the thought of what her life would have been like if she had married Joe. "That was a long time ago."

Joe scoffed and shouted, "Two weeks, Delores! Two weeks before we was to be married, and you break it off with me to marry him." He walked around the room and looked at the family photos on the wall. "Must've been the pictures he sent you of him in his army clothes, huh?"

"No. I'd always loved him, and I saw what kind of man you were going to become." Delores paused, studying the mess of the man before her. "I was right."

Tremors vibrated throughout Joe's body. "Jada is mine. I'm gonna take her."

"No! She's my baby now. Under my care! You've messed with two of my babies today. You're not doing it no more." Delores gripped her hands under the quilt.

"You little whor…" Joe took a step. He felt the burning in his chest. The bullet moved through his body like an angry hornet, stinging and singeing muscle fibers as it splintered into fragments, nicking the artery to his heart. He took in a deep breath and saw the swirl of smoke where the bullet had come through the quilt. Joe looked at his chest, and the dark red streak that seeped out.

Delores tossed the little Ruger LCP .380 to the floor and put her hands to her mouth. She had picked it out of the gun cabinet when McKlusky disappeared. It was the one Harvey had taught her to use, because she felt it was the only one small enough for her.

"De-Delores." Joe struggled as he put his hand over his heart to hold in the blood.

"Joe, I'm sorry, but they're my babies," she sobbed. "May God forgive me."

Joe collapsed to his knees and looked up. "He…," Joe breathed, his lungs bubbling in blood. "He will." Joe took a final breath and fell over dead. His face slapped the floor.

Mrs. O'Malley and Jada rushed out of their rooms, stopping at the sight of the dead man and the blood making a small pond in the middle of the shiny hardwood floor. Relief swept across Jada's face as Mrs. O'Malley stared blankly and latched onto Jada's arm. Delores stepped toward Joe, her eyes still teary, praying under her breath.

Epilogue

The media infested Marco Island like a horde of rats the day after we walked into the police station with the three missing girls. You'd think we would've become heroes, but we were under immediate suspicion as the actual kidnappers. It didn't help that we only had a busted yacht on a reef to show for it and no bodies.

The Hippie's body was never found on the oyster bar. The Albatross was shattered. Her insides were gutted out from the constant bombardment of waves, taking Karam and Marcus' bodies. The sea has a way of cleaning up after us and making everything pure again.

Of course, the girls' testimonies helped prove our innocence quickly. But our biggest advocate came from the grainy film footage from the parking garage underneath the movie theater. When the police chief's son is murdered by a drifter, people take notice. Brad's father would have bulldozed every mangrove down if he could've to look for The Hippie's body. But tides come and go. Grandpa knew the tides sunk The Hippie's body deep in the Ten Thousand Islands' muddy bottom to be ravaged by the crabs. As for Karam and Marcus, I like to think the tiger shark finally got its fill.

The media was insane and about as intrusive as the traffickers themselves. They showed the tearful reunion with Jada and her parents, cameras pressed so close they nearly wedged in between their hugs. Chloe heard through Kaitlin that Jada's father and mother were trying to reconcile. Jada never warmed up to me, Grandpa, or Becker. She grew distant from men after her experience. However, she sent my grandma cards and letters and referred to her as "Granny." Grandma said she was welcome any time to come and visit.

I Googled Jada nearly a year later. A picture popped up of her crossing the finish line in the Tennessee State Champion Track Meet. She won the state title. A smile, spread across her face, showed victory over more than her competitors.

Kaitlin went to the University of Florida. On holidays, if she wasn't going home, she drove to Marco, stayed with my grandparents and hung out with Chloe. She became one of the family. I joked with her that she quickly replaced me as the favorite grandchild. She broke up with her boyfriend and mostly consumed herself in her studies. She decided to forgo medical school and become an anthropologist. Once she heard about Becker's sister, she decided she wanted to go to Afghanistan and find the rest of the girls the drug lord had bought. She hoped that identifying their bodies would bring peace to their families.

I talked to Amber a few days after she went home with her parents. She told me in a hushed voice that she was doing well. We were interrupted by her mother yelling, "Amber, you no talking to boys, are you? You already see what happen when you talk to boys." Amber sighed and I laughed. Amber whispered, "I should've let the shark eat me."

"I'm glad you didn't," I said.

She hung up the phone. We do keep in touch from time to time, but it's difficult. Her parents don't allow Internet access at her house. And unless Amber picks up the phone, I'm greeted by her mother's voice, which shouts, "No boys call!"

Chloe asked me if I had a crush on her. I told her Amber was easy on the eyes but no crush; I just couldn't thank Amber enough for saving my life. She could have easily kept swimming and let the shark have me.

Becker didn't stick around long, a couple days. Before he left, he slapped me on the back, making me yelp in pain, and said, "You're alright, kid. Keep learning martial arts. Maybe one day you'll get in a fight and not get hurt."

"You're one to talk, Becker," I responded. "Have you seen what The Jamaican did to your face?"

He laughed. "Smart ass kid. He did do a number on me."

"It's alright," I said. "I think you look much improved."

Grandpa heard from him a few days later. Becker acted a little awkward, like there was something he needed to tell Grandpa but couldn't. Grandpa ended with the invitation to come fishing anytime.

Politicians made their empty promises about cracking down on human trafficking and child prostitution. But the media never stuck around long enough to force them into seeing any legislation through. A few shark attacks happened on the Atlantic side near Sebastian Inlet.

"Are sharks hunting humans?" the newsman said. Every news van left Marco Island and headed to the east coast, forgetting about the girls who had survived a little known human species of shark.

I spent a lot of time with Chloe during the rest of the summer. Because of the stitches in my hand and back, I couldn't fish or get in the water, but I couldn't get enough of her either. She didn't shy away from me after her ordeal like I feared she would.

"I don't want to remember how it felt when he touched me," she said. "I want to remember how it feels when you hold me, kiss me, and pull me close."

Her mother allowed the occasional sleepover. Not in the same room, of course. Mrs. O'Malley felt safe with me there, and she liked the smile I brought to her daughter's face. But what Mrs. O'Malley didn't know wouldn't hurt her. She took medication to help her sleep. If she didn't, she spent the nights awake listening for Chloe.

On most nights I crawled into bed with Chloe. She wanted me to, for nothing more than to hold her, so she could battle her own nightmares of The Hippie trying to catch her. Nothing more happened than the two of us, lying close to one another, trying to purge the dismal memories of the experience we had been through.

I thought of sex with her on nights I couldn't sleep. I would watch her, eyes closed, her breath gently blowing across my chest. The thought of trying to push her, to destroy something she valued so much, made me no better than The Hippie. I was already jaded enough. I didn't need to be like him.

* * *

The day summer came to an end, I stood with my grandparents and Chloe in the Fort Myers airport. I felt myself drying up and my roots becoming brittle. Chloe and I kissed one last time, and my grandparents gave me hugs.

"Take care, boy. Stay out of trouble," Grandpa said.

I smiled, Chloe's hand still in mine. "Ha! You're the one who gets me in trouble."

Chloe dried her eyes and kissed me on the cheek. "Okay, I'm going to be a big girl now and believe that all of this will end up for the best for us one day." She put on a brave face.

"It will." My heart climbed up to my throat, and I had to swallow it back down. "In the end it will." I turned to go through security but stopped and walked back to her. "Ten months, right? Maybe even Christmas. Who knows?" I said, a twinge of hope in my voice.

She nodded her head, not speaking, her face damming the tears behind her eyes. I left empty.

Of course, the kids at school regarded me as a hero. It made me seem tougher. It made for a smooth ride, until it all came crashing down a couple years later.

* * *

Becker walked across the pavilion. The dusk danced to the chatter in the bars and the music coming out of them. The pink and red sun dipped itself into the Gulf as if taking a refreshing dip. Becker's shoes barely scraped the pavement.

He stopped off at Sloppy Joe's bar to have a few drinks and wait for the night to enshroud the freaks that inhabited Key West. He caught glimpses of the hippies every so often as they walked past the bar, parrots or iguanas on their shoulders. He studied their faces just to make sure. A transvestite took the stage and sang Jimmy Buffet songs about margaritas and pirates. A fat, stubby man wallowed through the crowd and took a seat next to Becker.

"You took your sweet time getting here," Becker said.

"I've been here for a while. But this is the most relaxed I've seen you since I've known you. I really didn't want to disturb it." The fat man wiped the sweat breaking out on his forehead with his handkerchief.

"True, I'm in a good mood." Becker took a sip of his beer.

"You put yourself out there. Your face is all over the news." The fat man shifted in his stool, trying to place his sandals inside one of the rungs of the barstool. "You sure you want to know? It might be hard for you to get to him now."

Becker considered the fat man's words for a moment. "Why wouldn't I? Marcus said he worked for someone before he died."

"Died? Or you killed him?"

"Does it matter?" Becker asked.

"No." the fat man took out his cell phone and Becker followed suit. "Your phone secure, Becker?"

"Of course, Kirk. You trained me well."

Kirk sent an encrypted file to Becker's phone. A face appeared on the screen. He read the name under it. Becker stared silently, biting the inside of his cheek. His complexion turned white, his stomach tightening. "Does Harvey know?"

"No."

About the Author

Mitch Doxsee was born on Marco Island, Florida, into one of the founding families of the Island. Descended from a long line of clammers, fishermen, and even a pirate or two, Mitch spent his childhood days hanging around the docks and on his grandfather's charter boat. Even after moving from Marco Island to the North, he always returned during the summers to run the Ten Thousands Islands with his grandfather.

During his days in college, Mitch worked with Youth at a Mission in Amsterdam, Holland, where he witnessed the horrors of human trafficking first hand.

Mitch holds a B.A. in Secondary English Education from Lee University and a M.Ed. in Secondary English Education from the University of Tennessee at Chattanooga. Now settled in Chattanooga, Tennessee, with his wife and son, Mitch and his family make frequent trips to his native state of Florida to fish and hunt.

Dismal Key is Mitch's first novel and has been awarded the gold medal in the 2013 Florida Authors and Publisher Association EBook category.

Staying Safe
in an Unsafe World
by
Robert Parke

A common sense approach for young people to the threats of today's world. This text offers basic education on possible dangers. It then offers practical strategies that can help individuals avoid trouble.

Former Sheriff Ken Katsaris endorses the book and says, "Mr. Parke arms the reader with a plethora of easily implemented safety measures"

Can be purchased at www.syppublishing.com or most online bookstores

BJ Hathaway is a busy anthropologist teaching in New Mexico. Unexpectedly she inherits an old house on the St. Marks River and an ecological restoration project. This forces her to return home to North Florida. Upon her return, she enters into the work of restoration, resumes old friendships, and works on unresolved relationships from her past. In the process, she encounters dangers she did not know were there.

As she begins to re-establish herself in North Florida and work on the conservation project, she is met with surprising resistance from some resentful members of the Board. An angry person from her past, spurned in her youth, threatens both the project and her life. She must defeat her nemesis or lose all. In the process, she finds love in the arms of a man she once knew but never forgot

Available at www.syppublishing.com and other online bookstores.